PRAISE FOR *KOKO TAKES A HOLIDAY*

"This futuristic wild ride starts out quickly and doesn't really slow down until it's over. You would think such a breakneck pace wouldn't leave much time for character development, but you'd be wrong; Shea skillfully weaves characterization into dialogue and into the thoughts and actions of the people in the novel. The use of the present tense certainly helps make the story feel urgent and immediate, too: we get caught up in Koko's predicament and are carried along with her as she desperately tries to keep herself alive until she can track down her would-be assassin. Great fun and a fine introduction to an author with a distinctive voice. Expect more from Shea."
Booklist (starred review)

"Shea takes us 500 years into Earth's future, a place apparently decadent and war torn in equal measure. Reminiscent of Takeshi Kovacs from Richard K. Morgan's *Altered Carbon* with a dash of Tank Girl attitude, Koko is a memorable character." *Library Journal*

"...vigorous anarchic pulse... sheer velocity keeps the story rattling along like a big geeky pinball machine." *Publishers Weekly*

"A vivid and brutal old school (in the best sense) cyberpunk headkick." Richard Kadrey, *New York Times* bestselling author of *Sandman Slim*

"Big, brash, and ambitious as all hell. Fans of white-knuckled science fiction, welcome to your new favorite novel." Chris Holm, award-winning author of *The Collector* series

"If Hunter S. Thompson and Elmore Leonard got together and wrote science fiction you'd get *Koko Takes a Holiday*. Brutal, smart and wickedly funny... a jet-powered, acid-fueled trip of pure, rocking insanity." Stephen Blackmore, author of *Dead Things*

"Not since Richard K. Morgan's *Altered Carbon* have I felt so completely immersed in such a perfectly realized world of the future. Kieran Shea is the breath of fresh air the science fiction genre has been looking for. I want more Koko, and I want her right now." Victor Gischler, author of *Ink Mage* and *Go-Go Girls of the Apocalpyse*

"The tempo of the storytelling is near on perfect. The action picks up speed like a jet fighter going in to attack – and it twists and turns with the same agility… No holds barred, just plain fantastic fun." SF Signal

"A fast-paced cyberpunk fantasy with all the anarchic energy of a graphic novel. Newcomer Kieran Shea's debut novel moves at breakneck speed, and it's teeming with colorful characters and a joyfully black sense of humour… a fun and action-packed read." SciFi Now

"A nonstop bloody thrill ride with all of the subtlety of a rocket launcher, and I loved every minute of it." My Bookish Ways

"Darkly funny, intelligent and a little ultraviolent… action packed and humorous pulp science fiction at its best." The Book Bag

"An incredibly fast paced, zany rollercoaster of a ride… A quirky, gritty, humorous, and incredibly visual stylized book that would be perfectly at home in graphic novel or movie formats, *Koko Takes a Holiday* is an absolutely amazing debut." Portland Book Review

"Plenty of explosions, bullets, wise cracks, and surprises will leave you wanting more… Yippee-Ki-Yay… this book completely rocks." Geek Dad

"An amazing read that wonderfully mixes the works of cyberpunk and sci-fi space operas with a dose of acid and unapologetic violence to create a compelling and hard-to-put-down novel." Pop Cults

KOKO THE MIGHTY

Also available from Kieran Shea and Titan Books

KOKO TAKES A HOLIDAY

KIERAN SHEA
KOKO THE MIGHTY

TITANBOOKS.COM

Koko the Mighty
Print edition ISBN: 9781781168622
E-book edition ISBN: 9781781168646

Published by Titan Books
A division of Titan Publishing Group Ltd
144 Southwark Street, London SE1 0UP

First edition: August 2015
1 3 5 7 9 10 8 6 4 2

A CIP catalogue record for this title is available from the British Library.

Printed and bound in the United States.

FOR ALL THE HEARTBROKEN WHO GIVE A DAMN ANYWAY

"WHEN YOU THINK OF THE LONG AND GLOOMY HISTORY OF MAN, YOU WILL FIND MORE HIDEOUS CRIMES HAVE BEEN COMMITTED IN THE NAME OF OBEDIENCE THAN HAVE EVER BEEN COMMITTED IN THE NAME OF REBELLION."

C.P. SNOW

(ESPRESSO SHOT) THE STORY SO FAR*

Once upon a future time in the year 2516, retired corporate mercenary Koko Martstellar believed she had quite the life. Running a bar and brothel operation on The Sixty Islands, the world's most violently decadent South Pacific resort—honestly, who wouldn't believe they had it good? Of course when Koko's piously phony boss tried to have her killed for an unspeakable crime she no longer recalled, the easy life for Koko deep-sixed pretty fast.

Pursued by a lethal trio of eye-eating bounty agents and fleeing to the atmospheric sky barges of the Second Free Zone, Koko teamed up with Jedidiah Flynn, a Depressus-afflicted former lawman who'd been readying himself for a live-broadcast mass suicide, known as Embrace. Matching equal amounts of grit and pluck, together the two evaded Koko's hunters, executed revenge on Koko's boss, and ended up more or less living happily ever after back on The Sixty Islands, running a new saloon. Or so they thought.

One ruthless bounty agent, Jackie Wire, survived Koko and Flynn's eluding efforts, and Wire is still determined to collect the price on Koko's head no matter the cost.

This is where their story continues…

* *Koko Takes a Holiday* recap. (Book purchase warmly suggested.)

THE SIXTY I

IF YOU CHECK THE GUIDE

If, by chance, you're considering vacation travel to The Sixty Islands and you happen to be perusing the latest core-loaded version of *Nessim's International Almanac of Recreational Excursions*, under the NIGHTLIFE/ACCOMMODATIONS silos you will notice an addition to the usual roster of offerings. The addition reads as follows:

SALOON, ISLAND 13
RE4589769-DS7-8.2
SI Facility Endorsement Rating—Pending
Proprietor: Martstellar, Koko P. (Penelope)
House Manager: Flynn, Jedidiah
Staff: (Incl. Certified Release Specialists) 16 (M/F)
Availability: [*Unknown*] (Under development, scheduled for business late 2516)

If you have secured your own shuttle transport or one of The Sixty's new air-conditioned tuk-tuks, this soon-to-be-opened S.I. saloon offers boutique accommodations, soothing libations, and carnal entertainment on the very-very. Situated approximately fifty meters above current adjusted sea levels and tucked away on one of the resort's more sheltered islands, this delightful spot is a quaint yet alluring option for patrons seeking sensual satisfactions in a laid-back garden atmosphere. Exquisitely replicated to historic Polynesian architectural standards and situated near two of The Sixty's ceasefire quadrants, this concern boasts eleven chic rooms with a full bar, gourmet fare, lap pool/spa, as well as a recreational gambling area with unrestricted table limits. Rosters of both male and female release specialists are available for companionship with negotiable rates and group packages offered. Upon its opening, advance reservations are recommended and full medical records *are required.*

AND AWAY WE GO

As she mashes down a bundle of white bar towels, Koko Martstellar's mind redlines.

"Stay with me, sweetie."

In what must be mindboggling agony, Jedidiah Flynn lasers her a look. The towels pressed against the wound in his leg quickly soak red on contact, and he throws open his jaw and bays like a stuck hound.

"You keep pushing on my leg like that, and I'll stay with you. I'll stay with you long enough to rip your damn head off! God, who trained you in field medicine, Koko? A butcher?"

Koko peeks under the bloody towels. Flecked with dark leg hair, the pulse-round wound in Flynn's leg is a warm trench of glistening pink gore. Damaged and cooked iliotibial band muscle for sure, but at twelve oozing centimeters the wound is totally survivable if measures are taken, and taken soon.

"Listen," Koko says. "You need to keep compression on this until we get a chance to stitch it up, okay?"

Flynn whips his head and grimaces. "Sheesh, who *is* that? Is she the one who shot me? I thought all the violence on this resort is supposed to be simulated."

Koko needs to keep Flynn's mind occupied, so she takes one of his trembling hands and places it on the bloody towels.

"Here, firm and steady pressure. Got it?"

"Yeah."

Koko quickly kisses the top of his sweaty head and then snaps her blood-slickened fingers. She points at the release specialist, the one in the gold lamé hot pants who cold-cocked the intruder just after she opened fire.

"Get that ugly bitch's weapon and give it to me. Frisk her, check her pockets and inside her boots. Be thorough. I want everything she's got. Identification, currency, that holster and belt she's wearing, the works."

The young man in the gold hot pants quickly kneels and does as Koko says. It takes some work to reach underneath the intruder, but he rummages through all of the woman's pockets and finds only a single additional power clip for the weapon the intruder dropped when she fell to the floor. He pulls off both the woman's boots. The boots are empty.

Koko wipes her fingers on her pink T-shirt. It's a small challenge for her to get to her feet without using her cane, but when the young man hands over the intruder's belt she lashes it around her hips. After pocketing the power clip in her camouflage shorts, Koko checks and sights the weapon. It's an HK U-50. Naturally she's handled one before, but at a formidable twelve hundred plus grams the weapon is definitely not a personal favorite. Setting the safety and seating the weapon in the belt's holster, Koko then orders two other release specialists to retrieve a set of bug-out backpacks she's stashed in the saloon's kitchen.

"Look in the crawlspace next to the walk-in fridge," she says. "You'll see a huge green plastic bin labeled 'Used Commode Parts.' The backpacks are in there."

The two release specialists move out on the double, and, not missing a beat, Koko instructs three more to bring the electric cargo ute around to the front of the building, as well as her terra-sled from the rear storage sheds. Koko looks down at Flynn.

"I hate to say this, baby, but you and me? It's time to vamoose."

"Vamoose?"

"Yeah, like, scram on the pronto."

"What, *now*? Are you crazy? I've just been shot."

"Doesn't matter. An incident like this sort of voids our amnesty deal with the Custom Pleasure Bureau and The Sixty. Not only that, but we're kind of being recorded right now too."

Flynn's head flops to the side. "What do you mean, we're being recorded?"

"Look, I'm sorry I didn't mention it before, but a few weeks ago I got a weird feeling so I executed a top to bottom sweep of our new building and the surrounding perimeter. I found at least a half-dozen camerascopes imbedded in our rooms and three more secreted away in the brush outside. Someone must've come in and set them up when we were off the islands looking for staff. I guess you were right not to trust The Sixty's management team and CPB board of directors. Insisting we have biometric identifiers inserted in our skin and recording everything we do—after all that went down, I suppose they still want to keep an eye on us."

"Sheesh, I'm your damn partner here, Koko. You could've said something."

"Well, it's not like I could disable the camerascopes or anything. Biometric identifiers and a few visual recorders—I figured, meh, maybe it was just better to let sleeping dogs lie."

"Where?"

Koko looks up and gestures. "Right now there's one fixed directly above us at twelve o'clock. Ceiling fan, dead center. You see the raised bolt? On it there's a lens about the size of a pharaoh ant. I'm just guessing, but it probably takes in the whole bar area."

A bead of sweat drips into Flynn's eye. "Oh, man. I guess that means—"

"Someone else saw you bawling like a baby? Yeah." Koko motions with her chin to the burly-looking intruder knocked out on the floor. "So tell me, do you recognize her?"

Flynn shifts a bit. "I can't see her face."

"Lift that gorilla's head so Master Flynn here can give her a look."

Another two release specialists scurry over and shovel palms under the unconscious woman's forehead. When the intruder's crew-cut head tilts back, Flynn scrutinizes her features and a pair of zonked-out eyes.

"Oh, no. It can't be," he says.

"What?" Koko asks.

Flynn swings back. "She's one of the two bounty agents I saw back on *Alaungpaya*. She was in the terminal area right before we escaped the Second Free Zone."

Koko bites her lower lip. "Hmm, I thought so."

"She was with that redhead, the one with the neck extension bands. What the hell is she doing here?"

"Ruining our lives, apparently."

Wiping her brow with her forearm, Koko turns to yet another one of her employees—a female release specialist—and whips off the silk belt cinching the girl's kimono together. Koko lowers herself down and gets busy securing the wad of towels to Flynn's thigh.

"But Portia Delacompte is dead," Flynn says. "I was there, Koko, remember? We both were. How can a dead woman still have bounty hunters after us? It doesn't make sense."

Koko finishes tying off the dressing. There's no time to explain, but the logic is starting to add up to her. When they were fleeing the lower atmospheric sky-barge *Alaungpaya*, it's true: she did take out two of the bounty agents who were pursuing them via her ex-friend Portia Delacompte's brutal elimination order. The first was a suspected former professional athlete she plugged in Flynn's quarters, and the second was that dolled-up redhead with the neck rings she decapitated on *Alaungpaya*'s flight deck right before they hijacked the septic freighter. At the time of the second agent's demise, Flynn advised Koko there were two operatives on their immediate six, so now Koko forces herself to replay the whole deadly sequence of events in her head; how after the redhead's head slammed down the portal shaft, Koko heard the bellow of someone crying out below. There wasn't a lot of wiggle room for due diligence at the time, but her hunch is the unconscious woman who just shot Flynn is, in fact, the third bounty agent who was in the portal shaft. She must have survived the flight deck's high altitude depressurization somehow.

"Listen," Koko says, "all things being even it might be a matter of ego with this one, you know? If I were in her shoes I know unfinished business would have stuck in my craw. Back on *Alaungpaya* you told me there were two bounty agents on our immediate tail. For this one to survive an emergency depressurization at that altitude, I mean, I thought we were in the clear. What matters now is the payout on my elimination looks permanent."

Flynn droops. Koko pats his arm.

"I'm sorry, sweetie."

"Oh, sure. You're sorry. Is that somehow supposed to make me feel better? Goddamn it, I really hate all this."

"I know, getting shot really hurts."

"No, not getting shot. I mean, that hurts, yeah, but I really hate all *this.* You and me, how when things start going good, everything just turns to shit."

"Can you stand?"

"Did you miss my whole getting shot thing?"

"I'm serious, Flynn. You need to get up. We've a chance of getting out of here, but it's a slim one at best."

Flynn dabs at the blood-soaked towels secured with the kimono belt. Without being asked, several employees in the saloon rush over and, with some orchestration, get Flynn up on his feet. Somebody picks up Koko's white walking cane and holds it out to her, but Koko waves it off. Even if she's still recovering from the damages inflicted on her by Portia Delacompte, Koko is definitely of the mind that now is not the time to be relying on props.

Flynn hops and Koko drapes one of his clammy arms across her shoulders. The two release specialists Koko sent to retrieve the backpacks from the pantry return while, outside the saloon, the electric motoring sounds of the cargo ute and terra-sled draw near.

Flynn notices the backpacks. “What are those?”

Koko shifts Flynn’s weight against her body and discomfort twangs down her leg. “Bug-out packs,” she explains. “A few thousand credits, minimal rations, a couple of side arms, NBC-protective suits, potable water, stuff like that.” Together they limp around the fallen bounty agent. “Here, watch your step.”

Flynn looks over his shoulder. “Wait, we’re just going to leave her like that? But she could come after us. Shouldn’t we, like, do something?”

Koko stops. “Oh, so you want me to kill her, is that it?”

“Well, I know it sounds cold-blooded, but it seems sensible.”

“Sensible? Oh, really? Hmm, maybe you want me to bite out one of her eyes for good measure while I’m at it.”

“I didn’t say you had to go to extremes.”

Koko resumes dragging Flynn forward, adding sarcastically, “You know, I seem to recall a short time ago a certain somebody complaining about how I should turn over a new leaf. Gee, how did he put it? Broaden my emotional capacities? Embrace my softer, gentler side?”

“I was talking about with us. I mean—”

“You know what, Flynn? I don’t want to hear it. Not now. If SI Security is on their way here that bounty agent is their problem, not ours. They’ll deal with her. Priority one for us is to get good and gone.”

Flynn looks over his shoulder once more at the saloon’s main bar area and hesitates. Fleetingly Koko wonders if he’s stalling because he wants to take his chances with SI Security. Koko supposes she really can’t blame him for being freaked. Yeah, sure, he used to be a cop, but being hunted down on a dead woman’s orders, this sort of psycho scenario is in Koko’s wheelhouse, not his. As the traumatized saloon staff watch them leave, a few of the release specialists start to cry.

“What about them?” Flynn asks.

Koko knows who he means, but she keeps her mouth shut and

her eyes fixed straight ahead. Before she met up with him in the Second Free Zone on *Alaungpaya,* Koko had fought her way out of a whole smorgasbord of hellacious situations and not once in all those times has looking back ever helped.

"They'll be fine," Koko says. "Somebody will take over this joint. I mean, all the work we've done getting the saloon ready and all the promotions? The whole operation is practically turn-key."

She resumes getting Flynn out of the building with as little pain as possible. Passing through the batwings and making their way across the broad boards of the front porch, Koko fully expects to hear the hooting blares of SI Security sirens at any moment. Lightning flashes and after a deafening thunder crack, the savage downpour that had been threatening all afternoon cuts loose, and the straight-nailed monsoon rain sounds just like a round of applause.

COCHON DE LAIT: HORACE BRITCH

Horace Britch is about to sink his teeth into a kebab of suckling boar meat when his shoulder's epaulette mic warbles.

"Britch-3493? SI Security priority message. Please respond, over."

Britch neglected to pick up napkins at the end of the buffet line, and grease drips down his arm in a warm rivulet.

"Britch-3493? Repeat, SI Security priority message. Please respond, over."

Britch aims the kebab away from his body like a fencer's foil. Sweating, he flattens his chin on his epaulette and keys the mic.

"This better be good," Britch answers crustily. "I'll have you know, I'm on dinner break."

Dispatch is unsympathetic to his concerns.

"BOP event, Island Thirteen. Confirmed report involving unidentified female and a male resort manager, over."

Britch flattens his chin on his epaulette again. "Oh, for the love of—a breach of peace call? What, somebody got punched in the snot-locker again?"

A long fizz of static and then, "Uh, that's a negative."

Britch kicks an empty bamboo *masu* box at his feet. With both hands he then lifts the kebab and quickly chomps down the meat lanced in between. Hand-seasoned with turmeric and basted with coconut water, the fatty pigskin snaps in his mouth with each bite and is so delicious Britch's head actually starts to swoon.

As luck would have it, Britch is supervising officer for SI Security response that evening, and nearly everyone on The Sixty is throwing down big time on Island One. It's The Sixty Islands' weekly luau—an open-invitation, all-out bash publicized heavily by the CPB's promotional and marketing departments. Counting the stuck-up vacationing patrons, the full-time SI employees, and the high-priced pyrotechnic entertainment (DJ Rajini Superwong and the Slavectors doing percussion duels, don't you know), an eyeball estimate puts the luau crowd at nearly fourteen hundred and change. Most are scantily clad and nearly all are blitzed out of their minds on fortified rice liquor and God knows what-all. Between flame-spouting, caterpillar-tracked kulkul watchtowers, blade-juggling trapeze artists soar from catch bars as a tethered aerostat drifts overhead like a massive, gas-swollen dong. In the aerostat's gondola, go-go dancers use hoses to disperse hallucinogenic rainbow-colored dyes over the crowds. The wilding masses below hail their approval and extend their tongues upward to catch a taste of the sweet narcotic mists.

All in all, The Sixty's luau is an apotheosis of hedonism multiplied to the tenth power. If anything were to go wrong on the archipelago tonight, the sands of Island One are the odds-on favorite for ground zero. As Britch chews and swallows bite after bite, his beady eyes mirthlessly dart in their sockets. Eastward, past the flickering torches and garish massage tents, he can make out the smaller humps of The Sixty's teen-numbered islands. More than a dozen kilometers away, the crepuscular contours look like the backs of dozing animals, and the storm front forecasted for that afternoon looks to have finally cut loose in their vicinity. It's not raining just yet on Island One, but Britch can smell a charged fried-ion scent as a crimped vein of lightning marbles the darkening sky. The luau crowds cheer. Thunder rolls.

With almost two years' tenure on the resort, Britch appreciates his position well enough and knows, given his morbidly obese liabilities, he's damn fortunate to have it. Unlike most of his peers in SI Security, Britch didn't come from a hardcore battle-tested soldiering or policing background. Initially, yes, he'd been bred in one of the collectives and applied for such training, desperately hoping for field work—all that squashing of the de-civ ilk and shoring up economic interests and such—but his practical test scores indicated he lacked a certain amoral fortitude to serve as an active duty solider or law enforcement officer. A squeamish washout the recruiters said. Though he marginally passed the physical examinations, the recruiters were adamant Britch needed to perform without mercy to be of value as a soldier or policeman. Three months of extensive virtual-reality training pretty much ferreted out his lack of brutal grit. Crushed, Britch protested and begged for another chance, but the recruiters told him no way. However, they did inform him he wasn't completely worthless. While Britch didn't have the coldblooded makeup to be a full-time policeman or soldier, his cognitive assessments demonstrated he'd prime attributes for administrative duties.

It was so humiliating. Reluctantly, Britch took the offer and to his surprise he discovered, in time, that the recruiters were right. Purchasing and actuarial logistics were the robust pillars of his ken, and for a spell Britch secured work as a quartermaster for long-haul projects in quarantined resource regions. Regretfully, though, with his ass parked behind a desk ninety percent of the time, a freakish genetic anomaly in his thyroid kicked in and prompted a dramatic if not startling weight gain.

Britch had always been a mite pudgy, but his sudden monstrous growth spurt was something else. The cataclysmic megalo increase in weight whittled away at the tenuous underpinnings of his fragile ego, so to counteract the condition he first sought out medical options and then attempted to bulk up with weights. Both solutions, however, only seemed to aggravate his problem, and Britch finally decided to take his condition in his stride. He defended a position that it did not matter how he looked because his intrinsic values rested with his managerial proficiencies.

As things turned out, several of the Custom Pleasure Bureau's recruiters took notice of Britch's fastidious knack for logistics and sought out his expertise. Naturally, in person the CPB and The Sixty's personnel recruiters had their reservations regarding his physical detriments, but they hired Britch anyway with the assurance they wanted him for his talents at cost-slashing, supply management, and the like.

For six months on the resort Britch hardly needed to remind himself how good he had it. Honestly, a job on The Sixty Islands? One of the most lavishly insane resorts on the planet? Some people would murder for a slot. Working air-conditioned days at the resort headquarters, shuffling the provisions hither and yon and burnishing the bottom line—life was sweeter than sweet and more than cushy. But then SI management made a shift in policy. All security personnel (no ifs, ands or buts) were now required to pull patrol assignments regardless of their responsibilities.

For Britch, the sudden policy deviation was awful. Hoofing about and keeping an eye on people having the time of their lives was a sheer burden on his knees, not to mention insulting. He requested several times in writing for permanent excusal from patrol tasks, citing unabashedly that it was imprudent waste of his obvious strengths. Management did not appreciate his candor, and as punishment they upped his patrol count and drastically reduced his pay by half.

So now he's being tagged with a priority BOP summons from Dispatch. Britch considers forwarding the call to one of the other officers also on patrol duty this evening and scans the crowds for someone else to lay the call off on. Dropping his spent kebab skewer in the sand, Britch sucks his fingers and keys the epaulette mic again.

"Clarify event specifics, over."

"Initiating camerascope playbacks to your data tab now. Non-simulated shooting. SI saloon facility, one Martstellar, Koko P., proprietor."

Britch's head snaps: a wobbly double-take. Pork-slimed fingers be damned, he clutches his shoulder and nearly rips the epaulette mic free from his uniform.

"Dispatch, can you repeat that, over."

"Transmitting…"

Britch yanks his data tab from its clip on his duty belt. He knows damn well the saloon's exact location and recalls reviewing directives from the CPB and The Sixty's executive offices that all security personnel should make an extra effort to keep an eye on its owner, a former professional mercenary known as Koko Martstellar. Something to do with a recent senior administrative upheaval. Of course Britch had heard the rumors about the skirmish on The Sixty's runway apron several months back, when a late SI executive was blown to bits, but the files regarding what had actually transpired, or why it had even happened in the first place, had been scrubbed clean from the available archives. Word was Martstellar had been involved, but since then reports on the woman's activities had been unremarkable. From all outward appearances Martstellar was just another vendor getting a saloon and brothel operation online to service vacationing clientele.

After the costly flak Britch received for requesting excusal from patrol duties, he knows better than to go kicking a skunk. Nevertheless, he has to wonder. Something like this? A non-simulated shooting connected with Martstellar? This sort of cock-up stinks of leverage. If he handles it well, Britch might even be able to get his compensation back on track *and* free himself of patrol obligations.

Smearing a greasy forefinger on the data tab's screen to activate the interface, Britch cues up the transmitted visuals from Dispatch. With resolution enlargements, the event images are distorted, but they reel out dramatically in an edited playback loop. Britch adjusts the data tab's audio controls for volume, but hearing anything above DJ Rajini Superwong and the Slavectors on the main stage is impossible. Doesn't matter. What Britch sees on the tiny screen is more than enough to gas his butt into high gear.

"This is Britch. I'm on my way."

EVASIVE MANEUVERS

Flying down the access road in the cargo ute, Koko slams on the brakes, and the two release specialists trailing behind on the terra-sled come to a halt behind.

Climbing down from the cab and stepping out into the hammering rain, Koko grabs the bug-out backpacks from the ute's bed and quickly tears open a pocket.

"You two, shut that terra-sled down," she shouts.

The two young men do as she says, and Koko pulls a first-aid kit from the backpack. From the kit she retrieves a laser scalpel and without warning she stalks over to the two release specialists. Koko grabs one by his right arm and from his wet wrist quickly slices out his biometric identifier.

"Owza-wowza, Koko-sama! What you doin'?"

"Shut up."

After cutting out the identifier, Koko cuts out her own and sticks hers into the whining release specialist's shorts.

"Get back on the terra-sled and head straight for the airfield."

"Me, Koko-sama? No-no, me stay with you."

"No! Airfield! Now!"

Sheepishly, the young man does as Koko orders, loops a leg over the terra-sled and takes off. Koko then grabs the second by his arm.

"Come here, hot stuff. Help me get Master Flynn out of the cab."

Together they head to the front of the ute. Flynn is in the passenger seat and Koko opens the door. When they drag him out, Flynn howls.

"Wait! Hang on, my leg!"

"Give me your right arm!"

"What?"

"I said, give me your right arm! Your wrist!"

On the ground, Flynn looks up at Koko, baffled. Reluctantly, he holds out his arm. Koko pulls it close and works the laser scalpel.

"What the—? *OW!* Do you mind telling me what the hell you're doing?"

Koko finishes slicing open his wrist. "Evasive maneuvers, sugar."

Picking out the bloody identifier from Flynn's wrist, Koko flicks the tiny device on the floor of the cab and tells the second release specialist to drive the cargo ute as fast as he can to the farthest island on the resort. Visibly glad she didn't take the laser scalpel to his own wrist, the young man spins around to the driver's side of the ute, climbs in, and zooms off in a spray of mud. Koko takes a breath and looks toward the brush alongside the road.

"There's a maintenance access tunnel about twenty meters from here," she says.

Flynn holds his bleeding wrist. "Maintenance tunnel?"

"Yeah, to the islands and resort's support infrastructure. Right here there's a gap in the archipelago's scanners, so they'll think one of us is still in the ute, and the other is on the terra-sled hauling ass for the airfield. I'm trying to buy us some time."

Flynn swallows. "God, Koko, I don't think I can make twenty meters."

"Fifty milligrams of morphine says you will."

Koko pulls a morphine injector from the first-aid kit, and sticks it into Flynn's wounded leg. She then snatches the two bug-out packs and loops one on her back and the other one off her shoulder.

"Holy smokes," Flynn says with softening wonder, "that's what morphine feels like? That shit is amazing."

"It's reducing your brain's awareness of pain, but it won't numb it completely. Now get the fuck up. Let's go."

A minute and a half later they arrive at the maintenance access tunnel door. The door is rusted and covered with thick vines, but with a good pull, it opens with enough room for them to squeeze their way through. Inside, the passage is pitch dark, and Koko drags Flynn down a ramp.

"Where are we going?" Flynn asks.

"You'll see. Keep moving."

Soon the sound of sloshing water can be heard, and the dark passage they are in opens up to reveal a massive, cavernous space, replete with gangways, monstrous pipes, conduits, and overhead lights. Beneath them, on a series of docks hedging a large body of slopping seawater, are the humped backs of a dozen large and small winged submarines.

"Oh, you've got to be shitting me," Flynn says.

"You get seasick?"

"I've never even been on a boat!"

"Now's as good a time as any."

Together they cross a series of zig-zagging ramps down to the docks. A maintenance technician spots them approaching and instantly Koko sizes the man up. Tall and ropey, he carries himself a bit too heavily to his right side, which to Koko means the big galoot favors it. The tech caustically starts spouting meaningless words of how it's a restricted area and they don't belong there, and Koko screams at him in a strange foreign tongue. The tech is so startled by Koko's outburst, he falters and steps back clumsily. It's what Koko intended; get him off balance. She charges and lands a haymaker right into the tech's temple. Tottering, the galoot fights back with a series of wild hooks, but Koko slaps away each blow and uses a three-punch cross and kick combination to drop him to the dock. She shoves Flynn toward the submarines bobbing in the quay.

"Which one?" Flynn cries.

Koko points to the largest winged submarine tied to the dock pilings directly ahead of them.

"There, the one with the open hatch. Take the gangway."

Gingerly and quickly as he can, Flynn limps ahead and makes his way up the gangway. Koko has the bounty agent's weapon drawn and she checks the periphery. More technicians have noticed the ruckus and are headed their way. Someone hits an alarm, and an earsplitting horn screeches.

Koko aims and opens fire at the surrounding electrical cables and delivery conduits, anything that might short out or explode. Like schoolchildren on a bee-streaked playground, the advancing techs scatter. Flynn is struggling his way into the sub's open hatch.

"Hurry, Flynn!"

"I'm trying!"

There's no time for niceties. Koko leaps onto the gangway and storms up to the hatch. Planting a boot on Flynn's shoulder she forces him down inside. Flynn falls and lands spread-eagled on the deck below with a loud *OOOF*!

"Sorry, baby!"

Koko drops the bug-out packs on top of him, one by one, climbs in, and pulls the hatch closed. Spinning a wheel to lock the hatch off, she can hear muddled footsteps and shouts above her. When Koko looks at Flynn, she sees he's passed out.

She steps over him. Truth be told, Koko has never set foot on a submarine and hasn't the first clue about how to run one. All manner of flight craft and armored land vehicles, maybe a few amphibious watercraft now and then, but a submarine? Never. Her brain zips briskly through ephemeral, fragmentary notions. Something to do with positive and negative buoyancies and hydroplanes. She ducks under a riveted seam and makes her way to the sub's small bridge. As she's slipping into the vessel's pilot seat, a round yellow button marked POWER looks promising, so she jabs at it. There is a sharp click and then the submarine's powerful fusion engines roar to life.

Crap, Koko thinks, *I didn't have time to cast off the dock lines. Oh, well.*

Running her eyes over the controls, Koko grabs what looks like the throttle and slams it forward. The lurch from the stern is explosive, and the sub rips free of the dock in a shattering opus of destruction.

When Koko glances out the thick, bathyscaphic bow screen in front of her, one of the shouting technicians from above tumbles off the hull and falls into the water. Tugging back on the throttle, Koko throws a quick look back at Flynn. He still looks passed out, but she shouts at him anyway.

"Hang on!"

Chugging up and onto a plane, the submarine careens across the open water. Koko suddenly realizes that the only way out of the subterranean docking area is down. She needs to figure out the vessel's submersion functions and hydroplanes, like, fast.

On the sub's steering wheel there are two green- and red-colored toggles. *Green and red mean starboard and port, right?* Koko flicks the toggles, but there's no response. The far vertical wall of the cavernous docking space looms closer so she starts hitting and flipping every lever and button in sight. One of the levers blows the ballast and auxiliary trim tanks and after a loud, whisking hiss a full sluicing chorus of rushing water follows. The sub descends.

Oh, man... maybe it's like flying?

No time for second guesses because they're about to slam into the far wall. Koko pushes the helm's wheel forward and miraculously the winged sub enters a sharp thirty-degree dive.

"Whoo-hoo! Now we're talking!"

Outside, a bubbling suffusion of seawater rushes over the bow screen. Through the bubbles Koko can make out yellow directional lighting leading down a long, wide tunnel, and up ahead a large algae-covered sign with yellow letters reads:

EASTERN PACIFIC

Koko eases back the helm, and the sub sways from side to side. Leveling out their angle and reaching neutral buoyancy, she notches up their speed. Five hundred meters ahead a wide ovate exit soon becomes visible, hooped with flashing white signal lights.

It's funny, but Koko suddenly remembers that old story about a fisherman being swallowed by a great fish-beast.

Great fish-beast?

The great fish-beast can kiss her ass.

Koko slams the throttle forward for all its worth.

KEEPING A LIVE WIRE DOWN

Hours later, stripped and humiliated, bounty agent Jackie Wire leans her muscled, naked buttocks against the pressure cell's far wall and crosses her meaty arms. The invisible force fields in the pressure cell strain the limits of her vascular system. Bulging blue veins, thick as baby snakes, rope her skin.

In a teal-tinted hologram in front of her, a portly security officer looks on, the edges of his mouth curving slightly.

"We can't keep you indefinitely."

Within the hologram the officer's dimensions are half life-sized, but his plump face broadcasts a certain slovenliness and has an extra dash of under-my-thumb officiousness. Pritch or Britch was what he said his name was. Officer Fatty might be merited with some kind of rank, but Wire pegs him as unequivocally bush league. With a slight swerve of her eyeball she records the man's butterball features on her ocular imbed for future reference. Pulling this intimidation garbage and wasting her valuable time—it's a small world, buddy. Given half the chance down the line, Wire would gladly take a measure out of her busy schedule to quietly choke the fat man to death.

"So, if you can't keep me, when do I get released?"

A measured pause. "In a little."

"In a little? Like, in a little what? A few hours? Days? By my count you've had me locked up in this cell for almost three hours straight, and that's after I woke up. Look, pal, you obviously know why I came to The Sixty so let's quit dicking around. I know my rights."

"No doubt you do," the holographic officer coos. "As a bounty agent, I'd think knowing the variances of your rights would be a priority for you in most parts of the world. But see, the Custom Pleasure Bureau and The Sixty have deemed your detention appropriate as you're in breach of your reservation agreement."

"My reservation agreement?"

"Yes, the one you authorized upon your arrival."

"You can't impede someone from engaging in her chosen field of commerce."

"I'm sorry, but I think we can. 'All commercial activities or business transactions by patrons within The Sixty must be disclosed and have prior CPB approval.' Neat trick having a subaqueous spider-bot deliver your contraband weapons ahead of your arrival. Very proactive."

Wire hocks back a long draw of phlegm, swallows it, and lets her eyes roam over the pressure cell's barren walls. It's not the first pressure cell she's been in, but this one seems to be a new-fangled model, its atmospheric stresses specifically designed to inflict significant discomfort. Typically for someone of fewer physical attributes, such measures would keep a person sapped of strength and whimpering on the floor. Of course it took Wire some work to get her five-foot frame upright, and even more effort to fold her powerful arms, but she wants Mister Third Helping of Carbohydrates to know she's not a pushover.

The holographic officer buzzes on insufferably. "You stated you entered the host establishment with the intent of terminating Koko Martstellar, to collect on an outstanding Ultimate Sanction elimination warrant. While the initiators of this contract are no longer with the CPB—or living, for that matter—I understand these sort of bids are irrevocable and rewarded with accrued interest."

"So what's it to you?"

"Well, by now the payout on this bounty must be quite substantial. Perhaps you should have exercised discretion and waited until your intended target was off The Sixty."

Wire hangs her head and concentrates on the space between her spread feet. Sweat drips from her body as she replays how the whole debacle with Martstellar went down.

After pursuing Martstellar on a residential barge in the lower firmamental orbits of the Second Free Zone with two other bounty operatives (both of whom Martstellar killed), Wire cut her losses and hightailed it out of SFZ altogether. Called it a day and chalked up the anomaly of missing her target to a loss. Sometimes, at least in her profession, you had to play the self-preservation card. The feed publicity surrounding the Second Free Zone fiasco had pretty much iced pursuing Martstellar for a little while anyway, so to keep herself occupied after abandoning her assignment Wire reprioritized. She took a secondary recovery job in the Rhodope mountain region with a follow-up elimination stint in nearby Bucharest. It was a safe enough play. Keep working while the heat surrounding Martstellar cooled down. Both job assignments ate up months of her time, and after Wire finished up, she almost even forgot about finding Martstellar altogether. However, a routine skim of backchannel intelligence revealed that Martstellar was still alive and the Ultimate Sanction status on her head was still collectible. The news just pissed Wire off all over again. Being bested by that has-been, it wasn't something she could stomach. No way, no how. Wire had a reputation, a nearly pluperfect capture/liquidation record. If word got around that she'd bailed on a second-rate target like Martstellar, Wire might soon find herself being passed over for additional gainful work.

She has to concede it was a bit of a conundrum why Martstellar ended up back on The Sixty. You'd think after your supposed superior engages a directive to wipe your mortal being off the face of the planet you'd choose some other locale rather than the terra firma that left a bad taste in your mouth. Not so. The spunky little scamp apparently got off on the resort's dissolute *mode de vie*. With some additional investigation, Wire learned that after Martstellar settled the score with the woman who had put out her kill order (quite the spectacular shoot-out, or so Wire had heard), she ended up cutting a deal with the CPB and The Sixty. Got herself set up with a whole new arrangement. A top-shelf saloon with a demimonde bill of meretricious sex hustlers, gambling options, and even a lap pool. Yeah, her and that gangly dork who'd helped her elude Wire in the first place. A former sky-cop Wire now knows goes by the name Jedidiah Flynn.

A second teal-tinted hologram larger in dimension appears in the air alongside the heavyset officer's image. The second display runs an edited playback from camerascope receptors placed in and around Martstellar's establishment. Expressionless, Wire studies the playback like the most cringeworthy of dreams.

First, she sees herself with her HK U-50 drawn as she exits the brush and heads toward the building. The playback then smash-cuts to assorted voyeuristic angles (above, ground-level, behind, and so forth) all of which take in her swift and deadly approach. The recording then cuts to a fish-eyed overhead view of the saloon as she enters. Wire relishes the next part when she pops the man called Flynn in the back of his leg with a pulse round, but what Wire sees next sickens her. Like a glockenspiel figurine, a skinny young man in shiny gold shorts smashes a huge glass jug right over her head. Wire wants to review what happened next as she was down for the count, but the second display darkens and disappears.

"You'd think with your track record you would've been, I don't know, less brazen? That young man who knocked you out? His record indicates multiple arrests for pub brawling back in Melbourne before he was recruited by Martstellar."

Wire seethes. "Brilliant. Taken out by some shabby-ass, Aussie boywhore."

"Tut-tut. Here on The Sixty we now refer to them as release specialists."

"Spare me the semantics. So, what's the story here? Am I being charged with something or what?"

"Well, in the midst of your recent escapade you did shoot one of our employees."

"Oh, come off it. Replay that footage. I only winged that guy. I bet he's doing just fine. Besides, I was just getting warmed up."

The image of the officer starts to weaken, and it seems he is getting ready to sign off, playing more of his sly power games.

"Hey! Hold on, you didn't answer my question."

The hologram strengthens. "We're trying to keep this incident under wraps, so no, you're not being charged, not exactly."

Not exactly?

"All right, so when *exactly* do I get released?"

"Tomorrow."

"Tomorrow? Swell. Then what?"

"Deportation from The Sixty Islands, officially."

"Deportation to where?"

"Surabaya. You'll be housed in the brig on a short-haul flight craft, I believe."

"But I don't know anyone in Surabaya."

"Whether you know anyone there is not of concern."

"Yeah, but couldn't you, like, I don't know. Pick someplace else?"

"Come, come, it's not the worst place to be deported to. Did you know Surabaya was once known as the City of Heroes?"

"What about all my gear?"

"You mean the weapons Martstellar didn't take? Those have been confiscated. A subsection of the aforementioned reservation agreement outlines property forfeitures. Zero reimbursement, I'm afraid."

At last the pressure cell's measures take their toll and cream Wire to the floor. The impact on the smooth concrete is jarring, but now that she's down the potent unseen energies sense her movement and grow stronger in intensity. Wire pants and grinds her teeth. Her brain might burst from her ears like runny pudding, but she wills herself to focus.

"Wait, is Martstellar… still here? On The Sixty?"

The officer runs the tip of his tongue over his thick lips as if tasting the mist of possibility.

"That sort of information might require a small measure of recompense, don't you think?"

Wire tracks the officer's image as it repositions in the air above her. Her head whanging like an unholy gong, it takes a few more seconds for his greasy innuendo to sink in.

Figures.

Everybody has his price.

WAY DOWN BELOW THE OCEAN

SEA MONKEYING

Surfing the Kuroshio Current like a pro into the greater clockwork coil of the North Pacific Gyre, Koko is in the midst of getting a few quick Z's when the submarine pitches hard to starboard. Like a flashing seraphic eye, a red bulb blinks at her on the forward console.

Making certain all the onboard tracking capabilities were disabled, seeing to Flynn's wound and securing him in a makeshift bunk fashioned out of a dropdown bench had Koko wiped, so she'd engaged the helm's autopilot in order to catch a nap. Koko chides herself for being so stupid. Still at maximum speed, the submarine has now hit something, and somewhere along the starboard side an unhealthy tremolo wails.

Koko kills the power to the sub's engines, and a profound silence descends. An immediate diagnostic check discloses that the sub has entered a large, underwater debris field and has thusly been snagged. With a depth reading of a little over twenty-seven fathoms, everything outside the dense bow screen is ominously dark, but pulling up and reviewing additional vessel analytics, Koko is able to pinpoint the problem: a floating cable jamming one of the starboard-side rudders.

Shitballs.

This is all she needs.

Whenever Koko has encountered mechanical issues (be it a finicky weapon or even a clogged privy) she's found that generally a quick, targeted shot of brute force can solve most problems. Engaging the power to the engines again, she throws the sub into reverse to see if a short redirection can free the cable from the rudder. Sliding backward, at first her fix seems to do the trick, but then another hard listing rocks and the terrible starboard tremolo sounds off yet again. Koko shifts the throttle back to neutral, and sighing heavily she kills the power to the engines once more.

Oh, man…

She dreads it, but knows what she has to do.

She needs to free the cable manually.

Unbuckling her safety harness, Koko heads aft and stops briefly to lay the back of her hand across Flynn's forehead. Feverish and a small mercy, Flynn is completely out, so Koko presses two fingers along his neck to check his pulse. His heartbeat is shallow but steady, so being careful not to wake him, she squeezes herself past him and into the engine-access area. Freeing a latch on a port-side locker, Koko drags out a heavy bag full of scuba equipment and returns to the center area of the sub.

It's been ages since she's gone full frog. Underwater infil/exfil techniques, egress methods, months of underwater NOYFB[†] demolition training; it's not as if she's uninitiated to the rigors of diving, and thankfully the underwater gear stowed in the heavy bag looks top-notch. Two full cylinders with eighteen liters of compressed air, weight belts, gloves, fins, masks, and a variety of secondary tools, regulators, and gauges. Sadly, the two wetsuits included with the bag are shorties—skinned flimsy at a meager two millimeters for tropical temps. With her legs and arms half covered, Koko knows she's going to be a virtual popsicle out in the open water, but she hasn't much choice.

[†] *None of Your Fucking Business*

Removing her boots, she strips and hauls on the smaller of the two wetsuits and is pleased to discover it's a snug fit at least.

Heading further forward to the console, Koko blows the ballast and the sub gradually rises to the surface. A floppy wash of water swishes past the bow screen, and she flicks on the sub's outside lights. Traipsing back to the gear bag, she pulls on a pair of gloves and cinches a weight belt around her waist.

There's a small mouthpiece alternative air-source, but given the unknown nature of the cable caught in the rudder, Koko decides it might be better to go with full gear. Attaching the regulator, she checks the flow from the cylinder, and the air tastes cool and slightly like plastic. She then searches the bottom of the bag for line. The last thing she needs is to get sucked away by some unexpected current when she's in the water, and Koko finds a small coil of line tagged at five-meter intervals. Taking a pair of black scuba fins, Koko attaches the cylinder with its affixed regulator to buoyancy compensator vest, clips a dive light to the vest's shoulder, and grabs a mask. From a large toolbox beneath the pilot's seat, she also grabs a stubby set of bolt cutters.

Climbing up the ladder with all the gear, Koko unlocks the upper hatch and shoulders it open. The fresh air tastes amazing, and the gentle, warm breeze on her face is percale soft. Under better circumstances, it might be nice just to hang out and enjoy being out of the freaking submarine for a spell. Above her there is a dazzling cape of indifferent stars, and outward from the still half-submerged flanks of the submarine twelve long shafts of light skelter beneath the ocean's surface.

Koko sits down, fastens her fins to her feet, and pulls on the buoyancy compensator vest. Using a set of recessed toe-holds with her heels, she sidles down the starboard side and rinses some spit in her mask in the slopping water. Compared to the air the water feels cold, but she tells herself to deal with it. Jamming her regulator into her mouth and releasing the airflow, Koko secures her mask and ties off the coiled line to a stud-mounted cleat to her right. Tying the opposite end of the line to her waist, Koko slides into the water and the expected shock locks up her muscles and takes her breath away. She not so much switches on the shoulder dive light as slaps at it. This shit—why did a technical issue have to be *beneath* the sub? Releasing air from the BC vest via a depressed valve, she slips beneath the rolling surface.

Fearing an impending metabolic shutdown, Koko swims along the sub's flank as fast as she can toward the jammed rudder. When she reaches the affected area, she is pleased to find the impacted cable is scarcely thicker than the diameter of her forearm. No big deal. So she lines up the bolt cutters' jaws to cut, and squeezes the rubber-gripped arms together. The brutal cold constricting her blood vessels has her skull feeling like she's been socked by a hammer, but after a half a minute's worth of exertion, the cable gives way with a dull snip and Koko peers inside the rudder's recesses. She assesses that nothing else looks amiss, just as a vermillion-colored blob of pulsating flesh zooms past her back.

Koko blows out a startled blast of bubbles and rolls over. The ghostly shaft of the dive light attached to the BC vest catches a spaghetti tangle and just as the tangle disappears another mass of rippling, metachrosic meat and suction cups swoops past her face.

Oh, you've got *to be kidding…*

Zooming through the surrounding sub lights, the attacking shoal of giant squid is staggering. Bioluminescent, most of the creatures are the length of Koko's arm, but some pumping through the light shafts possess massive winged mantles topping out at whopping meter-lengths or more. Koko realizes the submarine's twelve outer lights have keyed in the invertebrates' swarming, collective aggression. The creatures flash like bar lights, and Koko is so completely freaked out she nearly drops the bolt cutters.

Another mass of smaller glinting squid flexes through sub's lights and then a second larger-sized group shoots past in the opposite direction. Crisscrossing back and forth, the squid appear to be searching for the source of the lights and are closing in on the sub fast.

Koko kicks back, presses herself as close to the hull as she can, and her air cylinder hits with a dull clank. Deliberately slowing her breathing—*piff-ahhh... piff-ahhh*—she inches her way along the flank, and like a squishy overgrown trumpet one of the polypods wraps around her head and rips her mask and regulator free.

Koko flails. The frenetic sucking sensations pawing her face quicken, and the bitter sting of cold water blinds her eyes. With her free hand, quickly Koko yanks the dive light from her shoulder and wags it out at arm's length, hoping to distract the squid gripping her head. At once there is a notable slacking and Koko releases the dive light. The face-hugging squid cuts away altogether, and pumps after the bright beam as the dive light spins end over end into the blackness below. Unable to see, and using her attached line, Koko drags herself back along the hull until she reaches the spot where she entered the water. Surfacing with a rush, she tears her way up the toe-holds and is nearly out of the water completely when a fumbling tentacle loops her right ankle like a whip.

Man, she's had just about enough of leechy calamari bullshit. Twisting about, Koko kicks wildly at the tentacle as the suction cups rip her scuba fin free from her foot. Grabbing a higher toe-hold, Koko pulls her weight upward right as a second giant tentacle lassos her other ankle like a slick cuff.

Oh, for the love of—

Swinging the bolt cutters, Koko pounds at the slimy feeler and just below the waterline, a single rimmed eye stares at her droopily. Rolling over, the massive squid stretches and exposes its carnivorous, basalt-colored beak as its other squiggling tentacles attach to the sub's hull. Veering riotously left, one of the tentacles whaps Koko square in the mouth.

Call her Ishmael?

Call me Ahab, sucker-puss.

Koko jabs the bolt cutter tip right in the attacking squid's eye.

Detaching, the giant squid retracts backward with a huge, vociferous splatter. Spewed ink and frigid seawater splatters Koko's face, and she doesn't give the beast a second shot at grabbing her. Climbing topside to the open hatch, Koko skips the convention of the ladder and drops down to the deck below. Jumping upward she grabs the hatch handle and then locks the hatch off.

"*Son of a bitch!*"

Koko kicks off her remaining scuba fin. Reeling forward and dripping, she slaps at the helm's controls.

No messing around this time.

Koko fires the engines, throttles back in full reverse, and the sub is free.

Ten minutes later and cruising forward at surface level, however, Koko learns the distressed rudder has affected additional operational mechanisms. A subsequent software shutdown has led to a chain reaction, culminating in seizure of the sub's deeper diving capacities. Maximum submersion depth? Two and half fathoms, barely over four meters. Running shallow and unable to dive deep, she and Flynn will be dead meat so close to the surface. Koko rips through the operational manuals.

Three hours of forced system quits, runbacks, reboots… nothing works.

THE SIXTY II

DISCUSSING DIRTY DEEDS

The next afternoon, Wire and the heavyset security officer she now knows as Horace Britch ride in the rear compartment of an SI security transport hovercraft. A sole additional security officer serves as the hovercraft's pilot and is silhouetted behind a partition of ballistic soundproof plastic two and a half fists thick.

As the hovercraft enters a banking turn, through a window slit in the rear of the compartment Wire can see the tops of palm trees rustling. She's grateful to be back in some clothes—not her own, naturally—and wears a yellow hemp-weaved detainee jumper with hand-woven buttons. The jumper is a size smaller than Wire would prefer and itchy as all get-out, but the size and itchiness are not as infuriating as the chains shackling her bare feet and wrists. Britch adjusts the gelatinous spread of his thighs on the bench seat across from her.

"So, once we understood we were witnessing an unusual security event, containment procedures were activated. To be honest, I half expected Martstellar to make a break for the resort air fields, as taking any number of flight craft would've been the fastest way off of The Sixty, even with our long-range batteries. Alas, the woman's creativity—"

Wire interrupts, “Creativity like what?”

“Well, first of all she initiated some confusion by digging out biometric identifiers. One of the release specialists, her own, and the wounded man Flynn’s. Together the release specialists led us on dueling chases in a cargo ute and on a terra-sled. This diversion began in a dead zone in The Sixty’s scanners, and it’s obvious to us now that Martstellar must’ve known about the technical oversight.” Britch tames an eyebrow with a finger. “After that she and Flynn got into an outdated access point and entered the maintenance tunnels beneath The Sixty.”

“These maintenance tunnels, that’s where she stole the submarine you mentioned?”

“Correct.”

Wire tongues her cheek. “Oh, man, and you call this high-priced tourist trap secure? You should’ve expected Martstellar to know about backdoors like that. Evasive training is second nature to someone like her.”

“Indeed. But you must understand, The Sixty is a massive operation. Utterly massive. The maintenance tunnels and lower support infrastructure rivals some of the major European flood zones. Naturally, we secure what we can, but there are over five hundred passages laced beneath the entire archipelago chain. The access point was simply overlooked.”

Wire jeers derisively. “What a crock. I don’t care if it’s five thousand access entries or tunnels, it’s still sloppy. And cutting out biometric identifiers? What is this? Some kind of half-assed amateur hour? Platelet-tagging is more reliable.”

“Pardon the pun, but the ship has sailed on all that. Shall I continue?”

Indifferent, Wire wiggles her fingers—whatever.

Britch drones boorishly on. “To preserve and maintain the islands’ support architectures, The Sixty operates a fleet of solo and two-person helmed submersibles. The short of it is that Martstellar and Flynn stole one of the larger capacity payload units, the variety our technicians use to service the rest of the fleet. Equipped for larger loads, these submarines cost twice as much as some of the smaller units, so they definitely chose wisely. With advanced calibrated fusion-drive capacities, the submarine they took? Fully submerged it's able to reach speeds topping out at fifty-five knots and has a range that's nearly worldwide."

"Meaning they're in the wind."

"Well, in the sea anyway."

Wire's chains clink as she weaves her fingers together. She cracks her knuckles. "Well, seeing that the world is three-quarters underwater and then some, how is this even remotely helpful to me?"

"Oh, I'm getting to that," Britch assures. "Once we understood what occurred we initiated trans-oceanic tracing sweeps as the stolen sub is equipped with a reliable GPS transponder."

"Great, so you *do* know where they are."

"To a point, yes, and to a point, no."

"Man, are you always this annoying?"

"I say only to a point because they disabled the transponder shortly after they escaped. What they didn't sort out until a short time later was that we have distance reach access to all the submarine's onboard navigations. Retroactively archived, I have records of all of their chart research. Of course when they realized this had happened they fried out this link as well."

Wire lets her eyes almost glaze over, almost. Goddamn, the monotonous, self-justifying minutia crawling from Britch's lips—it's the sort of mediocre babble that has always bored her to tears. And really, why is this waddling tub of dick telling her all this? Wire leans her head back against the compartment's padded wall. If only she were free of her restraints for a few delectable seconds, she could easily coil one of her forearms around Britch's neck and punch him in the face until his teeth jellied inward.

"Just sum it up for me," she says.

Delighted, Britch rubs his hands together. "All right, this is what I am proposing. I'd like an anonymous credit asset transfer from you. I've all the proper account codes ready, and once this transfer is confirmed, I promise to upload all the collected intel, the tracking records, Martstellar's last known chart headings, and so forth to wherever you receive your data, in return."

Wire scoffs. "Why the fuck would I do that?"

"Think of it as a quid pro quo arrangement."

"Oh, yeah? How's this for quid pro quo arrangement? How about I let your superiors here know you're a weaseling extortionist?"

"Now, now… me? A weaseling extortionist? This is a simple business transaction."

"Ohhh… a business transaction."

"Mmhm."

"But what about CPB's pursuit efforts, huh? You're telling me the CPB and The Sixty are just going to let these two numbskulls duck out on whatever contracts they have, boost one of their priciest submarines, and just let it go at that?"

"See, that's just what makes this offer so attractive for both of us."

"In what way?"

"You see in the grand scheme of things the directive has come down from on high to let this matter pass. Too much bad publicity and such. As you can imagine, the CPB has had more than enough trouble with Martstellar of late, and given the thorny history with her, the board of directors has decided not to engage in this matter further. Besides, the CPB has more than ample insurance to cover the cost of the submarine."

"Insurance on a fusion-powered sub? Damn, it must be nice to have that kind of juice."

"Have you ever looked at the CPB's holdings?"

"Not really, no."

"You should have a gander sometime. Just incredible. Now then, you're correct. The two fugitives' actions have violated their contractor agreements, and as a matter of course the CPB acquired and froze all of their assets. Given their hell-bent departure from The Sixty this was something the two couldn't possibly take care of in time, and added all together it's a trifling amount. But even if Martstellar was prepared with a back door, as you say, it's likely the two have limited resources stashed on their persons. They might choose to sell the submarine to shore up their liquidity. And if they don't end up selling the vessel and elect to abandon it, sooner or later someone acquiring it by salvage will re-activate the disabled transponder to see if it's operational, don't you see?"

"Most salvage operators have more sense than that. Reactivating a transponder would be like ringing the dinner bell."

"Perhaps, but then again some in the world's more uninhabitable fringes might not be so savvy."

"You mean de-civs."

"My, you're such the smart cookie."

Wire scowls. "You're talking some long freaking odds here, Britch."

"But you must admit, it is possible. So, what do you say? Interested?"

"I don't know. Maybe. Depends on this anonymous credit asset transfer."

Britch rests his own head against the compartment padding and pauses. "Look, I'm not greedy. I think fifty thousand credits is more than fair."

Wire feels like she's swallowed a shot of hot vinegar. "For *this*?"

"I'm taking a substantial risk here even propositioning you. And this is rock-solid intel. It's more than adequate to jumpstart your pursuit."

Wire leans forward. "I've got a better idea. Why don't you take this fifty large rock-solid ho-ha of yours, tie it up in a pretty bow, and stuff it up your pucker. Even if Martstellar is at large, you're forgetting one thing: I can just wait her out. I've got a whole psych profile lousy with her habits. Eventually she is going to turn up somewhere, and my resources will cost me a hell of a lot less than some fifty thousand delusion of yours."

"Hmm, I suspected you might feel that way. But here's another thing. This Ultimate Sanction status on Martstellar?" Britch beats a glance out the rear window slit of the hovercraft and then turns back. "I've checked into this. The order is not exclusive. I can easily leak all this to other hungry bounty agents, if you find my offer so repulsive."

Wire's eyes move back and forth.

Shit.

"But what if they scuttle the submarine?"

"Scuttle it?"

"Yeah, did you think of that? If they scuttle the sub and no one ends up finding it, then where would I be with your weaker than spit intel offer?"

"At a solid starting point."

"I could just beat it out of you."

Like a deranged crow, Britch cackles. "Oh, really now? How outré. And when would this supposed torment take place exactly? Do you really think you'll ever set foot on The Sixty again after this monumental bungling of yours? Again, you should've read the finer details of your reservation agreement. There are at least five paragraphs covering deportation proceedings with follow-up restrictions. Despite whatever vitriolic judgments you have of me, The Sixty or the CPB, the terms of your deportation includes a fatal consequence clause. If you ever appear again within The Sixty's confines or even our airspace, make no mistake, this will be acted upon. Expediency is the marrow of my position here, and the choice is now yours. We should be arriving at your transport vessel shortly."

Wire shakes her head. There is no way in a cold, deep, stinking hell she's giving this jerk-off fifty thousand credits, not even if it gets her Martstellar's head on a silver platter tomorrow. True, it'll probably take her a little more time to locate her and close out the contract, but seriously, is this guy totally out of his mind?

"I think I'll pass."

"You're not interested at all?"

"Nope. Not at all."

"Oh, I really think you should reconsider."

Wire lifts her fists and gives Britch the finger—both barrels. "Eat shit and die, piggy."

Britch sighs. The hovercraft's engines whine, and the craft enters a twenty-degree turn. After a long pensive moment, Britch slowly lifts up his right hand as though he's about to take an oath. Given the back and forth spirit of their talk, the gesture is weirdly atypical, and Wire's eyes flit briefly to the hand. Seizing her lapse in judgment, Britch quickly leans forward and stabs a pressure syringe with his other hand into Wire's knee.

Wire heaves back. "GAH! What did you just stick me with?!"

Britch tucks the spent pressure syringe into the breast pocket of his uniform and sits back. "That," he says, pointing, "is an incentive."

"A what?"

"A neural toxin. Untraceable, the serum is designed to spread severe damage to all four major lobes of your brain. When the toxin takes full effect it'll render you into a vegetative state for the rest of your miserable life. You ought to feel the initial effects, well, right about now."

Wire thrashes against her restraints.

"At first you'll feel some mild euphoria followed by momentary disorientation, and then an alarming weakening of muscle control along with a heightened body temperature. I've an antidote mixed with a powerful sedative that will keep you sedated until you reach Surabaya if you want it."

"Why you fat, slimy, four-flushing, piece of—"

"I tried to reason with you, but honestly you insist on being stubborn. If you want me to administer the antidote, act quickly and transmit the sum I've outlined via this handheld uplink to my private off-world accounts." Britch pulls his data tab from the sleeve on his belt. "Oh, and don't forget your flowcode address in the field at the bottom."

Wire squeezes her eyes shut. As the seconds pass, each sensation Britch just described passes through her body in terrible, creeping curls. The tingling paralysis spreads first, fingers then toes, and then her body temperature skyrockets. Despite her best efforts to remain upright, Wire slumps over in her seat.

"You won't get away with this."

"I won't? Please. I'll say you got free of your restraints and the use of force was necessary. Perhaps you hit your head as I valiantly subdued you and *voila*! Selective organ harvesting, here we come."

Wire clenches her teeth. "I am so going to kill you."

"Look, I don't get why you're being so obstinate. Just give me what I want, and I'll administer the antidote and forward our records along, I promise. Don't worry. Even a primate specimen like yourself can navigate the rudimentary interface on the data tab screen." He holds out the device and giggles. "See? All primed and ready to go. Just type in fifty thousand credits in the box marked sum and engage the transfer symbol on the bottom right-hand side."

Britch tosses the data tab at her and the device lands next to Wire's head. Awash in misery and half of her vision doubling, Wire barely musters together the coordination to pick the damned data tab up.

Goddamn it all to hell...

As she fixes her swimmy gaze on the screen, beneath Wire's breastplate walls start to smother her lungs. Looking up at Britch's dull, insouciant eyes, she has no doubt what the bastard told her about the neural toxin is true. Death feels close. It feels closer than it's ever felt before. Her ocular hangs on, but the rest of her vision grays as she realizes she doesn't have a choice. Using the numeric keys, slowly Wire thumbs in the right credit amounts and adds one of her shadow flowcode addresses in the address field.

Wire presses the icon on the bottom right to finalize the uplink and a trilling chirp confirms the transaction. Britch rips the data tab from her hands.

"There now, was that so hard?"

Wire's tongue swells like a sausage. "Thheantidoooooo..."

"Oh, right."

Britch removes a second syringe from his breast pocket and

pauses to check whether he has selected the right one. Parrying carefully in case Wire thrusts for his neck with a last ounce of strength, he leans over and sticks the second syringe into Wire's knee and frees the sedative-antidote with a quick *pfhht.*

As antidote enters her bloodstream, relief rides the rhumba beat of Wire's quickened pulse. Within seconds her heart slows and the soporific sedative starts to take effect.

Smiling with smug satisfaction, Britch sleeves the data tab on his duty belt, and when Wire's eyelids close he stands and kicks her in the face.

"Have fun in Surabaya."

THE COMMONAGE I

THREE DAYS LATER
(SO THIS IS WHAT IT'S LIKE)

STORM SYSTEM 61.9-Theta–Northern Pacific
Central Pressure — 964 mb
Forward Speed — 15-25 knots
Sustained Wind Speed — 80-112 knots
Storm Surge — 5.5-6 meters
CLASSIFICATION: **HAZARDOUS**

The worst storms are always monsters.

With a backpack slung across her shoulders, a girl of thirteen years runs through the screaming, rain-swept dark. Cutting right, cutting left, and cutting right again the girl weaves around the broken, piebald vestiges of what was once a modest manufacturing municipality fixed along the North American prohib coast.

Taking a slippery, moss-covered set of stairs two at a time, through the heavy rain and darkness the girl sees torch beams not too far behind. A quick count of the lights tells her there are least five groups, maybe more, and she hears muffled snatches of barking.

It's a search party. Someone must have seen her leaving the

Commonage. And they've brought along the compound's lone synthetic canine, a blue-furred Mastiff named Gammy.

It's bad news, but her pursuers bringing along Gammy makes sense. No doubt by now the diagnostic capacities hardwired in the dog's pronounced snout have all but confirmed her location and heading. Taking off again, the girl fights back her panic and runs faster.

Moving upward through the larger, cordoned sections of the ruined landscape, the girl is knocked sideways by a vertical downdraft. She tastes the dank toxic tang of the ocean on her tongue and with relief realizes she's now less than quarter of a kilometer from the cliffs along the sea.

You've come too far to stop.

You'll never have another chance at this.

Never.

A minute more of running flat out and she reaches the cliffs. The Pacific's booming violence is shocking and more than the girl could have imagined. Massive spellbinding troughs of churning froth twelve to twenty meters in height wallop the rocks and shoreline over and over. After hurrying through a thicket along the cliffs' edge, she locates her stowed-away gear lodged behind two boulders: a second lumbar pack that converts into a sleeping pouch filled with high-caloric rations, along with two canteens of water. The girl buckles the lumbar pack around her waist, clips on the canteens, and removes the backpack from her shaking shoulders.

From the backpack's main compartment, she withdraws a wound length of line and lashes one end around her waist with a double hitch knot, and then fastens one of four homemade hooks to the lead end of the line with another knot. The line and hooks are her safety apparatuses. Yes, it'll be a challenge to make her way along the cliff trail for sure, but the search party with Gammy in tow? Without securing hooks with tied-in lines, the gusts will be too much for them. They'd be crazy to follow.

As she jams her body sideways into the trail's first tight pass, the girl's thoughts pulsate. Imagine, no more Commonage. No more stupid collective edicts, no more spouting the hypocritical babble her parents are so fond of, and, most important, no more Sébastien or Dr. Corella. It's the last point that strengthens her resolve. No more Sébastien and his puzzling creepiness or Dr. Corella's phony compassion; those two and all their terrible, warped plans.

Eight meters in and the initial trail switchback is her first real test. Girding herself and pressing her body as close to the rock face as possible, with her right hand the girl lifts the hook end of the line. The switchback's turn is sharp and fully exposed on the rounding, and when she peers around the edge her eyes get stung by a full-on sock of whipping spray. The girl lifts the lead end of the line and reaches out for a crag when a deafening wail drills through the watery roar.

A quick glance at the storm-thrashed waves reveals an incomprehensible sight. A thousand meters out, a black-marbled wave of astounding size is pierced from below by a submarine. Skate-shaped with floodlights alight along its curved flanks, the breaching vessel bellies down the wave's face and, as its bow dips, lambent phosphorescent engines in its stern shriek with the sudden exposure to the air. Breaking, the wave becomes a dooming avalanche of white water and propels the sub forward.

Behind the girl, suddenly a beam of light splits the darkness and her heart leaps into her throat. Torn-away cries beg her to stop, and she can hear Gammy barking. Cringing, the girl adjusts her hold for only a second, and slips.

After all her preparation, after all her meticulous mental rehearsals, her failure to hook into a crag is a mortifying error. Like an invisible hand, a hard blast of wind yanks her backward and out.

Inexplicably, the final moments of the young girl's life are everything and nothing all at once—hyperconscious pulling the world together and apart at the speed of light.

Everything is fear.

Everything is loss.

Everything is beauty and sadness and regret with the possibility of unimaginable pain moments away.

No one will be able to stop Sébastien and Dr. Corella now. She's failed.

The submarine crosses the girl's line of sight twice just before it collides and inverts on the rocks below.

Last thought:

So this is what it's like to die…

AGROUND

With a jackhammering slam and metallic squeal the submarine's endless nauseating churning stops—*KA-BAM*! And like that, Koko's entire subaquatic world is upside down.

She's lashed securely in the pilot's seat in the sub's forward bridge, her legs and arms dangling out, a meat chandelier. Stupefied by the impact, she's still able to judge that she's intact. Bruised ribs, seasick to beat the band, and upside down, but, yeah, still miraculously intact. No dislocations or broken bones, she thinks, though there's no way to know for sure until she gets down from the bridge deck and pilot's seat that is now, in effect, the sub's ceiling. With a deflating croon, the sub's fusion engines power down and then cut off. Emergency backup lighting in the cabin sputters on and a pinwheeling tangerine wash cycles all around.

Like an ogre's punch, a wave hurtles into the sub's stern and one by one the cabin lights start to fail. Outside the bow screen, the view is blacker than black, with a re-forming slide of white bubbles shifting in abstract. Koko believes she can make out the edge of a surface of some kind. Greenish rock, kelp peppered with white.

Are those... barnacles?

Oh, shit—we've run aground.

Another wave hits and with a stomach-turning creak it slowly spins the sub around like a turtle flipped on its back. Koko then detects an unmistakable pressure differential and a shrill, cold whistle pouring past her ears. A briny stench and then another noise that's muculent at first and then rushing.

The hull has been breached.

Koko looks back for Flynn and sees he's still inverted and lashed into a makeshift berth in the submarine's narrowed stern section. All wadded up in his puffy lifejacket, he still mercifully looks out of it, as he has been for days with the spread of his infection. Like a morbid party balloon, Flynn's head hangs at a terrible angle.

A third wave erupts on the hull and terror grabs Koko by the throat. Beneath her feet, an eddying slosh of water rises.

Koko gropes for the clip on the pilot seat's safety harness. Freeing a buckled lever, she crashes brutally into the vessel's ceiling-now-deck. The impact sends an ache up her leg like it's been popped with a meat mallet, and she feels something hard pressing into her back. It's a ruptured metallic edge torn free. Koko rolls over and pushes up, scurrying hand over hand into the rising broth aft.

Water now seems to be leaking from everywhere, and it feels colder than Koko ever thought possible. Her fingers unsteady, she desperately claws at the knots of webbed lines holding Flynn in place. When did she tie him down? Was that two days ago? Three? It was just after they hit something and the submarine's steering went straight to hell, right before they entered the outer bands of the massive storm.

Flynn's weight keeps the lines taught, and no matter what Koko tries it's impossible to work the knots free.

She needs a knife.

But their bug-out packs and the rest of the vessel's maintenance tackle and tools are stowed in the lockers in the engine access area—now completely submerged under the mounting water. Koko can't get to it in time. Another wave hits and the blow drives her beneath the rising water. She springs up and clings to Flynn's bindings. Sparks snap and shower down.

There's no time.

Koko tears at the knots with her teeth. If she can just loosen half of them she could wrestle Flynn out of the makeshift berth. But then what? Wrestle him out to where? Where are they?

About to drown, that's where.

She stops biting and shakes Flynn's shoulders.

"Flynn! Baby! Wake up! You have to wake up!"

A feeble mutter and then nothing.

Koko falls back into the water. She trudges forward toward the bridge and studies the consoles above her. Just behind the pilot's seat, she sees a recessed rectangle with a scuffed patch outlining a set of emergency instructions. A red plastic lever is on the port side of the rectangle, and from flipping through an operational manual earlier, Koko knows the lever will trigger an explosive charge that'll blow an escape hatch just behind the pilot's seat. The escape hatch isn't the way Flynn and Koko boarded this miserable, sinking coffin a week ago, but now that they're upside down, it sure as hell is their only way out.

Koko braces herself against the starboard-side electronics. Clasping the handle with both hands, she takes a counterintuitive pull and releases the charge. When the bolts blow, in the sub's tight confines, it is like a small cannon going off. Ears ringing, Koko tumbles back to the ceiling/deck again as a weir of water cascades down from above.

Koko splashes her way back to Flynn as the overwhelming finality of their predicament sinks in. Even if she does get Flynn free from where he's tied in, he's unconscious and there's no way she can lift his body out of the submarine all by herself. Maybe with a strap or pulley, but it would take time to fashion such a measure even under the best of conditions.

Shit—this can't be it.

It can't.

I won't leave you.

But then—a loud sound clanging from above and a shout.

"*YOU!*"

Spinning around, Koko loses her footing and again slips under the mounting water. She lunges upward, pawing at her eyes and questioning whether what she's seeing is real. In a red poncho, half of a man reaches out to her through the newly blown hatch.

Before she can say anything the man throws a black snake at her, and then holds both of his hands to the sides of his mouth.

"Tie that off under his shoulders! Do it now or you're both dead!"

Dumbfounded, Koko sees that the thrown snake is not a snake at all, but a thick length of line. Quickly she picks up the line and yells back.

"I can't get him free!"

"What?!"

"His weight! The knots are too tight, and I can't get him free! I need a knife!"

Another wave detonates on the hull and the swirling tangerine-tinted wash of light goes black. The man in the red poncho slithers out just as another huge torrent of seawater floods down into the sub's cabin. A moment later he reappears, and on a hand-signal count of three, he tosses Koko a rod encased in black rubber. Koko catches the rod and looks at it with awe: a battery-powered ignition tool. She presses a button and a triangular-shaped prong slides out, glows yellow, then red, then hot white.

Eight minutes later Koko, a band of men, and a large blue dog are moving to higher, rocky ground away from the wreck and waves. With the incessant wind and driving rain, their progress is brutal, and they cover the ground mere meters at a time. Koko and the men share the load: Flynn's body and the body of a young, dead girl.

HE'S GOT THE FEVER

Delirium.

Haptic pulsing gyres of fevered misery.

A seeping chilly wetness, mouthing Flynn's clothes and flesh all over. And then hands on him.

Wait—hands? Whose hands?

A burn close to his skin and then the helpless sensation of a gallows drop. Next, a series of hard jerks and bindings across his chest and under his useless, limp arms.

Water.

So much water.

Cold, cold water and dragging.

A bitter taste of compounds in his mouth and an acrid, salted slurry funneling up his nose. A reflexive esophageal clamp and warm bile overflows.

More dragging.

Up. Up.

Over sharp shapes.

Up. Up.

The bindings tear at his body. Whatever or whoever has him

won't let go and now—*oh God*—it's up again. Up into a realm of expansive air and roaring water. He drops once more and each hoist, each knock, each drag amplifies the countless dull aches in his bones.

Flynn wishes for the boundless, sleek nothingness of all things dreamless. To be nothing, to just take one last, deep heave of the lungs and give up. But the torment has no end.

His ears sing and memory cells fire. A line Flynn once read or heard somewhere, some place long, long ago comes to him. Something about bells.

The bells of hell go ting-a-ling-a-ling for you but not for me...

Shakespeare?

No. Something else. Soldiers? No, that's not it.

Airmen. Yes, an airmen's song. Something sang in some long-forgotten war.

I was an airman of sorts once, wasn't I? Living in the sky?

But now there're no bells, only the keening in his ears, the unremitting roar of water and air, the slow thumping pump of his heart denying him oblivion's release.

Stupid heart.

More wracking tremors, and the air blowing against his face feels roomy and cold. Heavy rain rakes his body. Flynn hears people shouting, their words swirling and lost in the crashing wind.

Where am I?

Why oh why don't they just let me be?

When Flynn's spine twists in a way it was never designed to, his eyes fly open with pure anguish. Half awake, he realizes he's no longer in the submarine and is now being battered around on the cold, slippery steel of the outer hull. Such powerful deluges of water, so ceaseless. Flynn closes his eyes again and lets the groping hands take him. Stubby fingers pulling his shivering meat away in foaming water. Fingers pry open one of his eyelids and a fluid sweep of a light like a comet's trail scorches his retina and is gone.

A granule of brackish grit forces another vicious coughing jag, and Flynn perceives a face close to his own. For one last time, he dares a look and sees bright green irises, frazzled with exhaustion and worry. A perfect, sweet little nose…

Koko?

"Flynn, we made it!"

Koko… Kooookkkkk—

A smart smack across his cheek. Then another. And another.

"Don't you die on me, you son of a bitch! Don't you dare die on me! Hang on!"

Hang on? Hang on to what?

To this?

This sucks.

SÉBASTIEN MAXX

Propped up on his bed and stripped to the waist, Sébastien Maxx is listening to the raging winds outside his shuttered windows, when a series of quick knocks jerks him free of his thoughts.

The knocking is at the outer door of Sébastien's adjoining office. Fastidiously arranged and painted stark white, the larger adjacent area connects to his darker and more masculine appointed bedroom through a set of French-styled glass doors. Sébastien gets up, plucks his pale-brown tunic from the foot of the bed, and hauls it on.

"Just a moment..."

Now that he's answered, Sébastien takes his time arranging himself. It's nice to know that whoever is at the door would gladly wait one minute, one hour, one day if he so requested, because such is his cachet as the Commonage's alleged leader. After tossing back a mane of long, graying hair, he fastens the top button on his pants and crosses into his office in socked feet. With a finger swipe in the air, he kills the power feeding the blue projection screens at his desk and then switches on a floor lamp. Driven rain crackles against the room's shuttered windows. As Sébastien opens the door with a brisk snap, he prays whoever is calling is delivering good news.

Stout and lean like a pair of Greco-Roman wrestlers, two identical men in red ponchos stand just outside the door. It's Eirik and Bonn, colloquially referred to at the Commonage as "the twins." Their ponchos drip and Eirik, always the more confident of the two, is the first to speak.

"Our apologies for disturbing you, Sébastien, but the search party returned ten minutes ago."

Sébastien jogs his head once before turning around and moving toward his desk. After settling in a heavy wooden chair, he laces his fingers on his chest and sits back to absorb their report.

"I trust the search party was successful," Sébastien says.

Eirik looks briefly at Bonn and then back at Sébastien.

"I'm sorry, but something terrible happened. It's Kumari... She's dead."

The revelation is a nitrous-sharp shock. He sits forward, grasping the arms of his chair.

What? No—the search party had their instructions. They were supposed to subdue Kumari, bring her discreetly back to the Commonage... but dead? How could this be?

"Dear God, what the hell happened?"

"She fell."

"Fell? From what? Where?"

"The cliffs along the ocean just beyond the ruins," Eirik replies. "We were close, but something went wrong. We lost her before we could pull her to safety. I'm sorry."

Laboring to assemble his thoughts, Sébastien drops his head into his hands.

"Where is she now?"

"Her body is downstairs in the infirmary. We woke Dr. Corella when we returned, and he has her. The doctor advised us to inform you immediately."

Sébastien leans forward and places his hands flush on the desk. "Please tell me Kumari's parents haven't been notified."

"No, Dr. Corella thought it best that you saw her first."

Sébastien's eyes ping back and forth. Drawing in a deep lungful of air, he stands and swallows the hot bulge building in his throat.

"Thank you," he says quietly. "You two can go now. Tell Dr. Corella I need a few minutes. This, my God. I can't believe it. Kumari is dead? I don't want to believe it."

Eirik takes a step. "There's something else too. There's been a shipwreck."

"A shipwreck? Where? When?"

"Below the cliffs. The wreck occurred when we were trying to reach Kumari."

"But out here? Impossible."

"No, it's true. We don't know if it's commercial or militarized, but it's a fusion-powered submarine. It came in from the southwest."

"Are there survivors?"

Eirik nods vigorously. "Just two," he says. "A man and a woman, and the man is in bad shape. The female survivor, she attacked some people down in the infirmary when we returned. Dr. Corella has her sedated and Gammy is guarding her."

"Did you say *attacked*?"

"There were injuries."

Sébastien gets up and quickly moves around his desk. He steams toward his bedroom.

"Tell Dr. Corella I'm on my way. I want you two and anyone connected to the search party to assemble in the infirmary and wait there until I arrive. No exceptions. I want to debrief everyone. We need to figure out what happened and who these survivors are before the whole Commonage loses their heads."

Sébastien returns from his bedroom with a pair of laceless black boots. He drops into his desk chair again and pulls the boots on one after the other and then lifts his eyes.

"What're you waiting for?"

Eirik adjusts his posture. "Well, the search party also detected some unusual movement on their way out to find Kumari. It seems a band of de-civ migrants have taken up a position deep within the woods beyond the western edge of the Commonage."

Boots now on, Sébastien sits back in his chair. "How many?"

"A few dozen, maybe more. It was hard to get an accurate read, but it might be a larger group. The encampment is set up about a kilometer from here."

Sébastien waves a hand, indicating this additional information, while troubling, is not a priority.

"We've had de-civ transients cross through the area before. They've probably just been caught off guard and got disoriented by the storm. God, Kumari is dead, a shipwreck, and migrants? Let's take one crisis at a time, shall we? What time is it?"

"A little after three A.M."

Sébastien turns and listens to the wind outside again. "The models indicate the storm should be dying down soon. My bet is these de-civs will probably move on when the weather clears, but please keep me apprised if their status changes. I want a second search party ready to go back to this sub's wreck within the hour. We need to see what's what."

The two brothers bow and leave, closing the door behind them.

Sébastien drags a finger through the air and activates his projection screens. He cues up his personal communication links, and with several additional hand motions enlarges four sub-screens on his arrays. With a clawed hand he expands several satellite charts, checking the storm's present direction and rotation. His previous assessment of the weather's ebbing strength is accurate. The extended front shows dissipation and the storm is heading inland. He checks the surrounding area's offshore restriction measures, and is disturbed to discover that, because of the storm's intensity, there was a minor fluctuation in offshore communication uplinks. The break jibes perfectly with the timing of the wreck. Furious, he addresses his systems out loud.

"Priority assimilation of all known submersible crafts worldwide: commercial, private, and militarized with complete breakdown of onboard schematics. Addendums: retrieve a listing of all distress transponder communications filtered for the northern Pacific region for the past seventy-two hours before storm manifestation to present. Realign all and confirm all offshore and air-space restrictions."

SURABAYA, INDONESIA I

THE DEPORTATION SUCK

On a scale from one to ten, with one being pretty bad and ten being a grisly incubus of horror obliterating rational thought, waking up to a pair of rats gnawing your lower lip definitely levels Wire's dial at ten point nine.

Flopping over into a puddle, Wire screams. The rat hinged on her lip is nearly a kilo in weight and unflustered by the minor disruption to its meal. Its pinkish tail switching across her throat, Wire grabs the rat with both hands and with her thumbs she probes the creature's vibrating cranium. Sinking her thumbnails into the rat's eyeballs, she pops them inward like pair of pomegranate seeds.

A weepy shriek, and the rat spins off. There are dozens more rats swarming all over her, so Wire surges and vaults to her feet with a primeval snarl. Vermin drop off her in a dark sheet and she lurches left, collapsing into a mound of cabbage trimmings. She crawls backward on the steamy rot as four additional rats burrowed high in her yellow jumper tumble out and across her bare feet.

Wire's hand goes instinctively for her waist.

No gun. Fuck.

The disappointment of being unarmed is crushing. Picking

herself up, she reels from side to side down a smoke-strewn alley, the pack of rats trailing gleefully behind.

Howls of laughter above, and Wire looks up into an unwholesome revolution of dark faces. Beneath a hot, pearly cervical scar of sky and sagging laundry lines, slum dwellers—brown-skinned old women, deformed men, and children with hand-rolled chemical cigarettes chomped in snaggle-toothed mouths—laugh. They point fingers at her as they lean their scrawny bodies out of holes cut into stacked, rust-ribbed shipping containers. The alley is a nest of vermin itself, chock-full of the marginally re-cived and Indonesian damned.

Wire blunders ahead and soon the rats following lose interest in her. A hundred meters up ahead, the alley intersects with a larger road and Wire runs toward the gap. There's something wrong with her right eye, and she blinks to clear her vision, but the dull fog does not improve. A glass bottle hits her square in the back and shatters.

Reaching the mouth of the alley, Wire checks herself. In addition to no shoes on her gnawed feet, her pockets are empty. No credits, nothing save for the itchy, undersized jumper given to her back on The Sixty. A throbbing ache in her jaw telegraphs an additional misery. Using her tongue to probe, she realizes some enterprising scum has pried loose two of her molar fillings. She lifts a hand to the side of her skull, and it becomes apparent why her vision is muddled. The surface hardware of her ocular implant has been pried free and, like cacti needles, raw frays of ripped-out filaments barb outward.

A few meters in front of her and on her immediate right there's a dwarf pushing a bamboo cart on vulcanized rubber tires. The dwarf's head is strikingly disproportionate to the rest of his small body, and his tattooed skull is speckled with a raised paisley pattern. Laden with sealed packages of homemade candied foodstuffs and several tiered racks of multicolored tubes of super-tea, the cart is an oasis. Wire sways forward and grabs a tube of tea. She twists off the tube's cap and gulps all the warm liquid down as the dwarf barks.

Wire studies the raised paisley pattern on the dwarf's head: a shark and a crocodile circling each other in a dance of death.

Wire finishes her super-tea and looks around. The larger thoroughfare at the intersection amounts to a street market in full swing: a sweltering bedlam of marquees, makeshift stalls, and oily dung fires that run as far as she can see. Merchandise of all kinds. Reed rugs, repurposed electronics, bone bracelets, pickled baby fire lizards in huge translucent flagons, and hundreds of oversized baskets of rice. The choked ambiance is predatory and chaotic, and suddenly the dwarf gives Wire's hip a hard push. The hell if she understands the charmless, clickety vowels juddering from his toothy pie-hole, but Wire makes a motion that she's willing to pay for her tea and then drapes a hand around her back like she's going for a wallet. The dwarf grins expectantly.

Wire lets go of the empty tea tube, swings a *shutō-uchi* strike and breaks three cervical vertebrae in the dwarf's neck. Like a puppet cut loose from his strings, the small man shrivels to the ground.

Wire's earlier appraisal of the market's nature is right on the money.

No one cares.

She reaches down and hauls the dwarf up by his soggy armpits. The man's unctuous frame is heavier than she expects, but Wire sits him on the edge of the bamboo cart without his body toppling over. Wire pats his cheekbones a few times, mimicking an effort to rouse him as if he's just fainted and then ransacks his pockets. In a right pocket, she finds an electronic credit receiver and a satchel of fiber coins. Wire sets these items aside on the cart's ledge, and searching the dwarf's threadbare morning coat she discovers a cheap leather purse. When Wire draws back the talon zipper on the purse a crystal cube the size of a shot glass is activated and rises in the air. Within the cube there's an image revolving in a three hundred and sixty degree spin—a sickly woman and two children. It's a family portrait keepsake, and the soft, hollow notes of a bonang kettle can be heard.

Wire stuffs the cube back in the leather purse and discards it under the cart. Lifting the dwarf from the cart's edge, she looks for a place nearby to dispose of his body. She sees a pile of wooden pallets being broken down by a man who feeds the split pallet pieces into a fire. Wire props the dwarf against the pile of pallets, and the man doesn't give her a second glance as he cracks another board over his knee.

Wire takes up the cart's cloth-wrapped crossbar. As she pushes forward into the market throngs, her mind races—thinking: *priorities.*

First, she needs to access her personal credit accounts and data stores, and fast. The dwarf's fiber coins, his electronic credit receiver, plus all the merchandise on his cart should be more than enough to score her a basic ocular implant repair at a tech bodega, so she starts scanning the area for someone to lay the cart's merchandise off on. Once she gets her ocular back online and accesses her personal accounts, getting the rest of her immediate needs fulfilled should be a snap. Not far ahead, she makes out a clutch of people crowded around a street auctioneer. From the assorted wares being put up for bid, the auctioneer's circle seems a good place to start.

Second priority: medical attention. Rat bites equal infection, and who knows how long she had been left to die in that alley, or how long those noxious, greasy rodents had been feasting on her. With the ulcerating lacerations up and down her shins, she envisions viruses and whole seeping cultures of grotesque bacteria. Tasting the gash on her lip where the big one took its last taste before she blinded it, Wire shudders. Definitely a full clinical work up. Complete transfusions, arterial scrub, and super-sized antibiotic-vitamin cocktail to get her back on the mend. After that Wire pictures a long, disinfectant drench in a bath. Food might go a long way toward helping her deplorable state too, and her stomach burbles when she catches a whiff of garlicky bats frying in a nearby stall. Wire can't remember the last time she ate. Britch refused to feed her on The Sixty, so it's been more than a couple of days since her last good caloric intake.

Third and fourth priorities: clean clothes and a place to rest. After all she has been through, splurging on a first-rate hotel is a must. Room service with secure uplink amenities so she can scour her networks and see who the hell swings the big stick in this Surabayan hell hole. A soft bed sounds like a dream. A mini bar, heaven.

Of course, the rest of her priorities are pretty clear after that.

Get armed.

Get mobile.

Get Martstellar.

THE COMMONAGE II

WAKEY, WAKEY

When she comes round, the first thing Koko notices is a dim mosaic of lights overhead, row after row of alternating slates arranged like a massive chessboard. Realizing instantly she's strapped down from head to toe, Koko is definitely in no mood for games.

As she struggles against her restraints, somewhere off and down past her feet a dog barks three times. Koko figures it must be the blue synthetic that accompanied the group that saved her and Flynn, keeping an eye on her. The lights above grow bright and a door opens. She hears the hushed sound of rubber twisting on a tiled floor, followed by a doglike whine and heavy panting.

"Gammy, wait outside."

Trotting claws and the door closes. A second later there's the empty slap of an electrified latch.

"Ah, you're awake," a man says. "Good, that's good. Would you like a drink of water?"

A mechanism is engaged and whatever Koko is strapped to hums beneath her. Gradually, she's raised up in suspension, and when she catches her reflection in some tinted glass across the way she sees her clothes are gone and she's dressed in a cropped paper examination gown, trussed up like Frankenstein's monster.

Koko's bloodshot eyes roam the room. Handled glass-faced cabinets, two glowing projection screens that look to be running her vitals, and an assortment of additional chirring apparatus that all but scream medical facility. She recalls how earlier the group that rescued her and Flynn said they needed to take them to the infirmary, so Koko assumes that's where she's being held. A bleachy smell of disinfectant cuts through the crust in her nose.

Near the door, a man with long, graying hair stands. Early fifties or late forties, he's super lean and has the reserved, nonchalant look of someone who's used to being in charge. Dressed in a loose almost tan kurta-like tunic V-ed at the neck, and tough canvas pants stuffed into plain black boots, he wears numerous bracelets around his wrists and appears to be unarmed. The man moves forward and holds out a square, light-blue plastic container, its top pierced with a straw.

"I said, would you like a drink of water?"

Koko just stares.

The man continues, "First off, I want you to know that you are safe. We regret having to use restraints, but I'm told you put up quite a fight earlier. Not exactly appreciative behavior to those who've saved you. Two of those you attacked have subdural hematomas and hairline skull fractures. Dr. Corella relayed your diagnostics and confirmed right cranial scarring area consistent with ocular implant technology. From this I must assume you are or were once a soldier."

Koko blinks once and says nothing.

The man shakes the plastic container again. "Water?"

Running her tongue over her chapped lips, Koko licks a niggling cold sore and thinks, *When was the last time I had fresh water? Two days ago?* Her circadian rhythms are all screwed up, it might be longer. Her mouth tastes like it's been dabbed dry with sour cotton. She's so thirsty. Reluctantly, she nods.

The man treads forward slowly until he positions himself on her immediate right. With care, he lowers the straw to her lips and Koko draws hard. To say the liquid tastes better than kissing the astral plane would be an insult to the delusion of poets. Pure, distilled, and iodized perhaps, but then again—you never know about such things. The water could be contaminated. Koko's bodily needs trample her suspicions like a rodeo clown. She sucks greedily until the container splutters hollow.

So thirsty.

The man steps back, pulls up a caster-based stool, and sits.

"Call me old-fashioned, but I think it's best to start with introductions. My name is Sébastien Maxx and here are the facts. Your submarine wrecked on a restricted coastal area. By restricted I mean this place is located along the northwestern portion of the North American prohibs, and there's no good reason anyone on Earth should even be coming remotely close to these coordinates. If you cooperate, we're in a position to assist you. We mean neither you nor your companion any harm. Now then, I'll allow you a chance to speak. Can you tell me your name?"

Koko rolls her eyes upward and remains silent.

"All right, can you at least tell me where you're from?"

Koko licks her lips. "Well, hold on, let me think. Oh, yeah, now I remember. I'm from a little place called fuck off, ever hear of it?"

The man calling himself Sébastien presents an unruffled, tolerant gaze.

"Look, the storm you two just survived was gargantuan. We've been aware of this massive low-pressure system's approach for days, and the fact that you came through it in one piece is nothing short of astounding. Even now the storm's effects are producing a number of offshore waterspouts. You want to be glib? You want to be hostile? Fine, but make no mistake: you are both lucky to be alive."

"Is that so?"

"It is. And the man with you, while he's out of danger now, was very close to death."

Koko's brow crinkles.

Oh, hell—Flynn.

"Where is he?" Koko asks.

Sébastien shakes the empty water container. "Nearby. The wound in his leg has spread severe sepsis throughout his body and may have gone so far as to affect his cognitive functions, but is now being treated aggressively."

"Aggressively? Aggressively by who?"

"Trust me, he's in good hands."

"I don't trust anyone. Doctors especially."

"A common sentiment."

"So where the hell are we?"

"Our infirmary. This facility is part of the Commonage."

Koko blows out a breath and closes her eyes. "That means nothing to me."

"Nevertheless, it is where you happen to be."

Pulling together her best weapons-grade stare, Koko opens her eyes.

"Listen, *fuckstick—*"

"Sébastien."

"*Listen, fuckstick.* If you consider a beating heart essential, untie me and take me to see my friend *now.*"

Sébastien tsks. "I promise, you'll see him in time, but first things first, all right? I need specifics. Why have you come here? Are you from a corporate alliance? What are your objectives in the area?"

The water has loosened Koko's throat up, but her mouth is still gummy. She wants more water and could drink a couple of gallons without pause if she had the chance, but she resists asking for it.

No.

Stay strong.

Whatever they gave you before, your fatigue and everything else, it's affecting your judgment.

Hang on, Flynn.

Just hang on.

"Our situation isn't like that at all."

"Oh, really? Then what's it like?"

Koko sucks in a breath and holds it. "I want. To see. My friend. *First.*"

"You will, but only if you answer my questions."

"Man, you're making a big mistake."

"Am I?"

"Yeah. You've got us all wrong."

"But wrong how? Please, outside these walls there's nothing of commercial value in this area, and believe me, I would know. My people told me your craft looked to be of significant worth, but was incapable of flight, so that rules out the lower orbits of the Second Free Zone. Fusion-powered, it can't be yours personally." Sébastien sighs. "If you can't be forthcoming, you're putting me in a difficult position. More important, you're putting your friend in a difficult position. The safety of those within the Commonage is paramount to me. Outsiders are not something we readily accept. If you elect not to answer, I'll have to desist in helping you."

"I thought you just said you don't do anyone harm."

"Consider my position."

"So, what? You're threatening me now?"

"I'm being candid. Believe me, this was the last thing I expected to handle today."

"Maybe if I had some more water…"

Sébastien pushes the stool back, sways to his feet, and crosses the room. At a sink, he opens a spigot and fills the empty container with a stream of fresh water. Then he walks back, holds the straw to Koko's lips once more and she drinks.

"Once more from the top," Sébastien says.

Draining the container, Koko tries to picture Flynn. She imagines a fussy gaggle of medical personnel fawning all over him, monitoring his delicate, tenuous grip on life. *This Sébastien character mentioned a doctor just now, Corella was it?* As much as Koko hates doctors, she hopes the doctor knows what they're doing. She then hears a voice, echoing deep within her.

In the end, be fearless in the face of your enemies.

As a former corporate mercenary, Koko was trained by a long stream of hard-assed drill sergeants, constables, and sensei to withstand the rigors of restrained interrogation, to resist physical tortures she suspects would blow Sébastien's mind. Good thing Koko suffered all that training, too, because on more than one occasion the harsh, disciplined instruction prepared her for the real deal.

One time she and six other contract operatives were held for twenty-two days in a six-by-ten steel hutch deep within the subbasements of Manikin International's global headquarters outside of Bogotá. Her team had been recruited to surgically liquidate a production development group before Manikin International completed beta testing some deep mantle mining innovation. Little food, sleep deprivation, and repeated beatings were the pussyfooted opening acts before her captors moved on to the main event. Each member of the team, male or female, was systematically gang-raped in front of the others. Despite the incessant savagery, no one caved. Koko, because she was the youngest at the time and the most attractive of the lot, had been deemed to go last as a coveted prize. Koko can still remember the stink of that hutch. The crushing heat, the taste of the small mice that they ate raw to survive. Sometimes she still has nightmares of the tuneless, jagged clang of the hutch's padlocks being sprung. When the guards did finally come for her, she fought valiantly with diminished strength, but to her surprise the captors informed the team that they were free to go. Apparently Manikin International had entered into vertical integration negotiations with their competitors, the same ones that had assembled the team to execute the liquidation, and arranged their release. Total dumb luck. This dork's threats? Sébastien leaning on her was nothing.

"We're not from anywhere," Koko says.

"Everyone is from somewhere."

"We're totally on our own."

"Ah, so you're privateers then?"

Koko refuses to look at Sébastien directly and reruns a second movie in her head: a long river of images of her and Flynn's desperate flight from The Sixty. How they accessed the resort's lower infrastructure, how she and Flynn stole the submarine. With painful detail she recalls exactly how Flynn's screams of agony broke her heart. He begged her to turn back for his sake, but once at sea and at great speed, turning back wasn't an option. The bug-out packs' first-aid kits' suture threading was too weak to adequately close Flynn's wound so Koko stitched up his leg with stripped wire from a circuit panel. She was dismayed and distressed by how Flynn blamed her for everything. He wept and called her selfish, pernicious, and cruel. Of course soon after they passed the International Date Line, the floating underwater debris quadrant came next and that shitstorm of giant squid. While she freed the snagging cable, the starboard rudder never seemed to work right after, and Koko was forced to travel dangerously topside the rest of the way. Battling her own debilitating seasickness in the growing swells, Koko didn't take long to grasp that they were drifting far south and way, way, way off their intended course. The massive storm was almost a ludicrous, cosmic insult. The whole escape, it was one long voyage into pelagic perdition, and when they finally reached the continental shelf, the next thing you know—the wreck.

Be fearless in the face of your enemies.

"Very well," Sébastien says. "I suppose we should consider you two outlaws, then."

Koko has to admit, she's always liked the sound of that word, all rakish and beyond the straitlaced rules of law. Isn't that how she's always wanted to live her life anyway? An outlaw on her own terms? But then she pictures Flynn's poor face once more, his beard slimed with foamy drool, and her heart locks up.

Why not paint a thin truth?

"Not outlaws," she replies. "We're survivors."

The door to the room unlocks and opens, and a medium-built man in clean green surgical scrubs enters. Topped with a towering

Trotsky-like shrub of black hair, he sports a dark Balbo-styled beard on his chin, and holds a short diagnostic device in his hands.

"Ah, Dr. Corella," Sébastien says, turning. "Our guest is finally awake."

The doctor meticulously checks one of the projection screens, and when his face looms closer, Koko studies his startlingly porous, toffee-colored complexion.

"So, how are we feeling, Miss… Miss…?"

The doctor shoots Sébastien a tacit look, assuming he must have extracted the woman's name by now. Sébastien holds his hands open at his sides. Simultaneously they turn and look down.

"It would be easier if we could call you something," the doctor says.

Koko speaks through clamped teeth. "Koko."

Both men raise their eyebrows.

"Why hello there, Koko. My name is Dr. Corella. Tell me, do you have an assigned surname from your Oceania breeding collective?"

"My frickin' Oceania what?"

"Your cranial scarring indentations indicate you were at one time fitted for an ocular implant used by militarized interests. There was Oceania code alongside the indentations."

"That was a long, long time ago."

Dr. Corella nods. "All right. And your shipmate, the wounded man, I believe his name is Flynn? He's from the Second Free Zone lower atmosphere orbits, yes?"

Koko's eyes widen. "Wait, how do you—"

Without a shred of guile Dr. Corella clarifies, "While he didn't have cranial scarring like you, there were SFZ collective trademarks embedded in his DNA. After your immediate rescue, our people said you were quite frantic and kept shouting at your friend to stay awake and called him Flynn. You should know this was the right thing to do, otherwise he might have slipped further into a coma and possibly expired before he reached us."

"So you're the one fixing him up?"

"I'm the sole physician here, that's correct."

"And he's doing okay?"

"His status is no longer critical, I'll say that. Would you care to see him?"

If she could nod her head she would, but the restraints keep Koko's head fixed.

Her eyes shift to Sébastien, who looks concerned.

"Doctor, I think I have to caution you..."

"Oh, Sébastien, she's fine. The tranquilizer in her system only allows her the most rudimentary muscle functions anyway, and inhibited as such she won't be able to harm anyone. Not like her little scene earlier."

Sébastien takes Dr. Corella by his elbow and moves him across the room. The two of them whisper in conference for a moment, and then the doctor crosses to a cabinet and removes a sterile package containing a pressure syringe. After selecting a cartridge from the cabinet as well, the doctor loads it.

"Well, we'll err on the side of caution then."

Koko locks in on the syringe. "What the hell is *that*?"

"This? An additional response limiter. Not to worry, it's actually quite pleasant. You'll still be able to walk, but you'll experience your surroundings with a sluggish temporal shift. Have you ever had the sensation of déjà vu? It's akin to that."

Sébastien engages the table's controls again, and Koko motors up into a nearly vertical position. After lining up the injection on the tightened muscles of her neck, the doctor pulls back.

"It'll be easier if you relax," the doctor advises.

"That's what all the boys say."

He slides the pressure syringe into her neck and after a warm bite a strange sensation seeps into Koko's blood. Surprisingly, it feels kind of jazzy, all gluey and liquefied. Under better circumstances Koko might even enjoy the trippy, fugue-like buzz, but right now, being captive? No, she doesn't like it at all.

Sébastien moves toward the door. His lips open and close, but it's as if Koko is watching a poorly lip-synced video, his voice registering in her ears three seconds after he speaks. Sébastien ushers in a male and a female assistant who are also dressed in green scrubs like Dr. Corella, and tells them to undo the table's restraints.

Once free, Koko melts to her knees, and the two assistants catch her. Their movements taffy outward and reset, and she's guided forward in a controlled fall. Soon they're in a windowless hallway so brightly lit it makes Koko see spots. Sébastien instructs the blue dog to stay, and several more men and women in green smocks secure self-adjusting hygienic masks to everyone in the group—the doctor, the assistants, Koko, and Sébastien. When the mask gets sealed to her face Koko gets her first glimpse of Flynn behind a set of curtains. He's suspended and floating in a clear plastic tank. The surrounding ambiance is a reverent reduction and the two assistants move Koko closer to the tank. Dr. Corella steps forward and taps the translucent plastic.

"He's fit. Considering the spread of his infection, that's good. As you can see, we've done some intensive grafting and reconstruction on his leg. Naturally there will be a scar, but he's responding remarkably well given the circumstances."

Koko struggles to speak. "Can he… hear… me?"

"No."

One step, then two on leaden feet, and Koko shuffles closer to the tank. The number of tubes and wires snaking into Flynn's body are frightening, and a respiratory helmet covers the upper portion of his face. Koko then suddenly realizes they have shaved off Flynn's beard.

Oh, baby…

Dread stretches through her. She tries not to imagine the ragged chasm Flynn's death might slash inside her, and drugged as she is, she cautions herself not to let her affections show. But the stinging in her eyes can't be helped. Drifting on syrupy delay, Dr. Corella goes on.

"A full amputation of his leg from the hip down was considered, but it now looks like that won't be necessary. Being at sea is hardly an optimal treatment condition for amateur surgery. I imagine you did the best you could."

Koko turns around and looks at everyone. One of the medical assistants dabs her cheeks with a small towel and quietly suggests that it's probably better that they leave and let those who know how to care for Flynn do what they do best. Turning her to face Sébastien, the assistants take her arms. When they move back into the bright-lit hallway again two identical men in red ponchos approach.

"Eirik, Bonn, what is it?" Sébastien asks.

"We've an update regarding the situation beyond the walls," one of the men replies.

Sébastien doesn't disclose any alarm and bends forward as the other twin whispers something in his ear. Koko can't hear what is said, and after a moment Sébastien addresses the two men curtly, indicating Koko.

"Take Gammy and escort her to the open room on the third floor of Lodge Delta. Secure her there with Gammy until you receive further instructions from me."

Relieving the bookending medical assistants, the two identical men drag Koko away. The big blue dog follows.

ALL HE DOES IS DREAM... DREAM, DREAM, DREAM

Meanwhile, back in the warm, aquarium-like serenity of the IC tank, Flynn drops through a vivid, bottomless dream.

A tunnel, a rabbit hole, a monster's throat, he falls in an endless cavity of flight. Flynn thinks if he could just reach out and touch the walls that surround him he might be able to slow his descent and wake up, but he can't.

He falls.

And falls...

And falls...

A phantasmagoric jump and all at once the tunnel disappears. Flynn finds himself standing alone in a vast, hard desert. Looking up, he searches for the tunnel he just passed from but all he sees is empty blue sky.

With a flash of lightning a giant pyramid appears on the horizon, and Flynn is pulled magnetically toward its base. Up close, the structure is alarmingly huge and dark. Constructed of metal pipes, the pyramid hums like a massive, dense engine, and not knowing exactly why he's doing it, Flynn locates an opening, enters and climbs upward.

Seconds, minutes, hours seem to pass and when Flynn climbs over the threshold of a narrow passage he looks to the right and sees that the passage leads outside. Moving toward the light at the end, he discovers upon exiting that he's so high up on the structure that a sudden vertigo threatens to topple him off. He holds on and below sees a lone person dressed in white at the pyramid's base. From where Flynn is it's too far to make out the person's face, but when they wave at him he hears Koko's voice in his head.

Keep going...

Flynn feels stupid. Dream or not, he can't believe he does what Koko tells him. Pulling himself up along a vertical outcropping, he mounts the pyramid's summit seconds later and balanced up top he finds a small wooden box. When Flynn lifts the box's lid, he sees two black marbles. Intuitively Flynn realizes he must choose one of the marbles, but if he selects wrong he also knows he might just die.

LODGE DELTA

Outside, Koko's bare feet slip on the wet bricks as one of her escorts speaks.

"Watch your step. Please tell us if you're going to be sick."

Strength sapped, Koko nods her head even as she attempts to keep track of her surroundings.

Wambling off to her right are the whitewashed walls she remembers seeing when they came back from the wreck. Smooth-surfaced and thickened at the base, the ramparts are high and bank off in opposite directions—suggesting that wherever she and Flynn are being held is possibly a large, circular fortress. As they make their way across a courtyard, a woman in yet another red poncho scurries past and looks shyly at them. With her paper gown soaked like a tired flag, Koko imagines she must look quite the sight. The twins jar her forward and the big blue dog whimpers, keeping its head low to the wind.

Soon the four of them arrive at a brick-faced oblong building. After passing through a set of windowed doors, they turn left and climb a stairwell. Koko counts the levels. One, two... at the third floor they enter a dimly lit hallway that runs the length of the building. There are arched metal doors on either side of the corridor, all of which are closed. When they reach the end of the hallway, Gammy gives her damp fur a good shake, and Koko's escorts stop. One supports her slumped body as the other taps in a code on a keypad and unlocks the door.

Like the hallway, the room they guide her into is also dim—lit by a single floor lamp. A round Persian-style rug covers most of the room's polished, pale tongue-and-groove wood floor. One of her escorts points ahead.

"Here we are. You've got a bed over there on your left, and the door to your bathroom is just over there on the right. A desk and a couple chairs… the window is shuttered because of the weather. Sorry, but we're going to remove the floor lamp and any surplus materials in the desk and bathroom that might be used for other purposes. Can you stand on your own?"

It takes a long time for Koko to respond, but finally she nods, and the two step aside and watch her as she rocks from side to side. One of the men backs up and retrieves a few items from a single drawer in the desk and then something else from the bathroom. The other man then removes the floor lamp and the room goes dark. Sitting and waiting in the hallway, the dog observes everything.

Somewhere deep down in Koko's fuzzy brain a message surfaces. *Now.* Now would be the perfect moment for her to do something. But she can't find the coordination, the strength or the will. Dreamy seconds later she hears the metal door close and the secondary bite of its electrified catch behind her.

Koko urges her legs forward. It takes forever and a day to reach the window and she nearly falls twice along the way. Bracing her weight along the sill, Koko lifts a hand and blindly feels for the shutters' latch. The next thing she knows she's on the floor, her soaked paper gown bunched around her waist like a sad tutu.

Another five hundred years seem to pass before Koko crawls over to the bed. Curling up into a ball beneath a brown woolen blanket and cool sheets, her head spinning, she can't help but wonder one more thing before she gives in to sleep.

If this place is a fortress… then where the hell are the defenses? Why aren't these people properly armed?

CAUTION WORDS

"Sébastien, wait."

Sébastien rotates as Dr. Corella catches up with him in the hallway outside the infirmary.

"What is it? There are things I need to attend to, Doctor. I need to organize another group to head out to the wreck."

Dr. Corella palms a hand through his pate of frowzy hair. "Of course, I understand completely. However, I thought I might have a few words with you first."

Sébastien measures the doctor's insistence and then nods.

"First, I'd like to offer my condolences," Dr. Corella says. "I know, well, I know how special Kumari was to you."

Sébastien's eyes slit.

"Kumari knew," he whispers.

"Knew? Knew what?"

"What do you think?"

Dr. Corella's face goes ashen. "My God—why didn't you say something?"

"Too many people around," Sébastien replies. "And there hasn't been time. I thought the search party could bring her back."

"But how? How do you know she discovered everything?"

"I found an extraction signature on my personal systems," Sébastien says. "That's why I sent out the search party. When I first noticed it, I immediately went to Kumari's family quarters to confront her."

"When?"

"Around nine or ten. Her parents told me that Kumari had gone to bed. I didn't want to alarm them. I told them I was merely following up on one of her lessons."

"And?"

"And they looked in on her and she wasn't there. I told them not to worry, but immediately I had people search the entire grounds. Someone had noticed her heading for the tunnel, so I assembled a search party and had them take Gammy along. The real kicker is just now, while you were attending to Flynn, I found a needle drive squirreled away in Kumari's clothes, along with some of her mother's jewelry. She probably intended to barter the jewelry to back whatever it was she was planning."

"A needle drive?"

"Yes. I haven't had a chance to check it yet, but knowing her and the fact that she left an extraction signature, I'm willing to wager it has everything. The Tranquil Adaptive Modifier research, my pharmaceutical contacts and communications—a needle drive possesses ten psi-bits' worth of memory. That coupled with the jewelry seems a likely explanation as to why she was running away."

Dr. Corella swallows. "Do you, God, do you think anyone else knows?"

"I need to search her quarters. Her parents don't even know that she's dead yet. She may have left clues to her intentions."

"Sébastien, this can't, I mean, this *can't* happen."

"I know."

"I've risked everything to do this. We've risked everything. If my TAM research," Dr. Corella quickly corrects himself, "I mean, if *our* TAM research gets out prematurely, it could ruin five solid years of clinical trials. And if anyone outside the Commonage finds out what we've been doing all this time, using these people as subjects—"

Sébastien grabs the doctor's arm. "Will you calm down? No one knows anything yet. Yes, there was an extraction signature and I was damn fortunate I saw it, but there's no way Kumari could've hacked into our outside communications relays."

"She managed to get into your other systems, and those are supposed to be protected. How can you be so sure?"

"Our relay safeguards are different. There're crash-out, flush protocols that are impossible to skirt."

"But the girl is a genius, you've said as much yourself."

"*Was* a genius."

Dr. Corella looks down. "God, I can't believe you could've been so careless..."

Sébastien drags him toward an empty alcove across the hall. When Dr. Corella shakes himself free, Sébastien shoves him up against the alcove wall.

"You're a fine one to be calling *me* careless. If you'd started Kumari on the adaptive modifiers earlier, we wouldn't be in this mess."

"But she'd just started menstruating, Sébastien! I couldn't start her on TAM until after her first few cycles became regular."

"You said you were working on that."

"I have, but with female pre-pubescents the pharmacokinetics don't work. Everything I've tried has failed." Dr. Corella clenches his teeth, "God, if you hadn't been so enamored and taken with the girl's intellect..."

Sébastien fights the urge to push the doctor again, throws his head back, and slaps and kicks the wall in frustration. Peeking around the alcove corner, he looks down the hallway to see if anyone has noticed his outburst. So many problems all at once—Kumari's death, these shipwrecked strangers, the fading storm and the de-civs' encampment—his mind reels. Cynically, though, Sébastien remembers that he and the doctor are still partners. They need to diffuse their rancor and get all their thoughts together, en masse, because blaming each other right now isn't helping.

"Okay," Sébastien says, "Okay, I'm sorry. I'm sorry for grabbing and accusing you just now. Let's take a breath and step back, take everything in for a moment, all right? Each thing singularly and calmly."

Dr. Corella looks at him and then down thoughtfully. "You're right. Clear thinking. Address the problem. There's no need to panic."

The two pause for a long moment.

"So this needle drive of Kumari's," Dr. Corella says. "You'll look at it as soon as you can?"

"Yes. And Kumari is now gone. So if her parents are unaware of what she was planning, then for all intents and purposes TAM looks contained. What're your thoughts on these wreck survivors?"

Dr. Corella scratches his hair vigorously and paces to and fro in the alcove for another long silence until he looks up.

"I think discretion is the best call," he says.

"How so?"

"Well, Flynn is recovering. He'll be out of the IC tank in the next hour."

"Meaning?"

"Meaning, with a former soldier, posting guards and locking up Koko could be problematic."

"But she attacked people here earlier."

"Yes, she did, but she didn't know who we were."

"We just saved their lives and that is how the woman *reacts*?"

"I know," Dr. Corella says, "but I still think we ought to make a concerted effort to not present ourselves as a threat. Enflaming her obvious agitation and treating her like an inmate—if this needle drive turns out to have everything you think, drawing any excess attention to our efforts here won't help."

Sébastien bites his lip. "Couldn't you, I don't know, maybe *do* something about her?"

Dr. Corella stiffens and glowers. "Sébastien, Koko is a problem, but I am not, repeat not, deserting the greater potential of our long-term aims, however profitable they may be. Good lord, man, have you lost your mind?"

"I didn't mean *eliminate* her. I was thinking of long-term sedation."

"But for how long?"

"Indefinitely?"

"Indefinitely isn't recommended. No, look, she's exhausted. She's confused. Given the circumstances and her background, her reactions before were logical and expected."

Sébastien gives the doctor a dubious look and then retrieves a rubber band from his pocket. A few short years ago when Dr. Corella first approached Sébastien about the lucrative global applications of the Tranquil Adaptive Modifier program, and after he lent the last of his significant capital to move forward on the Commonage project, Sébastien had his notions about his partner's hoity-toity ethics. *Deserting the greater potential of our long-term aims?* Once they get TAM to market, Sébastien is sure such disinclinations will vanish. Using the rubber band to tie off his hair in a shaggy ponytail, he decides not to press the matter of sedating Koko further, at least for now.

"So you propose we do nothing about her."

"Not nothing," Dr. Corella says. "I mean, for now Koko is sedated, yes, but maybe it's better to simply keep up the face with her until we're able to further vet their situation."

"Keep up the face? How?"

"Display the Commonage's operative principles. We don't have to give anything away. Let the community and people's behaviors here speak for themselves. Listen, think of Koko as an inconvenient batch of strong acid. Without betraying our specific motivations with TAM, we can act as a neutralizing base. Besides, we're helping Flynn heal. That may count for a great deal for someone like her. I sensed a palpable connection when we brought her in to see him."

Sébastien puts his hands on his hips. "You're saying they're intimate?"

"Possibly. And Flynn, he has negative ocular implant trauma.

He isn't like Koko. While they both had cuts on their wrists congruent with the removal of temporary biometric identifiers, this deep connection, coupled with Koko's abrasiveness, may indicate they're merely in flight from something. There could be extenuating circumstances."

"With them blundering through the offshore restrictions I paid handsomely for, I'll bet there are extenuating circumstances."

"Oh, for heaven's sake. *If* Kumari did bypass the communication relays and some entity did manage to find out about our efforts here and sought to capitalize on them, do you really think they'd pair up a former soldier with someone who's obviously not?"

"They'd have been much more assertive."

"Right. They'd have sent a whole team. In all probability this could be a misunderstanding. A mere tempest in a tea cup."

Sébastien scowls. "Fine choice of words given the weather. So what else do you recommend we do?"

"Well, seeing that Flynn was born in the Second Free Zone collectives, I wanted to tell you that I ran some more extensive tests. In his blood I found trace deposits of powerful anti-Depressus medications."

"*He has Depressus*?"

"Well, the traces confirm long-term ingestions. Access to those kinds of medications are strictly regulated."

"My God," Sébastien whispers.

Dr. Corella gives him an expectant look. "Are you thinking what I'm thinking?"

"Why, all things considered, this could be the silver lining with these two."

"Precisely."

"We've only been working with terrestrial-based subjects with TAM. But the Second Free Zone confederacy markets with Depressus are enormous. My pharmaceutical contacts would be thrilled to know how TAM applies to Depressus cases."

"Right, and if we start TAM on Flynn, we could—"

"Aggregate the findings into our overall research."

"And here's another plus. With Flynn being from SFZ we could even suggest to your contacts the eventual application of TAM for the sub-orbital correctional barges and prison populations."

Sébastien rubs his chin. "God, I need to see what I can find out about them first."

"Of course, that's only prudent. But starting Flynn on TAM should balance things out. One less person to worry about acting out anyway. We can't use TAM on Koko regrettably."

"Why not?"

"Sébastien, TAM subjects need to be fully conscious to administer the first and second doses. Even if we could further sedate Koko and use response limiters, she's a former soldier who would do her utmost to resist. In its current form the TAM procedure is extremely delicate. If Koko moves even a bit—good God, I don't want to lobotomize the woman. But Flynn, well, he's already being cared for. I could say the first injection is part of his treatment. We could take things from there."

Sébastien pictures it.

"So, we're in agreement?" Dr. Corella asks.

Sébastien steps closer and places a commiserating hand on the doctor's shoulder.

"Okay, we'll play it your way. We'll keep up the face with Koko to put her at ease and get Flynn started on TAM. How long will the inhibitor and sedative last?"

"Given her already depleted state? I estimate four to five hours," Dr. Corella says.

SURABAYA, INDONESIA II

SHE'S BACK, BACK IN THE SURABAYAN GROOVE

Convalescing in her climate-controlled suite at The Grand Monggo-Monggo Hotel, Wire stands at her window, comfortably draped in a white complimentary robe. After shaking out a trio of antibiotic pills from a vial, she slips the pills under her tongue and chases them with a flood of potent, hot 126-proof arak.

While smogged, the view of Surabaya between the room's drawn blackout curtains is impressive: a blazing seventy-story high panoramic of unrepentant squalor and industrialized blight.

On the other hand, in the sepulcher-like air of her luxury suite, Wire herself feels outstanding. Rested, fine-tuned, and pretty much amazing. After she'd had her ocular implant and teeth repaired, the interns at the pop-and-op clinic advised her that beyond precautionary treatments, with rest and plenty of fluids she was good to go. No signs of a parasitic disease manifesting in larva-laying microscopics, no exotic sub-viral infections or internal distress. Diligent, the pop-and-op interns provided Wire with a full regime of antibiotics and cautioned her to refrain from imbibing any alcohol. Yeah, right… like *that* was going to happen. Medically minded twits—they may have their remedies, but Wire has her own.

As she polishes off the rest of her drink, from the king-sized bed behind her drifts a somnolent groan. Turning, Wire smirks as a young man and woman cower in a knot of blood-spattered sheets.

Color her seedy, but Wire believes a little exhilarative extravagance now and then goes a long way in the healing of whatever ails you. The fact is, she's never been one to eschew her own personal satisfactions, and at her request The Grand Monggo-Monggo's concierge sent up two prostitutes to her suite the previous evening. The tantalizing talent arrived just after her dinner had been whisked in by room service, and the meal itself was superb—a platter of braised mimicry proteins and hydroponically grown fruits. Even now the extraordinary tastes of the dinner linger in Wire's memory. Freshly broiled Sphynx cat with guava chutney, poached reptile medallions spiced with garlic, and a dome of sticky rice dusted with powdered cricket bacon. After finishing her meal, she gave the prostitutes explicit instructions to commence a full circus of carnal acrobatics while she drained off a magnum of solar ale. Later Wire brushed her teeth, stripped, and joined the two on the bed until they were all wrung out, beaten, and spent.

The male prostitute holds his female counterpart around her shoulders. Both have bloodstone-bruised jaws, and one of the female's eyes is completely puffed shut like a rotten fig. Fear bleeds the remaining color from their faces, and they scrabble out of the bed like a pair of frightened rabbits. Heartlessly aloof, Wire follows them as they pick up their flimsy clothes. She points to a credenza by the suite's door.

"There's extra credits for both of you in the envelope. It should cover whatever medical treatment is necessary. Please tell the concierge my compliments. Your stamina surpassed my expectations."

As if he's seizing a written stay of execution, the male snatches up the envelope, and the female flings open the suite's door. Seconds later, both of the prostitutes take off down the hall, running.

Wire chuckles and closes the suite's door. Cracking her neck, she unfastens her robe and lets the thick cover-up slip to the floor.

Wearing black compression shorts and matching sports bra, Wire begins her daily workout regime: a quick, brutal set of calisthenics that includes lunges, deep crunches, and two hundred straight pushups as well as twenty-five additional pushups, one-handed. Her goal is to max out her heart rate at one hundred and seventy-two beats per minute, and a short time later Wire feels fully limber and ready to rock her day. Admiring her sweaty, jacked build in a wide mirror affixed to the suite's far wall, she gives her nipples a brief, playful tweak.

Damn, girl, looking gooooooood.

After peeling out of her sweat-moistened garments, she then takes a ridiculously long steam shower, replaying her activities thus far.

Once she booked her room at The Grand Monggo-Monggo, Wire used the hotel's secure data-uplink amenities to kick her personal reboot into a higher gear. Her first matter of business was accessing her credit balances and investments holdings to see what she could quickly offload to get her back in the game at full strength. Of course, she immediately checked the status on the gnaw-ware program embedded in her shadow flowcode address. With the poison Britch injected her with, she may have been at death's door, but she wasn't stupid. She gave him a shadow flowcode address used for covert black-ops. Once entered, it launches an undetectable gnaw-ware program. When Britch eventually accesses his off-world accounts, the gnaw-ware will activate and present a 'dummy' account with a few thousand credits as a diversionary ploy. Meanwhile the rest of Britch's off-world savings and associated investments would be transferred into Wire's own accounts. As a bonus, the savage piece of programming would subsequently reach out, infect, and plunder any and all mainframes connected to the data tab before it vanishes completely. Sadly, when Wire discovered the gnaw-ware hadn't launched yet it made her wonder. Could Britch have figured out the devastating back-end embedded in her uploaded address?

No, that would be impossible. Once more, she felt stung at being compromised, but then when she noticed a message in her inbox from Britch with attachments she actually laughed out loud. What do you know? The fat tub of pus held up his end of the bargain!

Lord, Britch, what kind of dipshit honors a deal?

A dipshit sucker, that's who.

The data from Britch indicated that Martstellar intended to make a serious break for the flooded coastal fjord metropolises east of the Hecate Strait. Located just west of the Kitimat Ranges of former British Columbia, and well north of the deplorable New Vancouver supercities, the region was a twisted maze of strip mines, platform derricks, and mineral refineries primarily owned and operated by the new Canadian government's resource alliance—C-GRAP. Not exactly a hospitable destination given the unruly arbitrage fluctuations and governmental infighting, but when Wire thinks about it she suspects C-GRAP's bustling maritime ghettos are at least a decent place to go to ground. The real dripping cherry on the cake from Britch was that Martstellar downloaded a list of shipbrokers and recycle specialists in the region. Damn. Britch's speculations were on target: Martstellar and her cohort aimed to offload the stolen sub to keep their pockets flush.

With her mood significantly improved, Wire then forwarded a series of encrypted flowcode communications across her network to see if any of her contacts knew who was running the show off the books in Surabaya. This took a little more time, but within a few hours she had a bead on the whole degenerate briar patch. An associate of hers was well-connected throughout Indonesia, and he owed Wire plenty. The associate delivered new clothes via courier and put Wire in touch with a black market outfit that had a long-range personal propulsion aircraft for sale.

Used in Chile's Atacama Desert during the recent restructuring engagements, the bird for sale had some wear and tear indicated in its schematics, but was fully equipped with serious weapon capabilities. It did strike Wire as a bit strange that such an aircraft had ended up in Surabaya, but then some 3-D-rendered cross-referencing on conflict trade activities revealed the aircraft had been part of a larger geo-political transaction. Wire placed a deposit and made plans to check out the aircraft later that afternoon. If everything appeared to be on the up and up, she'd fly the hell out of Surabaya as soon as possible.

While she towels off, the suite's augmented intelligence screens engage and advise Wire that she has a visitor waiting for her downstairs in the hotel's lobby. After quickly selecting one of her new tailored tactical suits (the one with climate insulation settings and environmental recognition software), Wire dresses and pulls on her new field boots. She stuffs her pant cuffs into the boots' tops and pockets a new handheld uplink. Not one to take chances, she takes a steak knife from her room service tray and tucks the long serrated blade down her right boot.

After a plunging glide in a glass-walled lift, Wire arrives in the gleaming, marbled lobby. The Grand Monggo-Monggo's lobby is heavily palmed and decorated to a T, and as she looks around she identifies her visitor. Much older than expected, the visitor is a man of medium build who carries himself with a small, hidden defect in his step, as if he is attempting to hold in a fart. As he draws closer, the man's disturbing personal disfigurement becomes apparent. Wire assumes radiation scarring, but there's so much ulcerated scar damage on his face that his features resemble the bumpy, jaundiced texture of a dried apricot. He holds two gunmetal attaché cases and wears a plain collarless black linen suit over a white silk shirt. An old school, inert-connected translator is secured to the man's mouth and left ear with lamprey-like barbs.

"*Hpphshh*—Jackie Wire?"

Wire almost puts out her hand in greeting, but she notices the man is not making a move to offer one of his own.

"That's me," Wire replies. "The one and only. So, you got my shit?"

The scarred man lifts up the two cases, and Wire is immediately suspicious. If all the weapons she requested were present, the two cases would be heavier than her body weight on Jupiter. There might be nothing inside them at all, and this could be a shakedown. Then again, the man's ease at lifting them could mean his clothes are concealing powerful hydraulic prosthetics. Both cases are armed with tiny winking clip-on detonators.

"*Hpphshh*—follow me, please."

Wire holds up a hand. "Hold on a second there, sport. I thought we were going to go someplace for the transaction."

A long sputter riffs through the translator speaker as the man stares at her and then brusquely turns. Wary and checking her surroundings, Wire follows him and a minute later they enter a windowless conference room down an adjacent hallway behind the hotel's reception kiosks. The conference room is bare except for a long glass table with eight high-backed chairs lined up on one side. The man gently sets both of the cases down on the glass table, while Wire's eyes scour the room's corners for hidden visual receptors, listening devices, and possible weapons. The man's translator whirs.

"This room is safe. Please transfer the credits as discussed."

Man, Wire thinks, *all this overt pushiness is feeling a bit shady*. She wonders how quickly she could grab the steak knife tucked in her boot.

"Mind if I inspect what I'm buying first?" she asks.

The scar-faced man shakes his head. "When your credits are transferred and the receipt is substantiated, only then am I authorized to disengage the security measures on the cases. This was outlined in our flowcode message—*hpphshh*."

"Yeah, I know, but normally…"

"Please initiate transfer or this transaction will be terminated."

Fucker. Wire tries to read the man's flat eyes.

"You ripping me off? Feels like I'm sticking my neck out."

"*Hpphshh*—nature of risk. Need I remind you, you are the one who reached out to us, not the other way around."

Okay, Wire thinks, *so prune-face here is all business and a major-league dick.* Chest puffing and skepticism is getting her nowhere, so she unzips a pocket on her new tactical suit and retrieves her new handheld. Pulling up the interface, she lifts her eyes and asks the man for the transaction code—a twenty-seven sequence of characters interspersed with universal credit modifiers and numbers. She reads back the numbers, characters, and modifiers in order and when the man's head nods she engages the transfer icon.

The man touches the left side of his head as he receives verification via the translator's connecting earpiece. Without a word he then bends forward, disengages the clip-on detonators on the two cases, slips the detonators into his suit jacket, and leaves.

Wire opens the cases. Packed in several layers of gray ballistic memory foam are enough weapons to wage a small war. Pulse pistols, integrated ammunition sleeves and stocks, electronics, grenades, and combat field supplies, all polished and pristine. She may have gone overboard a little to round her barbarous accouterment, but Wire is the type to go big when she goes hard.

She shuts both cases, removes the steak knife from her boot, and tosses it on the glass table.

Carrying the heavy cases out into the lobby, Wire takes the lift back up to her room.

It's time to pack the rest of her things and get the fuck out of Dodge.

THE COMMONAGE III

BRAVING THE PARENTS

"Words cannot adequately express my sympathies," Sébastien says.

Regardless of his orders to keep the news of Kumari's death quiet, reports of the strangers returning with the search party and an unknown covered body swiftly flourished through the Commonage. Restless with speculation, a neighbor of Kumari's family knocked on their door close to dawn and asked if they knew anything about the mysterious goings on. Kumari's mother and father confessed they'd heard nothing, and after closing the door the unhealthiest imaginings froze their hearts.

Kumari's family had joined the Commonage shortly after Kumari's ninth birthday, just when the girl's precociousness and raw intelligence had started to burn bright. Insatiably curious about everything, Kumari soon lapped her young peers at the Commonage conservatory in nearly every conceivable subject. With her feeling marginally ostracized by the other conservatory children for her gifts, once she turned eleven, her parents thought perhaps private tutorage might be the better option for her, and they sought Sébastien's guidance.

Sébastien was familiar with the child. After giving Kumari a series of tests he was so impressed by the girl's aptitude and IQ that he told her parents he would be delighted to attend to her studies directly. Like most who discover their child is gifted, Kumari's parents were thrilled, and together they made sure the girl took her additional academic responsibilities seriously.

When they didn't find her in her room, Kumari's parents fell into a stasis of dread, until Sébastien came to their door and ripped their world to pieces.

"We've no idea why she was out along the cliffs," Sébastien continues as he sits across from them. "Of course we're looking into it, but tell me, did Kumari—"

Kumari's father looks at him blankly. "No."

"No, what?"

"No, we've no idea why she was out there. Climbing gear you said?"

"Yes. Hooks of hammered metal and line."

"But Kumari doesn't do things like that."

"I know."

"Of course, rope is easily had around here, but she's never been a physical type of girl. When she was small my daughter was always afraid of heights. I couldn't even lift her onto my shoulders without her throwing a fit. Why would she—" A raw impatience briefly coagulates and then passes. "After dinner, we talked about her lessons, what she'd been reading, you know, things that you've given her, but she told us she was tired. She said goodnight and went straight to her room."

Sébastien looks to Kumari's mother perched on the edge of her chair. Earlier when he arrived and shared the horrible news, naturally the woman broke down. It's strange, but now she manages her shock by silently knitting from a woven reed basket of yarn on the floor. They talk over the fervid clicking of knitting needles.

Chick-a-chick-a-chick-a...

Sébastien desperately wants to examine Kumari's room to pick through her things for clues or a secreted-away journal or perhaps even a second needle drive. Kumari's father cups the back of his wife's head.

"For her to run away like this..."

Sébastien bends forward. "We don't know that she was running away."

"But you just said she had supplies," Kumari's father says.

"I did. But if she was running away, she must've given you two some inkling."

Kumari's father quells a creeping palsy in his voice. "We had dinner together like we always do in the commissary. Nothing seemed wrong. No, I don't think we had any indication at all."

"Did she seem upset lately?"

Chick-a-chick-a-chick-a...

"No."

"More reserved?"

Chick-a-chick-a-chick-a...

"Not at all."

Sébastien stands. "Well, then. As our operational guidelines stipulate, I've scheduled Kumari's interment for later today so now might be the appropriate time for you to go and see her before Dr. Corella prepares her."

Chick-a-chick-a-chick-a—the knitting stops.

Kumari's parents look up.

"Go now," Sébastien says.

There is no reluctance. With venerate and almost liturgical meekness, Kumari's parents rise to their feet and do exactly as instructed. When they leave, the two don't even bother with a final look back. As soon as they close the outer door, Sébastien rubs his face and groans.

Thank God for TAM, he thinks.

It's been a night for the ages.

Working with sensible care and reminding himself to think craftily as a young girl might, Sébastien spends the next half hour methodically probing and examining every square inch of

Kumari's bedroom and the rest of the family's quarters. He looks beneath rugs, unscrews and peers behind each switch plate on the walls, and opens every cupboard and container he can find. As with all Commonagers' quarters, the rooms and cupboard materials are frugal and orderly arranged, but he is unable to locate any incriminating evidence whatsoever. In her parents' bedroom, he notices a jewelry box on a bureau and replaces the necklaces, bracelets, and rings Kumari took, and checks the time on a clock. Thoroughly frustrated, Sébastien is about to head out, when he sees something he hadn't noticed earlier and stops. Slipped between the balls of yarn in her mother's knitting basket is a small folded slip of yellow paper.

Sébastien crosses to the basket and snatches the paper up. A part of him hopes it's a pattern instruction or some sort of darning guide, but when he sees that the yellow paper has an unmolested seal of tape with a heart drawn on it, he hooks a finger and rips the paper open.

Papa, Mama

There is so much to say, and I don't know where to begin.

Remember when you told me how Sébastien recruited you to join the Commonage? How you believed, deep down, that his intention was to design a place for people who yearned for a fresh start and for those who believed the world had gone mad? None of that it is true. Sébastien and Dr. Corella have lied to you… to everyone.

I know it sounds crazy, but the Commonage is being used as a five-year early trial facility for a drug compound called TAM. Unable to ethically or legally study the applications of TAM because of its brain-altering properties, Dr. Corella and Sébastien have been using adult Commonagers as test subjects. Within months, if not sooner, their plan is to sell their findings to the highest bidder. It breaks my heart to tell you that both of you've been exposed to the TAM compound under the guise of a vaccination series just after our family's arrival years back. All adults have been exposed to it, and once the second treatment is administered the effects are irreversible.

I know you're confused, but I've never lied to you. I've copied all the TAM materials, Sébastien and Dr. Corella's findings, etc. and my plan is to expose or find someone who can put a stop to all this before it goes too far. I'd hoped there was another way, but since my body is changing and soon I will be considered a mature adult, time is running out.

I can't stand by and do nothing.

I love you.
K

THE PARTNER DOCTOR

"He kept mumbling her name."

Dr. Corella inspects Flynn's dressing and doesn't look up at the attending assistant. Flynn's wound is healing quickly with the deep muscle accelerants.

"Mmm. Seems to be sleeping now."

"Should we wake him, Doctor?"

"Heavens, no. Let the man rest."

Dr. Corella pulls the curtains around Flynn's bed aside and the assistant moves away down the hall. When Dr. Corella crosses the hall to his office, he pulls up Flynn's diagnostics on a projection screen and picks up a mug of cold, black coffee. Sitting down at his desk, he takes a sharp sip of the cooled bitter brew and studies Flynn's charts.

As men of science, for five years he and Sébastien have been so careful with everything. Naturally there's been bumps along the way, ebbs and flows and the like, but nothing so unexpected as a pair of strangers dropping in from the blind or a young girl right under their noses attempting to bring the project down.

Good lord… despite global malevolent tendencies for greed,

these days getting any new drug to market took decades, and with TAM's invasive nature had they proposed an extended trial from the outset they would've been hung out to dry by their respective thumbs. By utilizing the ruse of the Commonage and circumventing the usual jurisdictional foot-dragging, they now have the proof that TAM actually works—and in one fifth of the time it would have otherwise taken. True, the delivery system and quality controls need tweaking, but they now understand how TAM is absorbed and metabolized and what the safe dosage ranges are. With TAM's shocking lack of long-range toxic effects, Sébastien and Dr. Corella are nearly ready to offer their discoveries to the highest bidder. What the highest bidder does after they acquire the research is not really their concern, but the program surely contains loaded promise to change the world.

Rid humankind of its congenital and biological paradoxes, all of the predictable societal ills.

Bring peace, equanimity, and most importantly, social engineering at a price.

Dr. Corella knows if they both can keep it together for just a little while longer, a few more months at the outside, he and Sébastien will both be wildly, impossibly rich.

Of course for his partner the massive windfall from TAM will be surfeit fortunes on top of previous excesses, but for Dr. Corella the impending payday would change everything.

TAM is his life's work.

Agreeing to get Flynn started on the adaptive modifications verifies he and Sébastien at least are still on the same page. Point of fact, Dr.Corella actually finds it stunning that neither of them had ever considered TAM's use for Depressus cases before. While there may be some averseness given the commercial ratings on live mass suicide feed broadcasts, people's tastes in entertainment are hardly inexorable and, heavens, doesn't everybody love a good comeback story? Who's to say the Second Free Zone confederacies wouldn't be interested in a policy about-face? One thing is for certain though.

Patient advocates who backed the mass euthanizing events will undoubtedly have to change their tune.

Dr. Corella takes another sip of cold coffee and rises. After retrieving a large pressure syringe from a nearby cabinet, he unlocks a drawer and selects a local anesthetic and then a TAM cartridge.

It's time to wake Flynn.

HAVE A FRUIT PLATE

After calling on Kumari's parents, Sébastien returns to his quarters and examines the contents of Kumari's needle drive. Quickly he ascertains that his previous hunch was correct. The archived contents confirm that she accessed and downloaded every last TAM file and sub-file on his systems and found out *everything.*

Minutes later, the dispatched second group returns from the wrecked sub. As they enter, they report that they checked the sub's onboard systems and industriously removed what they could. After the group hands over all the recovered electronics and Koko and Flynn's bug-out packs, Sébastien advises them to keep word of what they've found strictly to themselves. Effectively compliant and obedient with TAM, the group respectively bow their heads in unison and then depart.

After their exit, Sébastien inspects the electronics and proceeds to transfer the sub's records into his systems for more penetrating analysis. When he examines Koko and Flynn's backpacks and finds what's inside he isn't surprised at all.

Keep up the face?

Well, in any case he now knows something about the two alleged survivors.

Taking the backpacks, Sébastien leaves his quarters and treads downstairs to the commissary. Just off the rear of the central kitchen, and used for miscellaneous waste disposal, are a pair of thermite furnaces. As he's unacquainted with firearms of any kind, it takes Sébastien a few minutes to break down Koko and Flynn's weapons, and when he's finished he uses a slot to feed the deadly hardware into the furnaces' forging heat. Checking the first-aid kits, he decides it would be sensible to destroy the laser scalpels and he slips these into the furnaces as well.

Taking the backpacks into the kitchen, Sébastien finds a tray and collects some food: a small loaf of bread, a plastic carafe of water, a bowl of mixed fruit, and a couple of milky-white wedges of hard cheese. Then he heads off to the Commonage's supply stores and gathers some clothes and toiletries. Minutes later he climbs the stairs in Lodge Delta and approaches Eirik, Bonn, and Gammy with calm reserve. He tells the twins to go, and they head for the stairwell.

Gammy, on the other hand, is delighted to see Sébastien. Setting down the tray of food, clothes, and toiletries he's brought, he praises his synthetic and gives Gammy's throat a good scratch.

"Good girl, good girl. Let's see if our visitor is awake, shall we?"

Sébastien types in a code to erase the door lock, and then, leaving the backpacks outside, he picks up the items he brought and opens the door.

"Hello?"

Koko is slowly stirring and tonging open her eyes with her fingers, but when she sees Gammy and Sébastien entering the room she sits up like she's on fire.

"I'll just leave these here," Sébastien says as he sets the tray and other items down on the desk. "Fresh clothes and some toiletries. I took a guess at your size and they're nothing fancy, but you should find them suitable to our climate. The clothes and boots you arrived in are still being laundered, I believe."

Koko glares at him. Briefly Sébastien wonders if she'll make a mad dash for it, but she remains still.

"I think we've gotten off on the wrong foot," Sébastien says. "I admit, that's partly my fault, but Dr. Corella suggested it might be better to extend a greater hospitality to you. Obviously you can understand our earlier precautions. So, all that said, how're you feeling?"

Koko eyeballs Gammy and responds churlishly, "Through the ringer, but just so you and your huge pooch are clear, I'm not exactly in a trusting mood right now."

Sébastien picks up a yellow pear from the fruit bowl on the tray and tosses it to her. Koko bobs right, and the pear bounces and rolls off the bed. Gammy looks at the fruit with big, dark eyes.

"Please, there's nothing spiked in that pear. Squandering food is discouraged here." Selecting a green apple from the bowl, Sébastien takes a large bite to demonstrate that nothing on the tray is tainted.

"So, where are your enforcers?"

"Enforcers?"

"Thugs one and two."

"I told Eirik and Bonn to leave. They're hardly enforcers." Sébastien takes a second bite of his apple and munches. Gammy watches their words, leaping from lips to lips. Koko rubs her temples.

"Damn, that quack of yours sure knows how to slip a girl a mickey. How long have I been out of it?"

"Only a few hours. Looks like you needed the rest."

"The rest. Right, so now what?"

"What do you mean?"

"With us. Flynn and me. What now? Is this some kind of game or are we free to go?"

"If you want to, I suppose you could leave, but your friend Flynn is still recovering from his surgeries. Fantastic progress with Dr. Corella's treatments no doubt, it's more than likely he's out of the IC tank already."

"Is he conscious?"

"That I don't know."

Sébastien lobs a second pear from the bowl on the tray to Koko and she snatches it from the air. For someone just coming around from a sedative and muscle limiters, her speed is nothing short of amazing. With her eyes cemented on his, Koko smells the fruit and tears off a small, hesitant taste. She gobbles the rest of the pear in six quick bites and chucks the core into a corner.

"See? It's good stuff. One hundred percent organic and grown right here. By the way, there's a rubbish receptacle in the bathroom."

Giving him and Gammy a short venomous look, Koko wraps the wool blanket and sheets around her waist and slowly gets off the bed. She shuffles to the window, unfastens a latch with one hand, and draws back the shutters. Slanted sunlight spills into the room.

"Where the hell are we?"

"As I said earlier, you're at the Commonage."

"No, pinhead," Koko says. "I mean coordinates. Longitude and latitude. Prohibs and the coast, yeah, I know that, but how far are we from the northern borders?"

"Was that where you were heading?"

"That's my business."

"Well, in that case, let's see. Give or take, the borders are close to nine hundred kilometers from here."

"Terrific," Koko declares bitterly. "What're you dimwits doing out here in the middle of the prohibs?"

Sébastien thinks of his earlier discussion with Dr. Corella. "That may be a bit difficult to explain."

"Try."

"You could call it a personal investment. A social petri dish could be another way of putting it. Perhaps we should start with some basics. Tell me, do you have any idea who I am?"

Koko splutters, "How am I supposed to know who you are? Right now, you're just some middle-aged a-hole holding me and Flynn captive almost a thousand kilometers from civilization."

"No one is a captive here, Koko."

"Says you."

"And I'm making an effort to be gracious." Sébastien looks behind him and gestures to the door. "See? The door is open, and the lock has been erased."

Koko looks suspiciously at the open entry and sniffs.

"Look, man," she says. "I'm not stupid. Us having a sub, I know how it all looks, but me and Flynn are survivors, nothing more. We just crashed here because of that huge fucking storm. I mean, who in their right mind would ever think about deliberately coming to a place like this?"

Sébastien takes a step, and Koko's eyes switch to the food tray. While he has Gammy to protect him, Sébastien is suddenly thankful he made sure not to include anything that could be used as a possible weapon on the tray.

"Lots of people actually like it here you know," he says.

"Oh, and are they hostages too?"

"Don't be absurd. Saying you're a hostage would mean we're holding you for some kind of ransom."

"But we're unarmed for fuck's sake."

Sébastien smiles. "I'll take that last opinion with a healthy grain of salt."

"What?"

"You see, I had some of the people go out to your wrecked submarine a short time ago. They found your stash of weapons. They've been destroyed."

Koko almost drops her blanket and sheets.

"*Destroyed?*"

A rocky growl slides up and down Gammy's throat as the synthetic senses a significant tensional shift.

"Shhhh. Everything's okay. Good girl."

Gammy quiets.

"You had no goddamn right to do that!" Koko cries.

"Balanced against saving your lives their destruction seems trivial."

Koko briefly looks at Gammy again. "So what about the credits in the backpacks, huh? The nuclear-biological-chemical suits? You went and destroyed them too?"

"Except for the scalpels in the first-aid kits, the credits and the rest of your things are in the backpacks outside the door."

"They better be."

"Hard currency means little to those within the Commonage. In any event, when the group found your supplies they also looked to see if there was a way to get your submarine back online. The hull was badly damaged and righting the vessel looked impossible. Some of the sub's onboard systems, however, were still operational. A Trang Xi Class submersible—can you tell me why you disabled your GPS transponder?"

"Please tell me you didn't re-engage it."

"Briefly, but only to see if it was still functioning."

"And?"

"It was."

Koko hangs her head.

Sébastien tells Gammy to lie down on the floor, and after the animal gets into position, he leans down and scratches one of her blue-black ears.

"From your reaction I take it that was a bad move on our part. I'm ready to listen to your tale if it's a colorful one."

Koko lifts her head. "Are you out of your mind? What, just because you're all friendly with me now and offering me food, you think for one second I'm going to just let down my guard? Hell, I can't believe you destroyed my weapons. I need those. *We* need those. What gives you the right?"

"We mean you no harm, Koko. How about a little trust?"

"Trust? Trust can suck it."

"Goodness, are you always this tetchy?"

"When people destroy my property, hell yes I'm tetchy."

Sébastien sits down on the edge of the desk and sighs.

"Okay, look. Maybe if you know a little bit more about this place you won't feel so threatened. Just now I hardly had a chance to elaborate, but up until recently I was what you might call a man of very significant means."

"Oh, yeah?"

"Yes. A few years ago I leveraged the last of my financial muscle to acquire a great swathe of this area and had the entire coastal parcel reclassified. You're now, in effect, within a privately owned Special Economic Zone."

"What's that?"

"It's a locale exempt from governmental, political, and multinational interference of any kind as outlined under the Baxter Worldwide Trade Treaty of 2476. Given the less than accurate ecocide assessments, nobody really cared to take the initiative here seriously, and since then we've been left alone to do as we see fit. Outwardly I know it may look peculiar, but our efforts here are ingeniously sound given the state of the world." Sébastien takes another bite of his apple and cheeks the flesh. "You're sure my face doesn't ring a bell?"

"Nope."

"How about PIWI? Pharma Impetus Worldwide Industries?"

Koko's eyebrows arch. "You mean the drug syndicate out of—"

"Northern Europe? Yes."

"Holy, hot buckets of snake whiz, that's *yours*?"

"No such luck," Sébastien replies. "I was merely one of PIWI's lead chemists. I helped synthesize an alkaloid that enhanced the company's consumer drug efforts. In on the fledgling ground-floor days as they say, back when PIWI was a start-up. The truth is, PIWI was insolvent and about to go under when I bumbled into my little breakthrough, and now the alkaloid is used globally in thousands of products. Domestic relaxers, anti-tumor agents, and the newer climate adaptive applications for deep space travel. Not to toot my own Mensa horn, but the Nobel committee was fairly impressed. True, Stockholm was never the same after the third wave of the Prion-22 virus, but pandemic contagions notwithstanding after securing the Nobel, PIWI paid me handsomely in market credit options before the alkaloid patent expired."

Sébastien sets his apple down and selects a wedge of cheese from the tray. He breaks off a tiny piece between his fingers.

"I was even a minor celebrity for a spell. Celebrated as one of the scientific golden boys of the new age, you know? Of course, I was much younger then and grew full of myself."

"You don't say."

A nibble of cheese. "Mmhm. The trappings of the credit-soaked playboy. I squandered great messy chunks of my fortune, but after a while one does tend to hit rock bottom with all that wealth without conscience hoopla. Thankfully when Dr. Corella and I met our combined ambitions were mutual." Sébastien spreads an arm in a wide arc. "Hence, the Commonage."

Koko shakes her head. "Man, what a waste. If I'd been rolling in that kind of bank I would've been smarter about keeping it. Built me a place near some action at least. Hell, maybe even invest in a sports franchise."

"Life is a terminal arrangement, Koko. Our motivations here are more proactive."

"Congratulations. You and Doctor Knockout operate a backwater fiefdom in the middle of fuck-knows-where."

Sébastien raises a finger. "Not a fiefdom, a community. A plausible kinship of like-minded souls cooperating peacefully under a shared and common authority."

"Being you and the good doctor, of course."

"I said shared and common, not absolute. The people here, they consult us just as much as we consult them… within reason."

"And they're here voluntarily?" Koko asks.

"All here were recruited for reasons far too extraneous to go into, but yes. The common denominator with all of them is that each sensed some equivocal deficiency in their lives."

"Welcome to the goddamn club," Koko says. "So, is it fair to say your pal Dr. Corella is rolling in the big PIWI bucks too?"

"No, but his contributions are different. We do, however, see eye to eye."

"Sounds romantic."

"It's not that type of partnership," Sébastien says.

Koko drifts from the window and looks around with disgust.

"So, you wasted all your money and built a settlement out in the prohib boonies. Great. Just great. I'm going to assume you've got outside contact."

"Oh, we do, but it's limited."

"Limited in what way?"

"Let's leave that for later."

Koko huffs. "So, if this Commonage joint is a settlement, where are your defenses? I may have been out of it before, Sébastien, but I've been vigilant. You're in the prohibs. You've got to have something."

"There's never been a need for defenses so there are none."

It's as though someone spilled a tall glass of ice water on Koko's retort gauge, burnt her toast, and dropped a sack of dead cats in her mental sink. Ten slow seconds later, she blinks once and then responds.

"None at all?"

"The specifics are much too intricate to get into now, but as a Special Economic Zone, let's just say nothing ever really bothers us here."

"But you've got walls."

"The walls were here previously. Two centuries ago when the republic tanked, this place was crudely designed to be a small township reservoir. Excellent bones. We customized the outer construction to fit our needs and had the compound filled in with enriched, contaminate-resistant—"

Koko holds up a hand. "You know what? Stop. Just stop because the colossal shit I'm not giving right now might start filling this room. I want out of here as soon as possible, understand? The next available transport when Flynn is stable."

Sébastien gets up from the desk. "That may take some time to arrange, but very well." He moves for the open door. "You know, it's been said that people are quick to judge others in order not to be judged themselves. Maybe you should think about that some. Come, Gammy."

Dutifully, Gammy pushes up and after giving Koko a quick sniff she trails after her master. When the two reach the open door Koko whistles and, in sync, Gammy and Sébastien turn.

"Yes?" Sébastien asks.

"Earlier when your guys brought us back from the sub, besides Flynn we were hauling along a dead body. Some kid."

Sébastien looks down at Gammy. Patting her head, he then carefully pokers up his gaze.

"Yeah," Koko continues, "if this place is so peachy, what was her deal, huh? Did she wise up and try to get out while she still had a fighting chance?"

Sébastien purses his lips. "That, I'm afraid, was an accident."

Koko sneers. "Right. Huge storm, a tra-la-la-la-la hike along the cliffs, an accident."

Sébastien tosses his ponytail. "Since you're electing not to be forthcoming about your plight, and we're helping your friend Flynn heal, perhaps it'd be best right now if you simply respect our grief. Come, Gammy."

And with that the two depart, and Sébastien firmly closes the door.

The second after the door shuts, Koko shimmies out of the blanket and sheets wrapped around her and sawmills the rest of the food on the tray. The cheese, bread, and all of the other potently sweet fruit—she even wolfs down the cores, including the one she casually tossed on the floor earlier, and the apple core Sébastien left behind on the desk. Brooding and gulping cool slugs of water from the carafe, she feels her strength coming back in slow waves. Koko then picks up the pear that fell on the floor and sticks it in her mouth.

Nine hundred kilometers give or take?

Damn, the storm blew the sub so far off course from her intentional heading, and now it seems it's totaled. Not only that, but they re-activated the tracking transponder which makes Koko wonder what, if any, additional electronics they may have retrieved from the vessel and what onboard files they might have looked at. It's a safe bet Sébastien and his doctor chum know all about her and Flynn by now or will soon: where they've come from and where they were headed. And none of this information sits well with her at all. All of this trying to be hospitable could be some elaborate ruse while they make contact with the CPB and The Sixty.

Sébastien's big show of the open door—*What, was that some kind of a test as well*? Does he actually think she'd even think of taking off without Flynn? Deeper personal emotions with Flynn aside, a fragment of her old private military code of conduct flips past Koko's thoughts—

Never abandon your wounded...

Fuckin-a right, so now is certainly not the time for Koko to sit idle. The clock is ticking, and she needs to get hopping.

After finishing off the pear from the floor she snaps out the folded clothes that Sébastien brought. A pale brown kurta-like top, just like the one he was wearing, tough canvas pants, two pairs of socks, and two single-piece Farmer John undergarments with functional snaps at the crotch. Koko runs the tips of her fingers along the seams and inspects the hems closely, searching for hidden software. The clothes appear clean. She lifts the material to her nose. Real clean. Targeting another whiff at her armpits, Koko frowns. Unlike her.

Checking the toiletries, Koko finds the items are basic. Four expandable chamois towels, a thick-toothed plastic comb, dental cleansers, and the usual pain-in-the-neck assemblage of feminine necessities. Unfortunately, Koko sees there isn't a razor in the supplies. Gray-haired bastard destroying her weapons and the first-aid kit laser scalpels. So much for trust.

Later, dressed in her new clothes (Koko opts to skip the undergarment—*yuck*), she retrieves her bug-out backpacks from outside the door in the hall. When she checks her wallet and counts out the credits, she finds that none are missing and that the NBC suits, while damp, are still intact. Koko pockets her credits, stuffs the suits back inside the backpacks, and tosses them by the bed.

It's time for a little Koko recon.

A QUICK SNOOP AT THE SPD&K AND SEC FIVE

In the tedious frippery of *Standard, Poor, Ding & Kwong's Worldwide Register of Corporations, Syndicates, and Multinationals*, Sébastien's former employer, Pharma Impetus Worldwide Industries, a.k.a. PIWI is listed as such:

PHARMA IMPETUS WORLDWIDE INDUSTRIES, LTD. - PIWI
PIWI Platz. 3426-A, Kastrup, Denmark 2787 FC – 09087655-75A.21
<>Entry: 1490;5643 - Volume 2, Silo 96553-A-87021 Current Geo Cycle Edition.
Chrm—Sutherland Vongas, III, Dep Chrm—Myrna Ngai Chen, Chief Exec Officer—Eliahu Solganik, Sr Exec V-P—Minnie Hoffenstern, Exec V-P—Rafael Mosier, Sr V-P (*Global Mktg*)—Mohammed Krantz, Sr V-P (Cor Devel)—Rocky Sinohara, Sr V-P (Engr)—Junxiong Gurkin, Sr V-P (Strat Bus Devel & Nat Rel)—Bashir Ali, Sr V-P (Cor Resources) Diedre Litwin.
Revenue: Over 80.00 bil world credit units
Market Saturation: 97.6%
Employees: 8,600-9000

WG INDEX TICKER – *PIWI*;
Primary Bank(s)—HICH, Credezbank AG, Landesbank Groupe;
Primary Legal Firm—Wolff, Deloitte & Tupper, LLP;
Defense/Acquisition/Risk— **CLASSIFIED**
Management Representation— **CLASSIFIED**
PRODUCTS: Adv. pharmaceutical technologies, diversified.
Ref. 45463278-90934231

As for Koko's aforementioned private military COC, Koko's former handlers, Global Resource/Syndicate Deployment Initiatives succinctly defines the code of conduct as follows:

SECTION 1. - [INSERT SOLDIER'S NAME], you have been bred, elected for enlistment, and have trained to your fullest potential. As such, henceforth, your fellow operatives in the field (whatever their origin, politics, or manner) should now be considered extensions of your own self. While contracts, business, and political objectives may fluctuate with field assignments, this extended kinship demands you demonstrate respect and solidarity within the frameworks of rank.
SECTION 2. - Your contractual obligations are deferential to the work statements, timelines, and project scopes of your employer(s) missions and/or assignments until your incapacitation, disciplinary actions, and/or death. Small or large, all operations will be carried out to their defined ends and, if need be, at the risk of your own life. Discipline, ruthlessness, and courage in the face of hardships—these are your strengths.
SECTION 3 - As you are now an elite military contractor/soldier, it is mandatory that you maintain your physical strength and combat preparedness at all times. Your most precious commodities are your skills, your powers of acute observation, and whatever weapons are at hand.

And, of course, last but not least…

***SECTION 4*. - You act with stealth and resolute purpose. You never surrender your dead. You never abandon your wounded. And under no circumstances do you ever, *ever* relinquish your weapons.**

WAS SHE HIS DREAMY LITTLE ROCK N' ROLL? (KIND OF)

After his vexing call on Koko, Sébastien returns with Gammy to his quarters. He then continues to pull together and examine all the assimilated research downloaded from resources worldwide, along with the extracted and analyzed information pulled from the acquired submarine electronics. It takes him some time, but he now feels he has a better bead on Koko and Flynn. Sadly, the lot verifies what Dr. Corella already suspected.

The two are in major hot water and definitely on the run.

All together it was rudimentary to connect the dots. The wrecked submarine was part of a fleet owned by the massive entertainment syndicate known as the Custom Pleasure Bureau. Of late, the Trang Xi Class unit had been used for underwater maintenance operations on the notorious resort archipelago known as The Sixty Islands. Several days prior, the CPB and the SI had filed a claim with their indemnification arbiters asserting that a vessel matching the sub's description had experienced an onboard electrical fire and subsequent implosion during a deep-water dive. A quick crosscheck of the CPB's less than adequately protected insurance companies' mainframes revealed that both Koko and Flynn had been employed on The Sixty Islands and that they'd perished in the wreck.

Odd.

Why didn't the CPB and The Sixty just report the submarine stolen?

Of course it would be a small challenge to orchestrate a fraudulent wreck site, especially at the claim's stated depth, but Sébastien wasn't so naïve to assume insurance assessors could not be bought, not with the financial resources at the CPB's disposal. In his previous luminous career at PIWI, Sébastien had been privy to the ingenious sorceries involved in public relations spins. If matters were suitably embarrassing perhaps the CPB meant to extract their retribution off the books. The idea of contacting the CPB briefly crosses his mind, but of course then he remembers the TAM research.

Koko's interest in the northern borders, Flynn's wound, a covered-up theft, a subsequent bogus insurance claim, coupled with Koko's prickly evasiveness—all of it suggests deeper problems.

The secondary task of finding and then sifting through Flynn's rather boring background turned out to be rather painless. Sébastien's systems confirmed Flynn, a former security deputy aboard the Second Free Zone sky barge known as *Alaungpaya*, opted out of his duties because of a Depressus diagnosis, just as Dr. Corella's blood work indicated. It's strange that Flynn never elected to follow through with his scheduled group suicide (something which nearly all the Depressus-afflicted commit to by contract), and the timeline of his predetermined commitment intersects and overlaps with some violent incidents aboard *Alaungpaya*. Intriguing stuff. Sébastien dwells on it and imagines that Koko was probably involved in some way.

In contrast, Koko's background was a bit more challenging to extrapolate. It took Sébastien's systems over an hour to hack into the intricate encrypted databases of three separate corporate military service providers until they hit upon a declassified Global Resource/Syndicate Deployment Initiatives file. Examining the data, Sébastien was horrified by Koko's gory career highlights: daring operations strewn across the planet with demonstrated skills at economic espionage and long-term combat operations. Never advancing much, Koko Martstellar apparently left her mercenary work to take a position on The Sixty Islands as a saloon and brothel operator, not once but twice.

Saloon and brothel operator?

So how did she partner up with Flynn? Their backgrounds were so drastically different. Were they or are they lovers, as Dr. Corella suggested? God, did it even matter?

Whatever the case, after the catastrophic incidents aboard *Alaungpaya*, both Koko and Flynn ended up on The Sixty Islands so the question is, what happened? What exactly prompted them to abscond with a submarine? All of the sybaritic violence on the resort is supposed to be simulated, but Flynn was shot. What other events had forced the two of them to do something so dangerous?

Sébastien time-tags and then saves all of his active analytics before terminating the blue-tinted arrays of his systems' projection screens and slowly thumbs his tired eyes.

Perhaps Dr. Corella is right. Perhaps the best way to keep handling Koko for now is to be hospitable and keep up the face. After all, Koko has just made it plain that her intentions are to move on and leave the Commonage as quickly as possible. Sébastien then remembers talking to Dr. Corella about starting Flynn on TAM to further whet the interests of his pharmaceutical contacts. Best to get on that, he thinks, so he opens a boilerplate document and spends a half hour spinning dispatches to those in the industry who have already expressed an ambiguous curiosity about some of his earlier communications. Indeed, previously, Sébastien shrewdly left out specifics as to what he and Dr. Corella have been working on (revealing your ideas and findings early in the pharmaceutical industry is like unzipping your own fly and having relations with a nest of fire ants), but since the project is so close to completion, now might be the suitable time to reveal a tiny bit more. With each message Sébastien makes sure to add the optimistic lines, "*While present exploratory efforts are now in the advanced stage and nearing completion, I am happy to report there may be applications for distressed Second Free Zone populations. Naturally, I look forward to sharing these new findings with you soon."*

Tactful. And just enough.

Once his dispatches are away, Sébastien then quickly types a message to Dr. Corella.

[MESSAGE START]
M/: Status/F?

Moments later comes a reply.

C/: Conscious. Recovery prognosis good. First TAM treatment initiated per previous disc. Status/K?
M/: KUTF.
C/: ?
M/: Keeping up the face.
C:/: Ah.
M/: K agitated of course, and some additional minor concerns.
C/: Elaborate.
M/: K/F originated from Custom Pleasure Bureau resort—The Sixty Islands. Stolen craft and circumstances cloudy. CPB, however, avows submarine destroyed @ The SI and K/F listed as killed. Insurance claim has been filed w/ CPB arbitrators.

A short pause and Sébastien waits for a response.

C/: Verified? Really, the CPB?
M/: Confirmed. Cover-up likely.
C/: Do we cease TAM w/ F?
M/: Negative. Note—if possible keep K/F separated.
C/: Separation will be difficult.
M/: Nuance req. Expect K but try. Eventual evac. imperative for K and present evaluation is she is of independent orientation. TAM/

Depressus opportunity too good to pass up. Cont. observations, etc. Note—brief comms to contacts regarding SFZ populations sent. Ambiguous phrasing but w/ TAM proj. nearing completion, preemptive luring appropriate.
C/: Any resp. frm contacts yet?
M/: No, but I'll keep you posted.
[MESSAGE END]

Sébastien signs off, stretches, and then looks toward his bedroom. Gammy is curled up on his unmade bed, so he blows a short two-count whistle, and the synthetic jumps down. As Gammy parades over and attempts to curl beneath his desk, Sébastien moves his chair back and rubs a boot along her ribs. Gammy lets out a contented blast of air from her dark nostrils and lies down. After a moment a bleak pall of sadness swells in Sébastien's throat.

Kumari…

So tragic and such a calamitous loss. He'd only shown the girl kindness, done his best to guide her, and this is how she chose to repay him? By hacking into his systems, running away, and attempting to destroy what he and Dr. Corella have sacrificed to build?

While admittedly Sébastien at first appreciated the girl solely for her aptitude, later on, he is pained to confess, it was Kumari's maturing exquisiteness that stirred something unassailably darker within him. Sébastien winces at the very thought of it. God, it wasn't as if he was some sex fiend or Nabokovian pervert; he knew such thoughts were wrong, implicitly, but still, from time to time he entertained other possibilities shamefully. If he were still back in the rest of the world, pursuing such corrupt inroads with any growing young girl, particularly if he didn't waste the remaining levels of his wealth, some may nary bat an eye. He knew of powerful people, men and women alike, who courted lovers with appalling age differences (typically vapid models or media darlings), but Sébastien's intentions were never like that at all. No, he was cleverer than that and had the stamina and judiciousness to wait. Still, people do make assumptions, and the prospect of bearing the corrosive burden of seedy suspicion from Dr. Corella makes him queasy—after all didn't he say something to that effect?

If you weren't so enamored and taken with the girl's intellect...

Sébastien replays some of Kumari and his times together. He questions whether he ever stepped over the line and let his more mischievous affections show. Encouraging light hugs and playful touches of camaraderie, of course, but did he ever present the rawer of his sentiments, even obliquely? God—women have a sixth sense about such things. Something suspicious misinterpreted could've set the poor girl off. Unspoken lechery and vile innuendos, equal parts decrepit and sexually hideous, did his unspeakable weakness for her motivate Kumari to pry into his systems and uncover the TAM research?

No. Sébastien definitely channeled his urges into her excessive tutoring, but damn it, he should have known better. The girl was a genius.

Climbing to his feet, Sébastien picks up the needle drive from his desk and then tosses it on the floor. With a quick succession of heel stamps, he smashes it to pieces and kicks the shards across the room. Gammy stretches, looks at him quizzically, and then barks.

Stupid, stupid, stupid...

THE TRICK AND GRUM SHOW

Meanwhile, three hundred meters outside the Commonage walls, two de-civs—Trick and Grum—conceal themselves in a thick stand of trees.

With small, obdurate eyes, Trick scrutinizes the Commonage's whitewashed walls. The smoky stench of campfire is strong on the morning breeze, and Grum drops a hand on Trick's shoulder.

"Porridge be primin'. Maybe you-me scram-amble back some now, huh?"

Trick turns his head and looks down at Grum's hand draped on his shoulder. A bearded troll weighing in at one hundred and twenty kilos, Grum quickly removes his hand as if scalded.

"Sorry," Grum mumbles.

Trick returns his attentions to the compound. "Put that meat hook on me again, I'll teach you hell from sorry."

As their nomadic group's leader, Trick doesn't entertain suggestions, not even with the friendliest of casual cajoling. No, sir, Trick is the chuffed and grizzled type, a fourth generation de-civ well-seasoned in pounding out a thin existence on society's disreputable edges. Lupine-featured, pugnacious, and sealskin brown, he'd sooner slice your throat and leave you for dead if you even tried to tell him what to do. Like targets in a carnival shooting range, two figures pace back and forth along the walled compound's parapets.

"How long we be at this, Grum?"

Grum bats a hand at a fly. "At what? You mean goonin' this place here?"

"No, dumbass, how long we be southin'?"

Grum runs his tongue over his abysmally brown teeth. His face knots up, and he counts his fingers in an attempt to tally the days.

"Been some time since we crossed the borders, I'll say that, right-right. Don't know. Two weeks now southin' for Sin Frontera, maybe?"

Trick rises from his crouch and leans his back against the papery bark of a spruce tree. Opening a flapped pocket on his waistcoat, he retrieves a jackknife and digs at some built-up grime beneath his fingernails.

"Wrong-o, doofus. Us be southin' closer to a month, nearly three and a half weeks on foot. Sick and hungry—hell, all of us nearly drowned in that big blow last night. But this place bein' out here, it gots me thinkin'..."

Grum looks at the compound and then back at Trick.

"Thinkin' 'bout what?"

Trick points with his jackknife. "Them. All this 'round me-you-me, nobody meant to be in these wasties. But here them be, big fancy castle-like on a hill."

Grum scratches his scalp and shoos off the fly again. Trick folds, stashes his jackknife, and then kicks him.

"Gots to lay it all out for you plain-like, don't I? All right, one... them being here, maybe it mean this place not so bad as they've be sayin' all these times. And two—" Trick's eyes squinch. "You smell that?"

"You mean the camp fire?"

"No, idiot—*dung*! There be dung on the wind. Stink like that means livestock. These wasties, if they be contaminated, how's that even possible?"

Grum shrugs. "I don't know. Maybe them be here before it be prohib."

Trick rubs his forehead like he's trying to smear back the biggest migraine in the world.

"Grum, the U-State collapse and Big China wars be a couple of hundred years oldy, don't you know nothin'? What, you think they be holed up here all the while livin' grid-wipe?" Trick shuffles his thumb in the direction of the compound. "You goon any corp-o or natty-like logos?"

"Uh-uh."

"Uh-uh be right-right. And y'know what else you no goon? No weapons. None. Not a single weapon stickin' out. Them two up there on them walls, they ain't even got pulse guns. I'm tellin' you, this place be reekin' oppor-tune."

Grum stares blankly at the compound.

"Oh."

"Damn, Grum, sometimes I swear you be dumber than them runts back at camp."

Grum moans. "Awww, don't be callin' them that, Trick."

Trick jeers contemptuously. "Oh, I know you're sweetmeat on the wee ones, you big clod, but I call them runts whatever I please. Hell, our group be southin' good clip before we picked up them breeders and they's whining broods. True than true, they be soft company, but if them want to south with us them best keep them runts squared. Got to say, still some places in the world where people eat babies, right-right."

"Oh, Trick..."

"'*Oh, Trick...*'—since when you be so putty-gutty?"

"I ain't putty-gutty."

"Oh, but you still be fond of them runts now, ain't you? Wee ginger one be, like, your big lovestar."

"Trick, stop..."

"Shut it."

Together, the two start off back toward the camp, pushing through webbed vegetation.

"And jaw this," Trick says. "If that compound be a real-deal, they'd got to have the scannin' tech, so why nobody take us out yet? Scannin' tech be SOP for a real-deal outpost. To the holys, no corp-o or natty-like logos, all nicely painted..."

"Maybe them be protectin' somethin'. "

Trick hoots. "Damn, boy, that's be the first smart thing you've said all day. Then again, walls might mean them be scared."

"Scared? Scared of who?"

"De-civs like us."

Grum laughs and quickly he cups his hand over his mouth. When Trick whips around and lands a punch in Grum's solar plexus, Grum drops to his knees hard.

Trick leans over him. "What'd I say about laughin' like that, huh? What'd I say?"

"Ow! Sorry, Trick. Really, I think it was just kind of funny is all. I mean, why them be scared of people like us?"

Trick picks up a branch and breaks it over his knee.

"Get up, we be wastin' time. The test at camp will get the smart of it. Got to make us a plan."

"A plan? But what 'bout southin'? What 'bout Sin Frontera?"

Trick hurls the two pieces of the broken branch off.

"Sin Frontera gots to wait," Trick says.

WANDER AND VISIT

Once she clears the windowed doors of Lodge Delta, Koko's ears immediately pick up a familiar sound—organized, regimented instruction. Moving left and rounding the building, she finds a group of thirty adults inside a pruned circle of ryegrass perhaps fifty meters in diameter. The adults appears to be in the midst of a session of guided exercise, and as they move harmoniously a strikingly tall woman with long black hair speaks in an even-tempered tone just off to the side. Noticing Koko's presence, the tall woman claps her hands together and crosses over to Koko.

"Why, hello! You must be one of the strangers. The one who calls herself Koko, am I right? I'm Pelham. It's super-great to meet you."

Super-great?

"Sébastien and Dr. Corella informed everyone about your situation," Pelham says. "My goodness, to survive such an ordeal at sea, you must be very brave. Would you care to join us? Our diurnal routines are quite invigorating."

Koko side-eyes her. "Uh, thanks for the offer, but I think I'll pass."

"Really? There's plenty of room. We're a friendly lot."

"Maybe some other time."

"All right then."

Koko points. "Hey, the infirmary is over there, right?"

Pelham tilts her head and follows Koko's hand. "The infirmary? Why? Is something wrong?"

"No, I'm fine, it's just that—"

Pelham leans back and taps her forehead with two fingers. "Oh, I forgot. Dr. Corella is still treating your friend. I'm so sorry to hear that he was badly injured. Flynn, isn't it?"

"You know his name?"

"Of course," Pelham replies cheerfully. "It's better for all within the Commonage if there aren't any secrets. Sébastien made a brief announcement earlier this morning, and an update was posted on the community message board. Everyone here is supposed to assist you as best we can." Pelham looks fleetingly back at her waiting group and then returns her attentions to Koko. "The infirmary is in the administration building right across the courtyard. Just take that path back around Lodge Delta and head across. Any door should suffice."

To Koko, Pelham's overt sunniness is almost galling. While she still feels it's important to keep her guard up, she harks back to how, when she was in the field, it often paid off to play the angles as they came at you. Koko figures now might be one of those times so she gestures to the exercise group.

"For what it's worth, you guys look pretty good. *T'ai chi ch'uan*, right?"

"Oh, do you practice?"

"I'm familiar with a lot of martial arts."

"I see. Well, being healthy is a priority for everyone here at the Commonage."

Pelham then claps three times before she turns and addresses the group. "Ready, everybody? Let's start from the beginning once more. First position."

Sallying off and circling around Lodge Delta again, Koko makes her way across the courtyard. Taking her time, she absorbs as much detail of the grounds as she can, and keeps an eye peeled for potential ground transport or aircraft. Now in the light of day she estimates there are more than a dozen buildings of varying sizes within the compound. Brick-faced with scooped solar-reflective roofs, nearly all of the buildings are hedged with serried vegetable-producing gardens, fruit trees, and plants of productive vines.

Beyond the central administration building, she spies four massive white tents and makes out the wooden edges of a large fenced-in animal area. She recalls coming through a dark tunnel when the group brought her, Flynn, and the dead girl back during the storm, so she tries to pinpoint the tunnel's precise location. Two larger support outcroppings on the westward wall frame a dark, arched gap, and it looks right. Koko decides to check out the tunnel later after she looks in on Flynn.

Entering the administration building, Koko sees one of the twins napping at an oval reception desk in the foyer. Now, less doped up, Koko struts forward and gives the desk a sharp kick to rouse him.

"Yo, where's the infirmary, Tweedledum?"

"Wha—?"

"You're one of the two guys who took me to my room last night, right?"

The man behind the desk rubs his eyes. "That's right. I'm Bonn. My brother is Eirik."

"I'm here to see my friend, Bonn."

"Of course. Just give me a second and I'll take you."

"I can find it myself."

Bonn holds up a hand and gets up. "Dr. Corella prefers a heads-up before anyone enters the infirmary." Now standing, Bonn is shorter than Koko remembers, maybe a hand or two shorter than her, and he comports himself solidly. "Follow me."

Two turns down two separate hallways and less than a minute later, Koko and Bonn arrive at a windowless metal entry. A plaque bolted in the center of the door reads INFIRMARY, and the door itself doesn't look familiar. Koko recalls exiting a different set of doors last night when she was all goofed up, so she assumes the door must be a secondary egress or entry. Bonn casually taps an adjacent keypad on the wall, and the door unlocks with a snap. When Bonn slips inside, Koko tries to follow, but he stops her with a hand.

"I'll be back in a few ticks. Let me make sure they're not in the middle of something."

"Take your hand off me. I want to see my friend."

Bonn retracts, seals the door quickly, and it locks off. Koko blows a lock of hair from her forehead and rebukes herself for not paying closer attention. She could've easily memorized the code when Bonn tapped it into the keypad. Hell, she could have barged past him, and now she has to stew. Five annoying minutes later, Bonn opens the door again and waves her inside. Dr. Corella greets her coolly with a pleat of slight aggravation on his brow.

"Ah, Koko. I wish you'd waited until I sent someone for you, but no matter. You're here. We've removed Flynn from the IC tank. He's fully regained consciousness."

Koko sucks in a breath. "He *has*?"

"Yes. His response has been better than even I expected. There were a few moments when you and he first arrived when I had some concerns, but I must say for what he's been through he's doing remarkably well."

"Flynn is tougher than he looks."

"Apparently," Dr. Corella says. "But now that you're here I'd like to ask you something. During Flynn's tests I found trace deposits of anti-Depressus medications in his blood. Tell me, were you aware of this?"

It doesn't feel right sharing anything with anyone, especially not a doctor who just recently felt it was no big thing to shoot her full of drugs. If Koko hadn't met him back on *Alaungpaya*, Flynn would have gone through with an elective mass suicide known as Embrace. Flynn had only registered for the mass termination because he believed he was ridden with Depressus, the severe psychosis acedia afflicting portions of the lower atmospheric orbits. Now that he's fully off his meds Koko thinks Flynn's temperament and despondent outlook has improved significantly, but still she's more than a bit wary of the doctor's interest. Once again she reminds herself to play the angles.

"He used to live up top," she says. "Flynn only thought he had Depressus. The whole thing was kind of a mistake. A big mix-up."

Dr. Corella looks at her and says nothing.

"So, where's my boy?" she asks.

Dr. Corella reaches out to take her by the elbow, but when Koko jerks her arm away the doctor immediately re-evaluates his gesture. Koko follows him and expects Bonn to tag along, but when she looks over her shoulder, he simply hangs back. Fifty steps later Dr. Corella shepherds Koko through a pale, floor-to-ceiling tracked curtain, and as they enter the space the lighting above Flynn's bed brightens. The myriad of tubes that were plugged into Flynn earlier are now gone, and a single yellowish catheter worms out from beneath the tight blankets covering him. Flynn's hair is combed and his repaired leg is elevated on a pillow. When his familiar musk reaches her nose, Koko is almost too overcome to speak, and a hot clot rises in the back of her throat. For some reason she can't immediately determine, Flynn's left eye is bandaged with white gauze like a pirate. When Koko looks up to ask Dr. Corella about the eye, the doctor parts the curtains and slips away. Koko moves closer to Flynn.

"Hey, baby… it's me."

Flynn's good eye flutters. "Koko…?"

"Hey, stud muffin, how's it hanging? You doing okay?"

Koko takes his hand, and Flynn's skin feels warm and dry like sun-dried paper.

"Mmmm…"

"Shhhh. They're taking care of you. You're doing fine."

Flynn licks his lips. "What… happened? I remember… I remember being in the sub and then being all wet. Man, I've been having the craziest dreams. Where am I?"

Better keep things digestible. "Our sub wrecked along the Nor'Am prohibs. It's not C-GRAP, but I think we're okay for now."

"The prohibs?"

"Yeah, ol' Northwestern United Shakes of Scare-merica."

"But I thought... I thought you knew what you were doing."

Koko sighs. "Well, we were doing fine, but then we hit a debris field while we were submerged, and the collision kind of messed up the sub's steering. I'm sorry, but I did the best I could. Do you remember the storm?"

"I remember getting jerked around a lot if that's what you mean."

"Yeah, well, you were pretty out of it. Anyway, the bottom line is we're both alive. We made it across the Pacific."

"But not to C-GRAP?"

"No, not to C-GRAP. We were rescued."

Flynn shuts his good eye and slowly licks the corners of his mouth.

"But by who? Where are we?"

"It's complicated, but we're at someplace called the Commonage."

"I'm so confused..."

"I know, sweetie, don't worry."

"And tingly," Flynn adds. "They gave me a shot before."

Koko clears her throat and fingers away a tingle creeping near the bridge of her nose. "You dumb bunny, you're probably too goofed up on painkillers to feel much of anything."

Flynn grins slushily. "Mmm, s'good stuff, but that's not what I mean. The shot... the doctor, Corella? He put it through my eye."

"*Your eye?*"

"Yeah."

"But why?"

"I don't know. He said something about sepsis."

Koko's ears burn. She bends forward and quickly kisses Flynn's forehead.

"You get some rest," she says straightening. "I'll be back as soon as I can, and then I'll see if we can get you out of here, okay?"

"Okay..."

As Flynn quickly fades off, Koko studies his face for a few seconds and the bandage on his eye, before she turns and rips back the surrounding curtains. Not far away just down the hall Dr. Corella is speaking with Bonn. A small analytic projection rotates in the air between the two men. Koko cruises through the display like a freight train.

"Okay, Doc," she says, backing Dr. Corella up. "This is what you're going to do. You're going to give me a complete account of Flynn's treatments, and I mean all of it. Blood work, that fucking eye injection, who here administered what, whatever you juiced into his system, right down to an itemized list of the manufacturers of his sutures and the width of the catheter shoved up his weenie, got it? You're going to give me this in both printed and digitized forms right now, no arguments."

Dr. Corella balks. "But, Koko, I assure you, everything we're doing for Flynn has been—"

Eyes like bayonets, Koko metronomes a single index finger back and forth like a switch.

"Just get it. Now."

SOMEWHERE OVER THE PACIFIC I

MORTEM DESURSUM

Blasting across the Pacific sky at a smooth altitude of ten thousand feet, Wire heads north-northeast at hypersonic speed without a shred of trepidation behind her newly acquired aircraft's controls.

Slope-surfaced and matted black for stealth, her new aircraft is a PAE Aerodynamics Goliath gunship. Primarily designed for long-range military theater engagements, the Goliath on first impression seemed a bit much for her needs, but now that she pushes the bejesus out of its twin fusion-powered thrusters, she's happy she reconsidered the purchase. All said and done, with dueling quad-racks of ASM missiles and state-of-the-art pulse cannons, the Goliath is absolutely badass, nose to tail.

Wire's munitions and clothes are stowed in a hold beneath the cockpit, but in one of her tactical suit's deep cargo pockets she carries her evasion and worst-case scenario gear. Bifurcated and sealed in two vacuum-pack pouches, this gear includes: a blowout trauma kit; two laser flares; a multi-tool gyro-motion-powered flashlight; a tarry of synthetic energy protein (toasted coconut); a rack of five pulse grenades; and a holstered Sig Sauer sub-compact pistol flush-fit with an extended power magazine.

Wire has been itching to try out the Goliath's pulse cannons and briefly she entertains a daydream of turning around and blowing by The Sixty, smoking every last inch of the resort just for spite. Yeah, lighting up those islands would be so satisfying. If she was lucky she might even take out that stupid fink Britch who deported her to Surabaya. But she left the resorts' greater coordinates hours ago so now her retaliation will have to take the shape of a carefully crafted flowcode message she types into the Goliath's comms.

Once her message is away, Wire checks her transoceanic navigational charts. Assembled, the lustrous arrays in front of her indicate a small commercial trawler up ahead, plugging northward across the sloppy seas at a steady twenty-eight knots. The vessel is of meager manifest value, hauling scrap metal destined for the offshore smelting rigs in the Sea of Okhotsk.

A closer examination of the charts reveals the nearest vessel to the trawler is over one hundred and ten nautical miles away. As the vessel isn't connected to any larger commercial syndicate that might cause her any future concern, Wire dips the Goliath beneath the clouds and increases her speed.

Soon the trawler is within range. Seventy nautical miles out now and in the next second—fifty. With a sweep of her finger, she syncs the Goliath's pulse cannon guidance systems to her newly repaired ocular, and half a second later a red-tinted overlay melts into her vision: ACQUIRED.

With a single blink of her eye, the pulse cannons fire. Strafing past, one of several rounds catches the trawler's stern fuel tanks and obliterates the vessel in a molten fireball.

Fuck yes!

Wire streaks past the flaming smear on the ocean's surface like a predacious black demon and pulls back on the Goliath's stick, grinning. Dragging g-forces instantly engage her tactical suit stress functions to modulate her blood flow, and climbing higher into the sky, the Goliath finally stabilizes. Soon Wire thinks—*Oh, why the hell not?*

She steers the Goliath into a victory barrel.

As the sun's glinting orb spirals over the translucent rind of the canopy, Wire lets out a bellowing whoop. Flying higher still, she whoops some more.

THE SIXTY III

HORACE BRITCH, IN REPOSE

Meanwhile, back on The Sixty, security officer Horace Britch sinks into a comfortable recliner and stares out the window of his residential quarters. The setting sun outside washes a golden shimmer across the ocean's surface and burnished edge, and the cheerless, dreadnought silhouettes of several massive Second Free Zone lower orbital barges can be seen in the distance.

Speculating on what has happened to Wire, Britch wonders if the bounty agent is still amongst the living. He's heard stories about how the poorest of the poor in Surabaya sometimes resort to cannibalism in order to survive, and he realizes the odds were certainly not in Wire's favor. Maybe he shouldn't have gone ahead and forwarded all of the records on Martstellar to her, but really—where was the harm? The Sixty and the Custom Pleasure Bureau's board of directors elected not to pursue the matter further, so it was no skin off his nose. Britch felt a certain meager obligation to keep up his end of the bargain, if only as a final, insulting taunt.

Switching his thoughts to his extorted credits, he tests a cocktail of rum and muddled lemon in a glass and wonders if maybe he should've taken more. After all, executing such a reprehensible play with Wire was chancy. If his superiors somehow learned of his less than honorable gains, the act would be grounds for immediate punitive action. With disciplinary infractions all staff on The Sixty receive a three-count tally before lethal measures are addressed, but dear lord… the extra influx of credits… it was so worth it. A well-deserved, welcome dividend; something for life's rare and precious luxuries for a change.

After Wire's deportation, Britch spent his first dip into the purloined credits on hard-to-procure foodstuffs. The luscious quadruple-distilled Himalayan rum he so shamelessly watered down with lemon for instance, and the tin of tank-raised Ossetra caviar spooned onto butter-crisps on a plate at his elbow. Ever careful, Britch prudently used back channels and scrambled these expensive food purchases via his private off-world accounts. It felt thrilling to round out his personal larder frankly, and with little things here and there, as long as he doesn't overdo it, he's confident he shouldn't attract any unwarranted attention.

As he leans over to select a caviar crisp, a ponging two-note at his door chimes. His quarters' augmented intelligence systems advise him on the callers:

"Three visitors, Horace."

Visitors?

Britch freezes. He has few friends on The Sixty (none at all, to be honest) and a chill drops through his stomach and shrinks his balls.

"Identify, please."

Before the AI systems can reply, the locks on his quarters' entry are bypassed—*kla-klack!*—and the door swishes inward with a reptilian hiss.

Getting up and turning, Britch sees three men. The first sports a slicked-back white pompadour, and the green rectangular badge fastened to the man's lapel is bad, bad news.

"Good evening, Officer Britch," the pompadour man says prissily. "Odin Riche, Chief Inspector with the SI Customs Office. Might I have a word with you for a moment?"

Britch doesn't move. The two men with Riche he recognizes as novices in The Sixty's security ranks. Hard, Gauleiter-like eyes and side arms at the ready.

"Um, I was just about to turn in," Britch replies, placing the caviar crisp back on the plate near his recliner. "Not feeling all that well, actually. Is something wrong? What's this all about?"

Riche starchily steps inside. "I'm sorry to intrude, but earlier this afternoon a distressing matter was brought to my office's attention."

Britch's face goes sheet white. "Oh?"

"Yes," Riche replies. "A flowcode message, actually, sent from an individual you recently handled for deportation proceedings." Riche flashes a neat reef of tiny teeth. "As you probably know, our office typically dismisses such messages from patrons who've experienced untimely expulsions from The Sixty, you know, sour grapes and all that. But SI management is electing to adopt a more hands-on stance with following up on any and all complaints. Part of the quality control initiative the CPB announced last week. Did you, by chance, happen to read the quality control brief circulated?"

Britch drains the rum in his glass. His hand shakes.

"Um, I'm not really sure..."

"I see. Well, there are so many briefs circulating these days I can see how you might've forgotten. In any case, this deportee, the one who sent the flowcode message? She alleges that prior to her expulsion you obtained a significant amount of credits from her under great physical duress."

Britch forces a short laugh. "That's preposterous!"

"Preposterous or not, this is her assertion."

"Can I see a copy of this alleged flowcode message?"

"By all means."

Riche produces a datatab from his jacket and hands it over.

After taking the device, Britch reads a neat, single-spaced, typed paragraph. Twice. The details within are devastating.

Why that muscle-headed...

"Well?" Riche asks.

Britch hands back the datatab. "I'm sorry, but this isn't true. It's a blatant lie."

Riche stuffs the datatab back into his jacket.

"So this is your position?"

"Of course it is my position!" Britch squawks. "Good lord, you know you can't trust a person like that."

"And why is that?"

"She's a bounty agent. They're not exactly known for their scruples."

"Indeed," Riche says, "but as you just read, the communiqué also listed violations of at least three security protocols."

Britch whines, "Oh, c'mon. This Wire person is just raw because I arrested her before she took out her supposed target. Wild allegations like that—she only sent the message to get back at me because I was the primary on her infraction. It's ridiculous. Nothing but sour grapes, like you said."

Stepping farther into Britch's quarters, Riche approaches the window and takes in the now darkening view.

"But this patron asserts you transferred credits from her to an off-world account. If this did occur, under the threat of death no less, it's my responsibility to verify the accusation."

"So?"

"So, once we received this message we confirmed some unusual purchasing activity from your own off-world accounts."

Britch's mouth falls open. "My accounts? But those, those are supposed to be private."

"Are you assuming I'm not taking the new quality control initiatives seriously?"

"No, sir, I'm not, but—"

"Given your depleted compensation package, which also is no big secret I'll tell you, these purchases were quite disproportionate to your means."

"But I've been thrifty."

"Thrifty?"

"I saved up and bought a few things to treat myself. It's not unheard of."

"At present the going market price for quadruple-distilled Himalayan rum borders on the insane."

Britch deflates. Dancing shoes or not, his stonewalling jitterbug with Riche appears up, so now what? The little pompadoured twerp and his novice flunkies are going to escort him back to resort HQ for a disciplinary hearing? Great. That is just fucking great. They'll probably stick him with extra patrol shift assignments and cut his pay again to send a message. They might even elect to sack him completely, the bunch of nit-picking jerks.

Riche then notices the plattered caviar crisps next to Britch's recliner.

"Ooh, is this the Ossetra you purchased? May I?"

Britch sighs resentfully. "At this point, why not? Help yourself."

Riche selects and slides a crisp into his mouth. Cocking an appreciative eyebrow, he emits a snuffle and then gently takes the empty glass with the smashed lemon from Britch's hand.

"Listen, had you waited to appease your gluttonous appetites, we might not even be having this conversation. The truth is I need to be somewhere in a few minutes so it would be better for us both if you just admit out loud what you've done. Forthrightness could bode well for you in regards to this evening's disciplinary measures."

Britch glooms. "Fine, whatever. So I shook that bounty agent down for a few thousand credits. Big deal. I bet half the security staff on The Sixty are guilty of worse chisels and then some."

"That may be true, but those malfeasances are not my concern."

"Sheesh, so now that I've admitted it, do you think we have time for one last drink?"

Demurely as a debutant Riche pats his chest. "Oh my, you mean the quadruple-distilled rum? Well, I really shouldn't, but yes. Thank you for offering."

Britch looks at the two security novices. Declining, the two steely-eyed men shake their heads, so Britch trudges over to a nearby table where the bottle of expensive Himalayan rum sits. He makes Riche a drink and when he comes back and hands it over Britch removes his glass from Riche's other hand and glugs out a hefty four fingers of rum for himself.

"This hardly seems fair," Britch complains. "I mean, so I went ahead and bent a few rules. This bounty agent, she's the real criminal if you ask me. I swear, the CPB and SI management's priorities are all out of whack getting upset over something like this."

Riche jerks the bottle out of his hand and rum splashes all over Britch's shirt.

"Seriously, you don't remember the quality control brief circulated last week? It outlined a new zero-tolerance policy."

"Zero-tolerance?"

"Mmhm."

The two novices draw their sidearms.

Britch barely registers the split second before the two open fire and his body bursts into flames.

THE COMMONAGE IV

AN IMMODEST PROPOSAL

Back at the camp, Trick leaps up onto a set of the mortared bricks half buried in the ground, and the rest of the gathered de-civs settle down. Weary, bloodshot eyes abound, and more than a few of them pick at festering facial lesions.

It takes Grum some effort, but he climbs up onto the half-buried blocks and takes up a bodyguard pose behind Trick. When Grum is set and Trick is sure he has everyone's undivided attention, only then does he begin.

"All right, I'll keep it short. As you know, our southin' has been longer and more difficult than most of us expected. After that storm, I bet lots of you probably flat out thinkin' just how much more of this southin' you can actually take. No lie from me. Be months yet likely, right-right, and I bet more than half of you will die." Trick passes his gaze over the sunken, diseased faces and holds a moment for dramatic effect. "So, here we be, in the godforsaken wasties and what do we goon here on this little pit stop on our journey south? Truer-than-true, I'll tell you what. A settlement, right smack in the middle of a place not supposed to have a livin' soul for a couple hundred years plus. Like you, when I gooned them walls, I thought, this can't be good. Best move quick, right-right?"

Trick is spouting gospel as far as the rest of the de-civs in the camp are concerned. There are more than a few sickly, bobbing chins.

"Yeah, we've known fortifications back north. Them and their paramilitary lapdogs, treatin' our kind like we ain't even human. Starvin' us, huntin' us down, some of you've even been kicked out of their so-called assimilation locales and damn well know what kind of hell those places be. Shit, it's why most of us lit out for Sin Frontera in the first place. I swear, this mornin' with that place I half expected armed squads roustin' us up, but no-no. Here we be, here we be."

A few heads turn to look at each other, but no one says anything. Trick pauses again, and when one finally raises a voice Trick is not at all surprised by who speaks up. It's a woman he's been keeping tabs on for a while now—a gap-toothed, former tar-sand pitter named Shirley.

Shirley claims she used to jockey an extraction crusher before she got reclassified as de-civ, and she's made no bones about how she's been gaming for Trick's leadership slot. Despite her coarse, corn-cobbed looks, Trick knows the woman has that unctuous, politicking charisma about her. Lately Shirley has been going on and on about how they're on the wrong track, arguing that their group should move off the coast altogether and head east for the mountains. When she brutes her way to the front of the group, Trick tenses.

"Judas Priest on a strat-sled," Shirley cries. "What we waitin' for then? We need to get a move on now while we still gots ourselves a chance."

Trick turns to Grum and gives him a calibrated look that he should keep an eye on Shirley before he turns back to address her.

"And where do you think we should go, huh? To the mountains? Oh, I know that's what you've been campaignin' for. Oh me, oh my! Run for the hills! Run for the hills! Be safer up in the mountains."

"Damn right," Shirley says. "We pack up now we could make

them foothills by sundown. That compound? We got no idea who they be and that means trouble."

Trick takes his jackknife from his waistcoat and unfolds it.

"Okay, okay… let me ask you a question then, Shirley. Do you know why walls like that be built?"

"Hell, man, I don't know and don't really care."

"Well, you should," says Trick. "Other than prisons, walls are for keeping things of value in or for keeping those seekin' those same things out."

"So?"

"So, if them got it in for us do you really think we could outrun them to the goddamn mountains?"

"Maybe they're fixin' to now the storm's passed."

"Doubt it. Grum and me, we be just up there and gooned no natty-like or corp-o logos. Not only that but we gooned no weapons neither. No logos or weapons? That compound might be independents, like down Sin Frontera."

Shirley glances back at the others. "Thinkin' like that could mean our lives, Trick."

"Oh, dry up, Shirley. Did you goon them up close? No, you be back here sucking down grackle-bone porridge and dandelion tea. I'll put it to the rest of you. When was the last time you ever heard of anythin' remotely natty-like with corp-o be unfortified?"

Someone else in the camp, a woman gathering a child close to her side, raises her voice.

"But they could be hidin' their guns."

Trick laughs. "Oh, c'mon! Hidin' their guns? Why'd they do that? Tell you what, though, they looked clean and well fed, that's for damn sure. If them people ain't armed and are independents, I say we jig that to our advantage."

Shirley says, "How?"

"Send out some of the runts to beg for supplies."

"Them?! Out there on their own? For all we know there be concussion mines surrounding the place."

Trick looks to the others. "How many of you be hungry?"

A lot of murmuring now and belly rubs.

"Yeah, me too," Trick says. "Stretchin' mealy oats with whatever creatures we can catch, washing it all back with bad water killin' us slow. Yeah, I know you think it be better to protect them runts, but this be about their survival too. We be dyin' out here. Them runts could goon the place out and get a drift of what's what."

Shirley steps closer and jabs an accusatory finger up at Trick.

"You. You're nothin' but a bald-faced, scheming liar. I knew you were a weaselly little prick the minute I laid eyes on you. Hell, you want to beg? You want to get killed or blown up, maybe you ought to do it your own damn self."

Trick has had enough. In a screaming burst, he launches himself off the bricks and tackles Shirley to the ground. At first there are so many thrashing arms, kicks, bites, and punches, it's hard to see who has the upper hand, but soon Shirley starts to buck as if she's having a seizure. When everyone sees Trick jiggling his jackknife across her neck, the entire camp lets out a collective gasp.

It's been some time since Trick took someone's life, and the great runny necklace of blood that pours out of the carved gash startles him. Stumbling backward, he catches his wind as Shirley desperately tries to stem the hot flow of life leaving her throat. When she finally goes still, Trick wipes the jackknife on his pants.

"Well, now. I guess that settles it then," he says.

THE INTERMENT CONTINUED

After Dr. Corella hands over the medical materials she demanded, Koko checks in on Flynn once more and finds him snoring peacefully. She needs him well so they can make tracks as soon as possible, so she leaves him and steams out of the infirmary and administration building to clear her head.

Once outside, Koko crosses the courtyard. Finding a low granite bench and with the data plug with mirroring information shoved into one of her pockets, she sits down and begins sifting through Dr. Corella's printouts.

All in all the medical nomenclature is insipidly dry, and it's difficult to make sense of the curative mumbo-jumbo. Subcutaneous and intramuscular dosage amounts, perplexing nano-surgery and grafting procedures, flesh mending accelerants, and lengthy compound descriptions that read like numeric and alphabet soup. When Koko demanded to know why he gave Flynn a shot in the eye, Dr. Corella quickly explained that the sepsis from Flynn's wound had swollen a forward portion of his brain and to relieve the pressure within, an invasive craniotomic procedure needed to be performed to relieve the edema. The doctor guaranteed Koko that, despite the slight discomfort, Flynn's eye was not affected by the injection. Koko doesn't like it (or Dr. Corella, for that matter) but in the end, in the cold light of day, she supposes the plus is in the upside: it looks like Flynn is back from the brink.

Taking a break from her reading, Koko raises her head and notices a group of twenty people walking in two lines several hundred meters away across the compound. It's a solemn procession and at once she realizes it must be the burial for the dead girl. A self-propelled wheeled plank bears a shrouded body, and there are about six in the lead portion of the procession, with Sébastien in front along with a bereft-faced man and woman. Middle-aged, Koko figures the couple must be the dead girl's parents. Born in the collectives and technically hatched in laboratory conditions, Koko's biological progenitors were nothing more than a deliberately selected helix cocktail of genetic code. Searching, Koko comes up short on sympathy.

Recent emotional growth spurts with Flynn notwithstanding, she still finds she cannot break free of some deep-seated personal convictions, one of which is that she utterly despises funerals. Death—she's seen more than her fair cut, inflicted much more for her bread and butter, but the archaic necessity of such ceremonies escapes her. Sure, she admits, you grieve for the loss that someone's death tears into your life, but she's always been of the mind that you beat the ground privately and you keep the orb of your sorrow brief. Taking the whole ghoulish spectacle public moves into some sort of maudlin narcissistic realm, so go ahead and ask the dead. If the dead could speak they'd probably look at you askance and say, why bother? Dead is dead, and gone is gone. They're not coming back. Let them get back to the primary six elements as quick as possible. Whatever… at least they don't draw things out here.

A voice, calm and observant, speaks beside her.

"Such a sad thing…"

Koko looks up. It's the t'ai chi instructor she met earlier, the tall woman who introduced herself as Pelham. Koko brushes a nonexistent piece of lint off her pant leg and folds up the medical printouts of Flynn's treatments. She stuffs the papers into one of her pant pockets, the one with the data plug.

"I wouldn't know," Koko says.

Pelham motions to the granite bench. "Do you mind?"

Koko makes room and Pelham sits down. "She was a rosy, creative spirit in every sense. Vivacious and wicked smart… her mother and father were some of the first to join the Commonage, back during the recruitment phase. Sébastien was her tutor."

"Oh?"

"Yes. And she was an only child too."

"Sorry to hear that."

"It's all such a mystery," Pelham continues. "Honestly, why would she be out along the cliffs during such bad weather? We'd all known for days the storm was imminent. Her parents are heartbroken."

"Got a name?"

"Didn't Sébastien tell you? Her name was Kumari."

"Pretty. I guess I owe her."

"Owe her? In what way?"

"Well, the search party. If they hadn't been out looking for her, Flynn and I might not have made it."

"Ah, I see. I suppose fate does present its roundabout gifts now and then."

Koko suppresses a short laugh, and Pelham turns.

"What's so funny? You're not the type who believes in fate?"

"Gee, whatever gave you that idea?"

Pelham looks back and regards the procession. "There's no need to be so cold, you know."

Koko composes herself, and together they watch the procession move off between two larger, oblong Commonage buildings.

Cold? What would you know about being cold?

If Pelham wants to see Koko cold she should try a stint looking into her eyes when she's really good and mad.

Still, however casual, Pelham's observation irks. Is she really that insensitive? Life has schooled Koko in harsh truths. Her thoughts skating back to Flynn, Koko supposes Flynn's outward considerate nature is similar to Pelham's. Always thinking about others, always flexibly giving people the benefit of the doubt. She's a little ashamed to admit it, but Koko has never been so taken with someone with such naïve convictions before. With Flynn (well, at least before that stupid bounty hunter showed up and everything went straight in the proverbial shitcan) it's been different. Real different. With Flynn it's as though everything in Koko's life has suddenly fallen into place somehow. Despite his softer gullibilities, life with him actually felt good for a change. She wonders if she was unhappy before Flynn dropped into her life. She doesn't think so, and frankly, she isn't sure what real happiness is. Weighed against everything that has fallen apart for her before, she imagines the ease she feels with Flynn could be called happiness. Hell, all the damages she's endured, the years of inexplicable destruction and horror, all for nothing but a stingy paycheck. But now with Flynn it feels like going through all that has been somehow worth it.

On more than one occasion Flynn has told Koko he could give a hot, high-flying hoot about her lethal history. Not only that, but he's always made a big effort to equalize and soothe the darker voids she tries hard to keep inside. Naturally, all this introspection begs a bigger question.

Does she love Flynn?

Koko loathes the conceptual underpinnings of love, seeing such declarations as lies of convenience to gussie up hot-to-trot chemistries. She's always been mortified to cop to such sappiness. However, what Koko does believe is that with Flynn these past several months she's felt like a better person with a shot at a more productive future.

The truth is, Flynn is kind of a fun guy. He makes her laugh, calls her out on her shortcuts, and tries with every sort of silly, awkward kindness to please her. Koko knows there are always risks with personal attachments, and sadly those risks tend to teeter you on a precarious verge. It makes her wonder. Would she be projecting such chilliness now if things had turned out differently? What if these people at the Commonage hadn't found them or given Flynn the medical attention he needed? *Hell*, Koko thinks, *maybe I should stop being such a frosty fish.*

"Look, Pelham," she says. "I know I come off hard, but I'm just used to seeing things black and white. You really don't know the first thing about why we ended up here."

"I'm willing to listen if you need a friend."

Koko looks at her.

Pelham smiles shyly. "So, did you find the infirmary all right?"

"Yeah, I did. Thanks."

"Not a problem. Glad to help. How is your friend Flynn doing?"

Koko stands. "He's conscious, but he's still a bit out of it. Dr. Corella claims he's making significant improvement, but then again I'm not the sort who trusts doctors."

"Oh, but Dr. Corella is an exceptional practitioner. He wouldn't tell you something if it weren't true. Before the Commonage, he was lauded as one of the world's leading authorities in muscular and regenerative neuropharmacology therapies."

Regenerative neuropharmacology therapies?

"Huh, and now he's here doling out aspirin in nowheresville."

Pelham shrugs. "I know the Commonage might seem peculiar to an outsider like yourself, but Dr. Corella believes in it. Anyway, it really is quite lovely here."

"I don't know. Maybe Kumari didn't think it was so hot. Have you considered that maybe she was running away?"

Pelham brushes off this observation. "Don't be silly. Kumari was a mere child. They can be so impetuous. When they're older, eventually children do adapt."

Koko gives Pelham another wry look and shakes her head, thinking, *Wow, just when you think this wishy-pishy weirdness is getting to be too much. Goddamn, is everybody here completely off their friggin' rocker?*

Pausing, Koko then has another thought. Maybe if she warms

up to Pelham, double-X chromosome to double-X chromosome, perhaps she can glean some more information about whatever transport options they've got at the Commonage. The angles... there are worse lengths to go to.

"So exactly how many Commonagers are there?"

"Close to two hundred."

"Wow. I guess your logistics must be a huge pain in the neck then."

"I don't follow."

"Well, with two hundred heads I've got to assume you have ground or air craft to secure enough provisions."

Pelham hesitates. "Are you being sincere with me or are you just fishing for information?"

"Maybe a little of both."

"I see," Pelham replies. "Well, by and large we try to grow everything we need within the Commonage boundaries."

"You mean food."

"Correct. Newer strains of improved micrograins, vegetables and fruits—with all the imported soil, at first we encountered sclerosis and mold infestations, but we've built up genetic resistances. And we have lots of animals too, and none are synthetics. Well, except for Gammy."

"But what about the rest?"

"The rest? I'm sorry, I don't understand."

"The infrastructure," Koko clarifies. "You can't possibly forge metals, construction materials, or rudimentary circuitry without advanced technology, so where does all that come from? Sébastien said this place was once a reservoir. Obviously it's been altered to suit your needs, so what about tools and such? What about Dr. Corella's medical supplies? Look, self-sufficiency is commendable, but be realistic. There must be ground vehicles or flight craft to support your efforts."

"Oh," Pelham says quietly. "We don't have any here."

As when Sébastien told her about the lack of defense, Koko is thunderstruck.

"But what if there's a crisis?"

"We haven't had any major issues since I've been here."

"But c'mon, there must be *something*."

"We've committed to being here, Koko, to forge a new way of life. Naturally, the Commonage's charter does stipulate we can retain outside assistance and even transport if an emergency warrants, but Sébastien or Dr. Corella would handle such a thing if an issue came up. And to your question of outside supplies, we get minimal materials and normal shipments arrive every two months."

Koko rocks back. "Every two months? You're joking."

"As I said, we strive for autonomy."

Autonomy? Herr Spent Capital and his doctor have these people at their mercy.

Creating a positive social initiative in the big, bad world, something is definitely off here. Communal ideal or not, the whole boondoggle doesn't make a lick of sense. And all that Special Economic Zone claptrap—free from governmental, political, and transnational corporate intrusion? That really gnaws. Why not set up the Commonage someplace more habitable if Sébastien and the doctor had the wherewithal? Pelham picks up on Koko's barometric swing and goes on soothingly.

"Sébastien and Dr. Corella are so kind and generous. They truly believe as I do that the Commonage is a saner model for how life should be." Pelham reaches out to give Koko's arm a light, solicitous touch. "You know what? I think you should take a closer look around and talk with some of the others. I believe if you open your mind and let go, you'll see the Commonage differently."

And with that, Pelham takes her leave and slowly walks away.

Koko sits back down on the bench.

Two months?

No way are she and Flynn staying here in this booby hatch for two months.

Flynn, baby. Get better.

Fast.

WITH THE WEE ONES

"Time to speak up if you got questions," Trick declares. "Otherwise I'm assuming you got it down crystal-like."

Kneeling on single knees beneath the trees on the edge of the weedy fields surrounding the compound, three of the camp's youngest cower before Trick and Grum. It's now early afternoon, and the children's faces are studies of relentless malnutrition and disease. Two boys and one girl, all are dressed in similarly tattered rags, so to identify them at a distance Trick has them tuck up their greasy hair beneath bandannas marked with wet soot. While Grum knows the children's names, Trick has no patience for such things. The soot markings are A, B, and C.

"Remember," Trick says, "don't skip at the first sign of static. You be de-civs, but them'll give in if you stick to the script."

One of the children, the same red-haired girl that Trick believes Grum is partial to, fidgets.

"The script?"

Trick cuffs her ear. The girl lets out a pained yip and Grum winces.

"The plan," Trick seethes. "Any damn fool can put their hand out and ask for rain. I chose you runts 'cause you got presence. You want to eat or not?"

The three nod and then look to Grum. The boys and girl like Grum. Over the past few weeks on the trip to Sin Frontera, Grum's pranks and antics have made their day-to-day trials bearable. Shirley's earlier talk of concussion mines weighs heavily on their fledgling minds.

"Nothin's going to happen," Grum says. "Just do as Trick says and you'll goon it, right-right. You'll come back to camp heroes."

The little girl adjusts her bandanna with a hand, her voice faltering.

"A-a-and you'll be right here? Waitin'?"

Trick glares menacingly at the child as though he's thinking about smacking her again. Grum speaks softly.

"Of course. Trick and me be right here. No fret, you bet."

"Just remember," Trick says. "Get a feel for the place, what it's made of. Goon for niches on the walls. Power lines, that sort of thing. If you end up gettin' nothin', you best be comin' back with some valuable info."

The three children stare out at the open field. Grum then gently places a hand on the little girl's shoulder and gives it a light squeeze.

"It'll be fine. You'll see."

A minute later the three children slink out of the trees and troop their way across the open fields. Trick and Grum carefully track their progress from the trees.

"I sure hope they get some rice," Grum says. "Rice goes a long way makin' grubs taste better."

Trick sniggers, "Rice nothin'. You best hope Shirley be wrong about concussion mines."

As the children get within eighty meters of the compound, one of two men atop the walls calls out.

"You there, please do not advance farther."

Fanned out with twenty paces between them, the children stop obediently as directed. The ginger-haired girl is between the two boys because that's the way Trick wanted it. Play up the pity, all waifish and framed. Straight ahead, the children can make out an arched entry and gated tunnel.

"Please, sir," the girl calls out. "We don't mean no trouble."

The first man looks to the second, who has stepped over to his side. There's an exchange between them that none of the children below can hear, and then the first man addresses the children sternly.

"This is a private facility," he says. "We're aware of your camp's presence out in the woods, so please turn around right now and go back the way you came. There's nothing for you here."

The girl looks at the boys on either side of her. She recalls Trick's warning about sticking to the script and how he hit her. The girl trembles forward on watery legs.

"We're just hopin' you could spare some tasties."

"I said, there's nothing for you here. Please, go back."

"But we haven't had any real tasties for weeks, sir."

"I'm sorry to hear that, but please do as you're told."

A third man with a small beard appears on the wall and sees what's happening. He crosses over to the other two men authoritatively and says something that none of the children can hear. All three children look up at the men desolately. Just as Trick predicted, when they start to tear up the combined theatrical impact is sucker-punch perfect.

Grum whispers, "What's goin' on?"

"Shh. Somethin's happenin'."

Twenty minutes later, the three children drag fat mesh sacks of food across the open fields. When they cross into the cover of the trees, their faces are aglow, full of excitement.

With startling force, Trick jerks the mesh sacks from their grasps and then orders them to sit still and keep quiet. The ginger-haired girl, thinking that the worst of their chore is now over and this might be some kind of spirited game, reaches for one of the mesh sacks. Trick backhands her brutally to the ground.

The girl shrieks and the two boys try to cover her with their bodies. Together they watch powerlessly as Trick delves through the sacks. Completing his inventory, he pulls out three bruised apples and holds them up in his hands for the children to see, a sinister gleam shining in his eyes like acid.

"Now then," he says. "Tell me everythin' you gooned and don't leave nothin' out. You speak truer than true, only then can you eat."

TAKING ACTION

Thinking that likely everyone is keeping tabs on her under Sébastien and Dr. Corella's orders, Koko leaves the bench and adopts a blasé façade as she circles and takes in the Commonage's central administration building.

Her basic scope of the premises reveals that, besides the infirmary and possibly Sébastien's quarters, the building houses the commissary and central kitchen. Following the heated smells of oil and steam, she locates the kitchen's rear entrance on the far north side of the building. Baskets of raw vegetables and three compost wagons are parked alongside a ramp, and the ramp leads up to a set of screened and kick-plated doors and a secondary disposal area with two thermite incinerators.

Once inside, Koko glides across the moist tiles of the kitchen with an indifferent air. Big chow assemblies are always in some level of chaos, so she reminds herself to act like she knows what she's doing. Nearing the far end of the kitchen, she passes a long prep table on her right where four cooks are peeling onions with their heads down. A quick look at the cutting boards, and Koko's mood improves.

Knives.

Any blade is good in a pinch, so she trips a worker carrying a load of bain-marie pans from the dishwashing pit, and the cymbalic cacophony has the desired effect. When the cooks' heads turn to see what's happened, Koko deftly swipes a serrated paring knife from the prep table, tucks the blade under her new shirt, and keeps moving.

She punches through a second set of doors at the end of the kitchen and enters the dining area. There isn't a meal in progress and the room is empty. Immediately she swings left and heads down a hallway toward a set of stairs.

Sébastien is the vain sort, and the likelihood of him grabbing a top-floor slot makes perfect sense to Koko. She climbs to the top of the stairwell and wonders, *Hmm, just how long should a burial take?* From their discussions she knows Sébastien is the long-winded type, so Koko sets her mental clock to a thief's window of five minutes in and out.

At the uppermost floor Koko enters a corridor. There's a blind corner on the opposite end, but the corridor is vacant. A quick jog and she locates a locked door slightly grander than the others, and it looks right. Oddly enough, a small strip of metal is on the door with the initials S and M.

Kinky.

The door has to be Sébastien's.

Adjacent to the door there is a keypad like the one Bonn used at the infirmary downstairs and for her room over in Lodge Delta. Taking the paring knife from beneath her shirt, Koko lines up the knife's tip on the keypad's casing and screws. Four quick series of twists and soon she's able to lever the keypad free from its backing. The wiring underneath appears standard—sheathed, color-coded wires: red, green, black, and yellow. God, how many times has she done something like this? Enough to know that even basic security measures can be wired deceptively. Loosen the wrong wire and an alarm could go off or worse. On operations, Koko's seen people burnt to a crisp or even blown in half from freeing the wrong wire. But lethal countermeasures? Here? In Commonage Cuckooland?

Unlikely. Rapidly, she bypasses the circuit. There's the sound similar to a carpenter bee shuddering off to her right, and the door lock pops free with a soft click.

Koko resets the wiring and keypad plate so nothing looks awry and tightens down loosened screws as quickly as she can. Checking the vacant hallway right and left, she slips inside and closes the door behind her.

Keeping the paring knife handy just in case, she takes in a neat white room. There's a library, various lab equipment, a desk, and a bedroom area off to the left with an unmade king-sized bed. There's a musty dog smell too and a bowl of nugget-sized dried kibble with a water dish set lapped clean. The rooms are definitely Sébastien's. After checking the bathroom and returning to the larger office area, Koko steps on something that gives with a crack.

Lifting her boot, she looks down and sees pieces of a shattered needle drive on the floor. She crouches down to take a closer look, and finds one broken piece is larger than the others, about the length of an almond. Using her fingernails she pries the piece open and gently removes the memory dot from the backing circuitry. Koko sticks the memory dot in her pocket, squeezes the piece shut, and places the broken piece on the floor approximately where she found it. Rising, she moves round Sébastien's desk and runs her fingers over the surface, looking for system activations. With the light streaming in from the windows she misses it at first, but a pale mauve projection icon the size of a gumdrop hovers in the air above the desk.

Three minutes, Koko, tick-tock, tick-tock.

Koko strokes the gumdrop icon with a finger and a dozen blue screens materialize in the air. All are blank, so she tries to engage each screen, working as fast as she can with basic operating gestures. None of the screens respond. Damn, of course Sébastien's systems are secure. Koko clears her throat, hoping for voice activation, but again there's no response.

Now what?

Drawers.

Maybe Sébastien lied to her before. Maybe her weapons haven't been destroyed and maybe, just maybe, the arrogant jerk has them tucked away in his desk to keep them close. She finds the drawers unlocked and, tragically, nothing of use. Some binders full of numbers and graphs, stuffed files, stationery supplies, and so forth.

Two minutes, Koko.

Tick-tock, tick-tock.

Focus. Find something.

She stops.

There are voices in the hallway.

Koko spins to the windows and looks out. No way—too visible, and she's too far up. Second option: hide, but quick. Hiding is always a bad choice and she fears she's now trapped.

But then again, if it's Sébastien coming down the hall perhaps she could just wait him out. If his systems are voice activated or if he uses a password she could wait until he's distracted, grab him, and put him in a choke hold until he orders a transport for her and Flynn, stat.

Koko remembers her quick patch job on the door keypad; did she reset the wires right? If the keypad doesn't work and it is Sébastien in the corridor, he'll know something is off. Quickly Koko engages the floating gumdrop icon at the desk to shut down all the activated projection screens.

Taking cover in a closet in the adjoining bedroom, Koko listens for the door. She runs one of her thumbs along the serrated edge of the paring knife and laments her choice. A longer blade would've been better for close quarters. Another brain-flash—shit! What if Sébastien has his dog with him? Synthetics can be fierce, and the dog will definitely sense her presence.

Damn, this little infiltration is turning into a real bust.

Koko's mind races. She thinks about Flynn and how he's in no condition to travel just yet. If she's found, yes, she could probably get away from Sébastien and Gammy, scale the walls, and take her chances in the wilds, but then what? Nine hundred plus klicks on foot without fresh water or weapons in the prohibs? That could take weeks, dangerous weeks. Even if she persevered and came back to spring Flynn, who's to say Sébastien wouldn't decide to sell Flynn out to the CPB in the meantime?

The talking in the corridor glides past the room, and she hears the sound of another door being opened and closed, followed by a hollowed silence. Koko eases from the bedroom closet, slips the paring knife into her pocket, and takes a deep breath.

Whatever, it's time to go.

Forty seconds later, Koko is back downstairs in the commissary and heads outside into the courtyard. She trudges across the pathways back to Lodge Delta, lost in a thick, dark cloud of her own thoughts.

SOMEWHERE OVER THE PACIFIC II

THE NOT SO FRIENDLY SKIES

Rugged constitution and all things being equal, conceits end up taking the back seat when you blow your lunch all over your new tactical suit.

Ensconced beneath the Goliath's cockpit canopy, Wire is chagrined to find her stomach is a disaster area, and it's been a disaster area since she crossed into the first fierce, fading bands of the storm. While the Goliath's onboard systems advised her that the bulk of the weather had already crossed inland, the systems also conveyed that the storm's lingering disturbances were going to be bad. Real bad. Wire initially thought she could handle it, but once she entered the unstable air proper, it was like she was thrown into a full-blown, three-ringed circus.

Chop.

More chop.

Bowel-siphoning, fluey rollercoaster draws of turbulence.

In all her years of pushing bad weather, she's never endured such an outrageous airborne assault. Wire begs the onboard systems to provide her with options to reach the C-GRAP region as quickly as possible, but the systems inform her that the only way to safely avoid distress is to land immediately or reverse her course. The storm's instabilities stretch across staggering spans, and neither recommendation is viable if Wire wants to stay hot on Martstellar's tail, so she decides to bear down and ride the weather out.

Hours pass. Very, very bad hours. Her airsickness morphs into a vinegary combination of dry heaves, tightened muscles, and jangled teeth. But then (lo and behold) a small miracle.

Well, maybe not a small miracle because Wire doesn't believe in such things, but eighty minutes outside the offshore boundary beacons of C-GRAP the Goliath's systems inform Wire that the GPS transponder on the stolen submarine has been reactivated.

Wire triple swots through the data. A sequence of vectors validates the sub's exact location with an accuracy of ninety-six percent. Exhilarated, Wire can't believe her luck. But it's so outrageously bizarre. The confirmed transponder coordinates are in a littoral, coastal region along the Nor'Am prohibs, and nowhere near C-GRAP at all.

The Nor'Am prohibs? Why would Martstellar head there?

With the urban breakup toxicities and radiation levels from decaying power plants, few, if any, still exist in the prohibs, so immediately Wire is suspicious. Maybe the reactivation of the transponder is some sort of a trick. Martstellar is a wily one, and she's used diversions before. Perhaps she's orchestrating a total double-back. Of course, when Wire considers the weather, another appealing scenario wickedly gels together in her mind.

Has Martstellar been dragged off course by the storm?

It could be.

Wire quickly uploads the transponder's latitude, longitude, and elevation coordinates into her ocular, and then re-plots the Goliath's navigations for intercept, just as the transponder transmission inexplicably ceases its signal.

What the—

A reactivation and now a subsequent shutdown? What the sweet fuck all is going on? Was it some kind of an error? No, Martstellar couldn't possibly be that stupid. However, if Martstellar willingly or forcefully changed her destination maybe the scenario that Britch suggested back on The Sixty—that a hapless salvage operator has found the sub and reactivated the transponder—could be the case.

But in the prohibs?

Fuck it. The contact is a positive lead, and Wire decides it's worth investigating. She ratchets up her speed. If the stolen submarine isn't there and this is, in fact, a ruse, she can easily power back north toward the original C-GRAP heading.

An hour later and she's nearly to the point of the transponder's last transmission. Closing in on Martstellar's immediate trail makes Wire feel almost giddy, but then the Goliath's systems deliver a thick, steaming bowl of bad news.

"*Owned*?" she says out loud, incredulous. "What do you mean owned? Since when does anybody acquire geographies and airspace in the Nor'Am prohibs?"

Chained by algorithmic logic, the Goliath's systems are incapable of candy-coating the information.

Airspace and terrain on the immediate heading are privately held by a denationalized title agreement and classified as restricted. See nav-screen three for details and activate enlargements on screen for review.

Using her ocular, Wire opens the nav-screen enlargements as directed. A set of three-dimensional topographical charts loom outward, and the dimensional details are nothing short of astounding. The entire restricted area encompasses one hundred square kilometers north, south, east, west, with an offshore limit of ten kilometers. Trimmed with scrolling data, the displays also indicate no-fly altitudes upward into the lowest commercial orbital heights of the Second Free Zone confederacies.

No way.

That's impossible.

"Clarify title agreement origin."

Repeat. Title agreement origin classified. Any violation of land and airspace restrictions will force an immediate and permanent shutdown of all aircraft functions per guaranteed arrangements with PAE Aerodynamics.

"You can't be serious."

Critical terminal boundary limit is now sixty kilometers and closing. Immediate course correction advised.

"Hold on, correct my course? But I'm nearly there!"

On the port side of Goliath's cockpit, a warning alarm blares a belligerent, undulating screech. Wire whips her head and looks for a way to shut the alarm off.

Repeat. Critical terminal boundary limit closing and engine shutdown sequence imminent. Shutdown to commence in twenty seconds.

Wire backs off on her airspeed, but she refuses to alter her heading.

"Manual override. This is an emergency. I repeat, an emergency. Pilot is in distress. I repeat, pilot is in distress."

The screeching alarm doesn't let up and a loud whirring noise starts to wind down behind her shoulders. There are two loud, flat snicks and then the ominous-sounding *thuh-thunk* of disengaged hydraulics.

Warning. Engine shutdown has now commenced.

Goddamn it, for the amount of credits she doled out for this stupid thing you'd think the double-dealing skells who sold her the Goliath back in Surabaya would have taken the time to counterprogram any bugs that PAE Aerodynamics installed. Mulishly, Wire disregards the secondary warning, and as she scours the charts vibrating in the air in front of her, a go-for-broke idea materializes in her head. Maybe if she lowers her altitude, yeah, maybe she can get low enough to bypass the agreement restrictions and get back in the pocket. She adjusts her flaps and compensates for trim.

Her ears pop as the last of the rainy cloud cover peels away and foam-laced heaves of the ocean below appear. At first it seems as if the seas are calm, but then Wire realizes she's dead wrong. Undulation and persistent, monstrous swells. Her crosswinds clock in at thirty-five knots.

Be advised. Fusion drive shutdown complete.

"C'mon, I'm in a jam here!"

A deafening whine revs high and then squelches silent as the Goliath's forward propulsion terminates. The sudden absence of sound is unsettling. The Goliath is now a sophisticated, sinking mass of metal hurling forward at a deadly rate of speed.

Pre-ejection advisory statement starting....

A bright screen superimposes itself over the navigational displays, and the portrait of a PAE Aerodynamics waxy-looking spokesperson appears. Unlike the Goliath's vocalizations, the timbre of the representative's pre-recorded voice is gratingly mellifluous. Standing before a backdrop of the PAE's iconic logo, the prerecorded spokesperson speaks:

"Greetings. Activation of this statement means an emergency engine shutdown aboard Goliath model number twenty-twelve dash seven has commenced. If your flight today has been ratified for wreckage identification, please make sure these location measures are prepped for extraction and/or retrieval."

Wire grinds her teeth and peers past the spokesperson's ghostly face. Outside the cockpit, overcast daylight is fading fast, and she detects a faint, distant agglomeration of crusted coastline. She isn't positive, but it looks like a long swim of at least eight kilometers, maybe more. The ocean's surface keeps rising, blooming bigger and bigger, and tapping her temple she switches on her ocular's night vision.

Those scum-sucking black marketers back in Surabaya, it'd be just like their sort to remove the parachutes attached to her pilot's seat and the Goliath's gear lockers too. The treacherous possibility is almost enough to make Wire despair. No matter how you slice it, death or ditch, whatever is about to happen is going to totally suck eggs.

"Please take a moment to be sure your pilot harness is tightly secured. Forward cockpit jettison in fifteen seconds. If jettison charges do not execute, manual override measures are located on the starboard side of your cockpit."

Wire looks right and finds the measures: a shaft with a finger groove handle and a bright red arrow indicating which way she needs to pull.

Duh. Like *that* isn't instinctual.

"While PAE Aerodynamics regrets the termination of your flight today, we do appreciate your patronage. On behalf of all of us, thank you for choosing PAE and good luck."

THE COMMONAGE V

PRESSING MISTER MAXX

Koko spends the remainder of the afternoon and early evening prowling around the rest of the Commonage's inner grounds and exploring other buildings, inside and out, looking for any kind of transport at all, and she comes up empty. Not even a bicycle.

The compound, indubitably, isn't the first walled complex Koko has ever seen. Before she banged out a relatively easy living on The Sixty for the CPB, Koko had been stationed at hundreds of firebases and forward garrisons, most of which could easily eat the Commonage as a light snack. Still, even with the frustration of no transport, she has to acknowledge Sébastien and Dr. Corella's little weirdo facility isn't totally lacking. The things that impress her the most are the structural economies. From what she can tell, the operative layouts are dutifully designed to service the occupants' needs without extraneous waste. Austere buildings, well-pruned pathways, module sheds, geodesic agricultural tents, all are exemplary models of functionality. But, man, dull as shit.

Stopping by the wooden rails of one of the livestock areas, she observes a half-dozen scattered men and women attending the animals. Each Commonager moves about their tasks with disciplined intent, and the permeating reek of manure, damp fur, and feathers is thick. Looking left, Koko spends a few minutes tracking the somewhat malicious movements of a small tawny-haired boy hitting chickens with a stick. Several of the terrified chickens try to sneak past the boy looking for sanctuary in a large wooden coop, but the boy viciously thwarts their frantic attempts with heavy swats. When the boy sees Koko watching, he opens and closes a gate, quickly running off. Sébastien comes up behind her.

"Ah, there you are," Sébastien says.

Koko turns and chucks a thumb over her shoulder.

"Guess that kid really hates chickens."

Sébastien glances at the boy who has run halfway across the grounds. A pulse of annoyance passes across his face.

"Oh, that one," he says. "I'll make it a point to speak to his mother. That boy is always after the animals. Children—they can be so cruel."

"A hatchet could give a real taste of cruelty."

Sébastien looks at the quavering birds that have resumed pecking the ground. "I'm afraid we try to refrain from eating animals unless it's absolutely necessary."

"Huh. Pelham forgot to mention that."

"You spoke with Pelham? Ah, so what else did she share with you?"

"This and that," Koko says. "She went so far as to tell me that despite all your avuncular baloney you and Dr. Corella are the only ones with outside contact and that you restrict supply transports to every two months, pulling in outside assistance only if there's an emergency. I've got to be honest with you, Sébastien. What? Flynn and I don't qualify?"

One of the goats in the pen pokes their head through the slats, and Sébastien allows the animal to lick his open palm.

"I've had other pressing matters to attend to."

"Oh, sure. Like that funeral for your little runaway."

Sébastien adjusts his posture and wipes his hand on his pants. He almost responds, but just then an older man with a strong, decisive stride crosses the grounds to them.

"My apologies for disturbing you, Sébastien… the twins said you wanted to be kept informed. There's been additional movement with the situation in the woods."

The fine brush of hair on her neck prickling, Koko looks at the new arrival.

Stepping with him, Sébastien guides the man by his arm and there are whispers, but a moment later the two break off. Sébastien returns.

"What's going on?" Koko asks.

"Some transient children approached the walls asking for food. Dr. Corella gave the okay to provide them some."

"Transients?"

"Yes."

"In the prohibs?"

"De-civs, unfortunately."

"You're kidding."

"No, part of a larger cluster. The search party noticed their camp when they were out looking for Kumari and found you and Flynn. This sort of thing, it's happened only once before."

Koko looks at the walls. "Guess your fancy-schmancy Special Economic Zone restrictions ain't quite up to snuff."

"While I've taken great pains to alter the perceived hazards of this area, it's nearly impossible to eliminate all generative map records, you know. In all probability this group are just disorientated by the recent bad weather and opted for a short cut that brought them through the area. Miserable creatures… You do know about Sin Frontera, don't you?"

"You mean the de-civ freedom warrens spread out in the southern deserts? Yeah, sure, of course."

"Persistent, apocryphal myth more than anything. Most de-civs seeking Sin Frontera elect for more eastward routes."

Koko clucks her tongue. "And Dr. Corella went and gave them supplies…"

"What of it?"

"Kind of a bad move if you ask me."

"Oh, stop. While they're de-civs, they were children, Koko. We're not monsters. And anyway, I'm sure the rest of them will move along soon."

Koko tilts her head. "If you guys are so community bent, I'm surprised you didn't just invite them in."

"Invite them in?"

"Yeah, you helped us."

"Don't be absurd. Your circumstances are different. You and Flynn are obviously re-civ and with de-civs there are significant disease concerns to consider. The specific trial parameters of our—" Sébastien stops himself.

Koko looks at him. "Specific trial parameters? What specific trial parameters?"

Sébastien looks away. "I misspoke. I was simply trying to articulate that the Commonage's greater—oh, why do you even care? It's not like you're staying."

Realizing she's rattled him, Koko pushes Sébastien against the fence. As he tries to move away, Koko dangles out an arm and fakes a punch. Sébastien covers up.

"Please, don't…"

"Don't what?"

"Don't… hit me," Sébastien says, puddling.

The left corner of Koko's mouth curls and she grabs him by his shirt. "Guess I have your full attention now, don't I?"

"You don't need to be so—"

"Insistent?"

"Let go of me."

"No, I've had just enough of your bullshit, so here's what you're going to do, Sébastien. You're going to take me to whatever communication systems you have, and I mean right now, and we're going to contact that transport, understand?"

"But—"

"No buts. You are going to do this, and I'm going to bird-dog every move you make. Once the transport is in the pipe, I promise not to beat you senseless."

"You don't need to act this way. I said I would take care of it and I will."

Koko lets go of him. Graciously, she fans out an arm.

"After you," she says.

Minutes later in the administration building, Koko strong-arms Sébastien up the stairs. Once they're unlocked and engaged, Koko is impressed by the scope of Sébastien's computer and communication systems. State of the art, one couldn't ask for more advanced personal tech, but given his background Koko expected as much. Upon entering his quarters, Koko was actually mildly tickled that her earlier patch job on the keypad worked without a hitch. Forcing him to sit down at his desk, Sébastien works quickly through the now activated screens.

"Who's your usual service provider?" Koko asks.

"Akotitiwin Air out of Calgary."

"Private?"

"Yes. They're reliable, and don't ask questions."

"Pull up their pilot dossiers."

Sébastien does as she demands, and Koko studies the records. "Most are ex-military, that's not cool. Wait. This one. Request him."

"Why?"

"Right there, subsection three. Guy trained only for distribution and shipping, and he has serious financial obligations. See? Right there. He has a spouse in the hospital and awaiting a skin transplant. Request that guy on a solo-helmed craft with no backup. A guy with those types of obligations will know better than to try to pull something funny."

Sébastien enters the request. "He's available."

"Good."

"Final destination? It's required to enter something."

"Moscow."

"Moscow?"

"Moscow by way of that's none of your business."

Sébastien shakes his head. "Tampering with flight plans... you're not planning to hurt this pilot, are you?"

"Not if I can help it."

Sébastien swipes a finger through a screen and ratifies the transport request. "There. Transport confirmed. Now... to the airspace restrictions."

"What airspace restrictions?"

Sébastien shakes his head contritely. "For someone trained to be in tune with her surroundings I'm surprised you haven't noticed. In addition to the SEZ maps, there's a no-fly zone covering altitudes upward into the lower Second Free orbits with blackout limitations a hundred square kilometers east, south, and north and ten kilometers offshore and to the west."

Koko beats a look out the window to the skies. Beyond a long swath of steely darkening clouds, there's nothing.

"That must've cost a bundle."

"That it did."

"How long until they take effect?"

"Seventy-two hours," Sébastien replies. "All time zones need to acknowledge the duration of the lifted restrictions, including every last SFZ orbital. Once the lift is locked in, the transport will depart Calgary, and the restrictions will resume after you've cleared the hundred square kilometers."

"Do it."

Sébastien types for a few minutes and then looks up.

"There. Happy now?"

"Not quite. There's still the matter of my reimbursement for the weapons you destroyed."

"Oh, that. Right, how much do you need?"

"A thirty thousand credit marker ought to cover it."

"Thirty thousand?"

"Dump twenty in the Universal Serial Holdings. I can access USH almost anywhere."

"Seems like a lot for a bunch of guns."

The truth is, thirty thousand is excessive, but Koko believes a little extra is due given the shit she's been through.

"Yeah, well, what do you know about the cost of hardware these days. Pull up the USH portal."

The Universal Serial Holdings portal appears on a separate cone-shaped screen. Sébastien drags and drops thirty thousand credits from a file, and then looks at Koko.

"They need an account number."

"Do you mind?"

Sébastien moves back in his chair and looks away. Koko bends down, types fast, and clicks an icon on the cone-shaped screen. The credits are transferred instantly.

"Now then," Koko says walking across the room. "I'm going downstairs to check on Flynn and give him the good news."

Sébastien stands. "So you're actually trusting me now?"

Koko slides her hand into her pocket and caresses the paring knife's edge with her finger.

"Trust has nothing to do with it."

"I could cancel these transport orders, you know."

"Yeah, you could, but look at my face. There are two hundred and six bones in the body, and seventy-two hours before the AA transport arrives. If you do anything, all those bones? Believe me, I will do my best to break every single one."

As soon as Koko leaves, Sébastien sends a message to Dr. Corella.

[MESSAGE START]

M/: Be advised. AA transport has been contacted/restrictions lifted. K coming to see F.

C/: When?

M/: Now.

BITTERBLUE

Downstairs, Koko finds the twins Bonn and Eirik talking just off the stairwell, and she demands that they take her to the infirmary at once. This time Koko makes sure she memorizes the keypad combination at the secondary door when Bonn types it in. When the door opens she quickly pushes Eirik and Bonn aside.

Heading down the hall, Koko finds Flynn up and balancing on his good leg next to his bed. His eye is still covered with gauze, and one of the green-smocked medical assistants runs a purring horseshoe-shaped scanner over the bandage on his lifted leg.

"The fuck is this?"

Loopy-grinned, Flynn opens his arms wide.

"A wonder of the medical arts?"

Koko stares at him before she crosscuts her eyes to the assistant. Gently easing down Flynn's elevated leg, the assistant is a woman of clear Eastern lineage and has silver-streaked black hair knotted in a tight bun on the back of her head.

Koko asks, "Should he be doing that?"

The assistant titters, "Dr. Corella's progenitor cellular therapies are astonishing, no? Of course big, strong man here only wanted to keep sleeping, but Dr. Corella was insistent. Oligopotent evolutions, they take quicker if the patient moves as soon as possible."

"Who are you?"

Flynn's paper gown rustles. "Oh, this is Ganga. Ganga, allow me to introduce my... um... my friend—"

Koko places her fists on her hips. "*Koko*."

"Right. This is Koko."

Ganga offers her hand. "Ooh, it is such a pleasure to meet you. There's been much talk around the Commonage. I'm sorry I wasn't here earlier when you arrived. You're the spicy one, yes?"

Koko ignores Ganga's offered hand and wraps her arms around Flynn. She looks up at his clean-shaven face and hugs him tight before she presses her cheek to his chest.

"She's kind of overprotective," Flynn explains.

Koko looks up. "Overprotective? You're damn right, I'm overprotective. You nearly died on me, you dumb dope. You're up and standing. Hot damn! You can actually walk?"

Flynn haws, "I'm a bit wonky, but yeah. We've been up and down the hall here a couple of times. Isn't that right, Ganga?"

"Indeed, several times," Ganga replies. "But we mustn't be too hasty, yes? The mending cells require a gentle step, step, step."

Koko looks at the assistant. "But how is this possible?"

Ganga busies herself with shutting down the horseshoe-shaped scanner in her hands. "The physiological abstracts are complex, but Dr. Corella's acute care skills are brilliant. I heard he gave you a diagnostic and operational précis, no?"

"I couldn't make much sense of it," Koko replies, "but yeah he did. This is incredible. I mean, I only left here a few hours ago and Flynn was still all laid out like a slug."

"Such states can be easily counteracted," Ganga advises.

Flynn interjects, "And it's not like I'm ready to run a marathon or anything, but I've got to say, I'm feeling a hell of a lot better. Of course my eye still smarts a bit, but Dr. Corella says that should fade soon. Where do they have you?"

"Some building called Lodge Delta."

"Sweet. Is it nice?"

"Nice?"

"Yeah."

"Flynn, this isn't some hotel. It's a room in a building. At first they even locked me in too, but now I'm free to move around as I see fit."

"So I guess you've met Sébastien then."

"Oh, I've more than just met him."

Flynn rubs Koko's upper arms lightly. "All in all he seems like a nice guy. Asked a lot of questions though, you know, about us, and he said us pulling through that wreck was a thousand to one shot. Talked on and on about the Commonage, the people here and how they get along. Pretty cool stuff, don't you think?"

Flynn notices the displeasure on Koko's face, so he gives Ganga an abashed look. Taking the hint, the assistant departs, and Koko jerks closed the curtains around Flynn's bed.

"Give me specifics, Flynn. What did Sébastien say? What did he ask you?"

Looking slightly puzzled, Flynn sits down on the bed.

"Sheesh, what's with the red face, huh? Here, you want some apple cider? They brought me some apple cider and cabbage soup before. The soup needed salt and I ate it all, but I think there's some cider left." He gestures to a pitcher and a cup on a nearby table.

Koko snaps her fingers in a dramatic three-count Z to reel in his attention. "Flynn, look at me. I'm not dicking around. Seriously, what did you tell Sébastien?"

"What's wrong? You look upset."

Koko pinches the bridge of her nose. "Listen, I'm sorry, but whatever glowing picture Sébastien laid out for you about this place, it's definitely not cool and he's definitely not some nice guy. There's something off about this place."

Flynn pats a hand on the bed. "Come here..."

Koko peevishly puffs out her cheeks and drops down on the bed next to him. When Flynn leans in to give her a peck on the cheek, she pulls away.

"Whoa, I smell that bad? I had a sponge bath earlier."

"Flynn… *your eye…*"

Flynn touches the gauze taped to his face and strokes a finger down his cheek. "Oh, that. That'll heal. Gosh, I'll tell you what though, it feels really strange not having a beard anymore."

"Damn it—just tell me what you told Sébastien, *all right?*"

Flynn raises his hands in mock defense. "Okay, okay… boy, why're you getting all riled? I told him I remembered being in the submarine, but I said the rest of it was a total blank."

"Good."

"He didn't press me if that's what you're getting at, but of course Dr. Corella was there too, and he started talking about dissociative memory deficiencies and short-term memory loss."

"And the two of them bought that?"

"I suppose. It didn't appear like either of them was all that concerned. Man, you're all tense. I might've been gummed up on painkillers before, but I thought you told me we were safe."

Koko scrunches the bed sheets with her hands. "Flynn, they know I used to be a soldier. Sébastien sent a second group out to inspect the wrecked submarine and they found our bug-out packs, and Sébastien destroyed the weapons."

"Destroyed?"

"Yeah, and they reactivated the GPS transponder too."

"So?"

"*So?*"

"I don't know what you're worrying about. This place is awesome."

Koko almost shrieks and grinds her teeth. "There're no land vehicles or aircraft here, Flynn. This place is completely isolated. Not only that, but Sébastien and Dr. Corella are the only ones with outside contact. Thankfully I just sorted that out and got us a flight out."

"We're leaving?"

"Damn right, we're leaving. There's this airspace restriction, but Sébastien got that lifted, and it looks like we should be out of here in seventy-two hours, tops. Anyway, Sébastien and Dr. Corella, I don't trust them. Those two might have a whole bead on our situation by now, I mean—who knows how the Custom Pleasure Bureau might've reacted to us stealing a sub? They might've contacted the CPB already and could be setting us up, but I think Sébastien knows better than to mess with me now."

"I think you're overreacting."

Koko leaps up and looks at him. "Overreacting?"

"Yeah."

"No, I definitely am not. At first I almost bought into the idea that this was some tribalistic, drop-out shtick financed by the megalomaniacal crackpot, but something else is off here. I swear, I can feel it."

"Financed?"

"Sébastien, yeah!"

"Gee, I think he mentioned that he used to be a scientist, but he didn't say anything about being loaded."

"Oh, he's a regular brainy Midas all right. Or was. Slimeball used to work for a huge pharmaceutical outfit and made a killing. Allegedly he blew his wad setting this place up. I mean, who in their right mind puts together a settlement in the prohibs?"

"Well, the well-heeled do have a tendency to be eccentric."

"What? Are you still stoned?"

"Maybe a little."

"Oh, terrific. No wonder you're talking all weird. Did either of those two mention the dead girl?"

"What dead girl?"

"God—you don't remember that *either*? They brought a dead girl back with us from the wreck site. She'd all this climbing gear on her and fell from the cliffs right when we hit the rocks. I bet she was trying to get away from this place. I mean, you've haven't seen the rest of it, but I sure as hell wouldn't blame her if she was.

Yeah, Sébastien and the doc might have been nice to you, but I'm not buying it. Damn, Flynn, they locked me up and sedated me."

"Well, knowing your temper you probably did something."

"Huh?"

"Look, all I'm saying is maybe you're blowing things out of proportion."

"I'm not exaggerating, Flynn. Really, I'm not."

"Fine. Okay, you know I trust you."

"Well, gee, thanks for that."

Flynn then looks off vaguely. "But ever since we first met I've never really had a choice but to trust you, Koko. You say there's something wrong here, that Sébastien and Dr. Corella aren't on the level, or that we might be in a bad spot, all right. I'll take that at face value. But I can't help but think that maybe you're all tweaked because you're not the one who's calling the shots. Maybe you should just chill out."

"Oh, now I know you're totally fucking high."

Flynn rolls his eyes. "Oh, c'mon… just look at the facts. First, no one really knows we're here, right? Yeah, you just said the GPS transponder got reactivated, but if the Custom Pleasure Bureau actually got wind of that or if Dr. Corella and Sébastien contacted them they'd be all over us by now, wouldn't they?"

"But we're in the Nor'Am prohibs."

"Uh-huh, so?"

"So they don't even have any weapons here."

"Oh, and do people always need to have weapons to be content?"

Koko's mouth opens in a perfect O of disbelief. "What the fuck is that supposed to mean? Cripes, Flynn, there's a frickin' group of de-civs in the woods outside the walls right now. There's no way we're staying here, not with disease-ridden de-civs on our fucking doorstep."

Flynn looks down and then picks at his leg bandage. "Well, can I at least get well first before you start barking orders at me?"

Going rigid, Koko pushes Flynn over on the bed with a harsh thrust. Flynn attempts to raise himself, but she then leans over him and presses a finger into his sternum.

"*How dare you.*"

"What?"

"I said, how dare you. I saved your life, you gloomy jerk. God, what the hell is the matter with you? You know what? I don't even know why I bother. After all this time I should know better. You going all namby-pamby on me like this and making excuses, honestly sometimes I swear I should've just—"

Flynn bats her finger away. "Just what? Left me to bleed to death back on The Sixty? Drown in the sub? Or maybe you're now wishing you left me up on *Alaungpaya* and allowed me to off myself in the first place."

Koko pulls back.

"Yeah, I've been mulling that over some," Flynn continues. "Your first instinct was to shoot me in my quarters, remember? Maybe that would've been for the best for you. More convenient—at least that's what you said anyway."

"I never said it would be more convenient."

"Oh, you did, but you just don't remember."

"Even if I did, that's not what I'm thinking now at all. What is all this? Where's this coming from?"

Flynn taps the space above his heart. "From here. This place. Where do you think?"

Koko's whole body trembles and she runs a hand through her hair.

"Look, I don't care what Dr. Corella or his people here say, you're definitely not yourself. No way. You've been shot and you nearly died, so I'm just going to put all this on your injury, whatever they've juiced you up with, because right now you're not thinking straight. Hell, this is probably just post-traumatic stress."

"I don't have post-traumatic stress."

"How would you even *know*? You've never been shot before. Are you even listening to yourself right now? You're not right in the head."

"See? That's exactly what I'm talking about."

"What?"

"You say I ought to listen to myself, but do you have any idea how self-absorbed you sound?"

"Me?"

"Yeah, you. All twisted up in yourself, always biting people in the neck and never giving anything or anyone even half a chance. Everything's great? Oh, no, not for Koko Martstellar. Koko Martstellar knows how things work. Things start going great, and everything and everybody becomes suspect. The real tragedy is you're the last one to admit it."

"Oh, and you being all post-suicidal, you're one to talk."

"Nice, real nice. Thanks for illustrating my point."

Koko looks at the ceiling and takes a long series of breaths. Temper past flared, her arguing with Flynn is definitely not helping.

"All right," Koko says tightly. "I'm sorry for bringing up all your sloughy Depressus horseshit, okay? Hell, maybe we should both stop talking right now before one of us says something we're really going to regret."

"Man, I really hate being micromanaged by you," Flynn grumbles.

Koko stares at him. Her mouth clicks open incredulously to respond, but what she's about to say, all her ire and frustration with Flynn, gets strangled in her throat like a damp rag. When she closes her lips, Flynn suddenly sits up and hops away on the bed.

"Someone's coming," he says.

Koko looks up just as the curtains around them are pulled back. It's Dr. Corella in his green smock, all smiles.

"And how's our favorite patient doing this evening?"

Flynn shifts his eyes sideways to Koko. In a flash, she leaps over the bed and pushes Dr. Corella across the hall.

"You bone-bagging hack! You leave him alone, hear me? Touch Flynn again and I swear I will lay you out flat!"

Shambling, Flynn circles the bed. "Koko!"

"*WHAT?*"

"Calm down!"

Koko spins. She grabs a chair nearby and hurls it. Running for cover, several medical assistants, including Ganga, screech and cover their ears when the chair hits the wall and breaks apart. Looking left, Koko then notices Bonn and Eirik approaching from down the hall.

"Oh, goody… here comes the cavalry. You two meatheads want to tango with me? Excellent, I'm up for a little asshole tearing."

Flynn eases closer. "Koko, please. Just stop it."

Dr. Corella steadies himself and stretches out a hand. "Bonn, Eirik—do not move. Leave Koko be."

The twins freeze as commanded, and Koko then shoves past them. Crossing to a nearby cabinet, she cracks out a leg and sidekicks the lock repeatedly until it splits. Keeping a flinty, distrustful eye on the twins and simmering like a brimstone-toothed demon, she tears open the doors and rummages through the contents. Koko tosses all manner of medical packages, vials, and containers over her shoulder; when she finds what she's looking for she turns and glares at everyone. The assistants, the twins and Dr. Corella, everyone in the infirmary including Flynn watch helplessly.

"Goddamn, bloodsucking piss-artists," Koko hisses. "Seeing that I'm fenced in for at least another seventy-two hours, listen up, buttercups. I'm making a withdrawal. Don't like it? Boo-hoo, you can bill me."

Flynn implores, "Koko…"

"Can it, Flynn," Koko says. "Do me a righteous favor and get your head out of your six and screw it on straight or I promise you—these prohib-living freaks won't be the only behinds I'll be kicking around here, *comprendo*?"

Giving them all a final poisonous look, Koko shoves the drugs into her pant pockets and then tramps off down the hall.

SPLASHDOWN

Wire drags a fluorescent orange rescue raft by its lifelines out of the breakwater and up the flotsam-strewn shoreline. Letting go, she totters backward in a complete drunken circle before she falls over.

Fried.

Kaput.

Smoked.

In other words, Wire's entire essence defines the X in *exhausted.*

With Geiger-counter intensity, her teeth clack nonstop beneath her purplish lips. Trying to get up again, she immediately collapses back down in a revolting pile of uselessness. As she hits the ground, a jagged rock tears the macerated flesh of her hands, but she's past the point of caring—so soaked, dazed, and cold.

Turns out, Wire's misgivings about the Surabayan black marketers cannibalizing the safety features on the Goliath were unfounded. Once she ejected, ancillary charges from the back of her seat deployed—*PU-CHA-BOOM! PU-CHA-BOOM!*—and the violent jerks of two parachutes were a portentous relief. As her plummet slowed, Wire was so pleased she nearly did a fist pump. However, her euphoria didn't last. Battered by strong winds, the parachutes insufficiently filled, seconds later the collision with the ocean's surface tension knocked her silly.

Seeing stars was nothing new to a woman in her elegant trade, but seeing stars as she rapidly sank underwater undeniably was another story. Fortunately, Wire had the presence of mind to control her panic, but then one meter became eight and she felt sure she was going to drown.

As she fumbled with her seat harness, her death's imminent reprieve came in the form of a muted belch beneath her legs and a flurry of rushing bubbles. Sensors in her seat registered her depth penetration, and releasing super-compressed air into inflatable bunting, the floatation measures shot her to the surface. Wire hit the air just in time to see the Goliath soundlessly slice into the ocean several hundred meters off. No fiery soufflé or thundering shockwave from exploding debris, just a single momentary *pssshhh,* and like a long-extinct leviathan the Goliath was gone.

Not knowing how long the inflated bunting would keep her seat afloat, Wire quickly unclipped her harness and kicked free. The bunting kept everything buoyant for about ten additional seconds before it too slowly vanished, dragging the parachutes down like a giant, matronly brassiere.

Looking around, Wire spotted a circular rescue raft fifty meters off to her left that had also deployed when she jettisoned. Equipped with a battery-enabled signal light lashed to a cleat, the raft was drifting away from her at a frightening rate. Wire clawed after it, and five aching minutes and half a gallon of swallowed seawater later, she swung herself inside.

After falling from that height she was fortunate she didn't have a full-on concussion. She quickly unfolded a collapsible paddle secured to the raft's ribbed air chambers and took her bearings. She couldn't afford to lose sight of the coastline in the dark, and having her ocular's night vision engaged she locked onto it.

People misjudge distances at sea. What appeared to be a reasonably attainable paddling span to the shore stretched into a nauseating three-and-half-hour ordeal. Huge foaming swells, heavy winds, and spinning currents on top of a counterproductive tidal retreat whittled away her gains. Blindsided by a rogue wave, she capsized, and it took her nearly twenty minutes to right the raft, locate the floating paddle, and stroke on.

Now Wire is finally on marginally dry land. Physically drained, however, she knows the worst danger is still close: stage-two hypothermia. If she reaches stage three, her core temperature could drop below sustainable level, and if that happens she'll only have hallucinations to keep her company on a very quick slide into cardiac arrest.

You're okay, she tells herself. *You've been in worse situations.*

Suck it up and remember your training.

Keep first things first.

Without warning Wire's whole body spasms uncontrollably, and she upchucks a hot wash of vomit and seawater. As she cups some of her splattered purge to her face to feel some of her own fading heat, she fears she may already be seeing things. The vomit dripping from her fingers looks like tiny yellow flower petals.

Wire slaps at her tactical suit and finds the temperature controls on her left side. A depressed button and soon warming and wicking measures start to dry-cure her flesh.

She flops over onto her back and stares up. Not a single star in the sky.

After a few more minutes of rest, Wire wills herself to get up again. She lugs the raft farther up the shoreline and sets it over a trio of boulders: an impromptu shelter. After a brief pick through the trashy flotsam, she finds some flammable plastics and wet scattered wood. She uses a laser flare from one of her vacuum-packed worst-case-scenario kits to build a small fire. The laser flare is capable of indefinite burn time, so she stuffs it in at the fire's base for maximum effect.

Wire squats down beneath the raft and draws off her wet boots and socks. She shivers in the smoldering red glow.

F-f-f-first things f-ffffirst...

Get warm, get dry. But then what?

Get moving. Locate Martstellar's sub.

She taps the side of her skull and pulls up the coordinates of the last transmission downloaded to her ocular. Given her bail out and the lengthy paddle to shore, she's actually amazed: Martstellar's submarine is barely ten klicks south of her position.

Wire draws out her Sig Sauer sub-compact from one of the vacuum packs along with her other supplies. She inventories everything to keep her mind occupied, fieldstrips the Sig, and then waits for her socks and boots to dry.

DR. SIMPATICO

"I must say, she certainly is a handful," Dr. Corella says.

Post-Koko freak-out, Sébastien came down to the infirmary with a parcel of Commonage clothes for Flynn. After a brief and stern discussion out of Flynn's earshot, Sébastien suggested that the doctor help Flynn dress, and now Flynn and Corella have moved to a conference table in one of the infirmary's auxiliary rooms for privacy. The two men sit across from each other and sip water from plastic cups. Still visibly shaken from Koko's looting outburst, Dr. Corella continues.

"Tell me, has Koko always been this way?"

Flynn takes a sip of water from his cup and sets it down. "I've only known her for a few months, but let's just say she can be a little unpredictable."

Dr. Corella drums his fingers on the table. "Well, it seemed best to let her do as she wanted."

"This whole experience has been very troubling for her. Can you tell me what she took? I'm sure I can get it back for you."

"Let's see... she took a bunch of opioid gel capsules and an aerosol tube of synthesized Xaniaphic-17, I believe."

Flynn whistles and shakes his head. "Man…"

"Is there something I missed?" Dr. Corella asks.

"Missed? With Koko?"

"Yes. Is she in some sort of pain?"

Flynn shrugs. "In a manner of speaking, yeah. But then again I suspect we're all in some sort of pain in our own ways."

"Ah. You're a philosopher."

"Hardly. It's just the way things are."

"Well, I suppose we're all born into a losing struggle. But still—back to Koko—does she really know what she's doing with those things? Medicines like that, they can be quite dangerous if not handled correctly."

"Oh, she'll be fine."

"But she isn't—what I mean to say is, I realize you've had your issues because of the traces in your blood samples, your Depressus and the Second Free Zone and all that, but she's not—"

"Looking to eighty-six herself? No, trust me. Suicide is about the last thing on her mind."

"I see. But I imagine she has other issues."

"Whatever she took it's recreational. Purely recreational."

Dr. Corella nods and turns his cup between his hands thoughtfully. "Soldiers… all that death and destruction, the constant exposure to violence. I know her kind are ameliorated from birth to handle the burdens of such employments, but substance abuse isn't exactly uncommon."

"She's not a junkie, if that's what you're implying. Or even depressed. Besides, she's not even a soldier anymore. She hasn't been one for quite some time." Flynn takes another sip of water. "If the Commonage had a bar I'm sure Koko would have left your supplies intact and found herself a private cubby to drink herself into a funk. To be perfectly candid, I know she has a penchant to smoke a little crinkle flake now and then, but no, she'll be all right. She's just blowing off steam. Again, I apologize for her behavior. It's my fault. I pushed some buttons I probably shouldn't have."

"If you don't mind me asking, are you two…"

"*What*?"

Dr. Corella lowers his head. "It's really none of my business."

Flynn smiles. "Wow, it's that obvious, huh?"

"Well, I had my suspicions."

"Koko thinks we're in a tight spot. She really doesn't like being here."

"No doubt," Dr. Corella says. "But what about you?"

"Me?"

"Yes. I'm curious. How do you feel?"

"My leg feels almost new."

"No, not that. I mean, your leg wound is healing marvelously, right on schedule. But the other thing you just mentioned; do you feel you're in a tight spot? Humor me. On a sliding scale, tranquility-wise between one and ten, do you feel more at ease? Do you like being here, generally speaking?"

Flynn looks at the table surface. He has a fitful awareness that he probably should withhold his thoughts and views of himself, but viscerally he senses portions of his willpower giving way. It's strange, but his mind and body are so relaxed, so mollified, so completely at ease he almost feels outside of himself. For the life of him he can't remember feeling so profoundly mellow and agreeable. And Dr. Corella? Well, he doesn't look like the sort of man who'd betray intimacies, so Flynn's willpower soon disappears completely. Oh, what's the big deal? Aren't doctors supposed to do that? Keep a trust and be a confidant with a patient and his secrets? Maybe. Flynn remembers how minutes earlier he felt substantially troubled by how he flubbed keeping things close to the vest and divulged quite off-handedly to Dr. Corella a few of his previous experiences as security deputy back up in the Second Free Zone. Flynn had to stop himself, knowing Koko would be livid with him for telling the doctor anything, but now it seems he doesn't care one way or the other. Anyway, Dr. Corella was so nonplussed by his babbling hubbub, and during their talk he's been genuine with all his concerns. It's like they're old friends.

"Uh, yeah, sure," Flynn answers. "I don't know. I tell you what, though, what you and Sébastien have shared, how you're choosing to build a way of living that's rational and sane out here, one could do worse. So ease? Yeah, sure. This place feels pretty grounded to me."

Dr. Corella smiles. "Grounded is a very good word. And how about content? Again, on a scale from one to ten."

"Right now?"

"Yes."

"Maybe a nine?"

"Splendid."

Neither of them say anything for a minute. Flynn finishes his water and then leans his arms across the table, open palmed.

"I know you're busy man, Doc, and I want to thank you for saving my life. The staff here, Sébastien, even though you don't know anything about us and even with Koko's outrageous behavior, you've helped. In this day and age, that means a lot."

"You're welcome. I swore an oath."

"Oh, yeah, that hippo thing, right?"

Dr. Corella shifts forward. "*Primum non nocere*, the Hippocratic oath, correct. But it's not just that, Flynn. It's much more. It's something that maybe Koko, because of her background and how she was bred for combat, is incapable of accepting. You see, Flynn, with specific guidance Commonagers here have successfully adapted to a model of how life was designed to be. Not an arrangement based on commerce, stratified beliefs, waffling loyalties or appalling states of anomie—they've taken to the responsibilities of a community. They've chosen a new path."

"Tough stand to take considering the rest of the world."

"Perhaps at first, but adjusting to such a path is quite easy if only with a certain… nudge. If you don't mind me saying, I think you're responding so well to it all because you were once a policeman."

Flynn laughs. "I guess I took an oath too."

"Oh?"

"Yeah. Uphold order and keep the peace, courtesy and regard for everyone, and blah, blah, blah. Seems sort of ridiculous now."

Dr. Corella's smile broadens. "You know what? I think that now you're better you should allow me to show you around and introduce you to some people here. Would you like that?"

The doctor's invitation feels irresistible, and a conflation of exhilarated sensations expands and fills Flynn's body. A state of giving over subjugates his sense of self like a warm, reassuring film, but strangely it feels okay, moreover, *right.*

"You know, that sounds pretty great," Flynn replies. "I think I'd like that very, very much."

CRUSOE-IN'

Just after a hazy, rotten yolk spread of dawn, Wire douses her fire, deflates and stashes the life raft, and starts picking her way south in the direction of the last known coordinates of the stolen submarine.

All along the shoreline, it's slow going. There are huge rocks, clotted tidal impasses, obscene nests of garbage in tangled clumps. Plastics of all shapes and sizes seemingly everywhere. With each section she traverses, she carefully examines all corners and blind spots, above and behind her, before she advances. Sensibly, she takes things a hundred meters at a time. Now in the Nor'Am prohibs, this is not the time to play things slack, but it feels great to be moving again.

Rounding a cove shortly before thirteen hundred hours, Wire finally tastes gravy. Latched on a grouping of barnacled boulders like a gigantic amoeba, the turtled submarine sits just ahead. She takes cover behind a washed-up steel kettledrum two hundred meters north of the vessel.

Waiting for signs of life, she gives her study of the submarine and the surrounding area a patient half hour. No movement, no smoke, no sounds except for a few wheeling gulls alighting on the hull and rocks. Employing the enlargement functions on her ocular,

Wire surveys the area for potential tripwires and booby traps. She deliberates whether she should wait until dark to make her move, but anxiousness trumps her reservations. She might as well get on with it. Daylight is precious, and she might need it.

Wire psyches herself up, scurries around the kettledrum, and advances on the wreck. In her head, she hears her own assertive boom.

Move! Move! Move!

Wire covers the distance in less than thirty seconds, stumbles once, and flattens the heft of her body near the sub's astern hydroplanes. After catching her breath, she picks up a handful of loose gravel and tosses the pebbles onto the hull. She listens and counts off thirty, but there's not a clang, not a rustle or peep from inside.

Finding inverted footholds in the sub's flank, she quickly climbs up top and approaches the blown hatch near the bow area, Sig out in a two-handed grip.

"Yoo-hoo, anybody home?"

Nothing. Not a sound.

Wire drops down on her belly and shimmies forward. After giving herself another short count, she then sticks the Sig down the open hatch and squeezes off three quick pulse rounds and pulls back.

Still nothing.

Huh, guess I'm going in.

A quick sweep of the vessel's innards using the torch function on her multi-tool illuminates a harrowing tale sticky with unrequited whats, hows, and whys. Given her milieu in combat operations, it does not appear to be a wise move on Martstellar's part to attempt an amphibious landing during a huge storm as the timeline suggests. What's more, why come ashore here? Why didn't Martstellar just crank the diving planes and stay submerged, break out a deck of cards, and wait the bad weather out?

A couple of scenarios brick together in Wire's brain. Perhaps Martstellar had no choice but to surface and head for the coast as fast as possible. After all, Wire did shoot her partner in the leg back on The Sixty. Maybe she needed to make up critical time and try for land if that Flynn guy's condition worsened. A second possibility might be an unforeseen technical issue. Yeah, Martstellar is resourceful with a hell of a skill set, but she certainly is not some seafaring wrench-head. Wire tries to recall some of the training portions of Martstellar's profile, and she's fairly certain rock star marine engineering wasn't part of her abstract. Wire slides the torch beam across the sub's hollow, fusty confines. No splashes of blood, but a blown safety hatch? Whatever happened, it seems possible somebody got out of or got into this inverted contraption.

Wire emerges from the sub and sits on the hull half in and out of the open hatch like a Panzer commander. She regards the waves, the cliffs, and then looks up and down the rocky debris-littered beach north and south. Massive, abraded basalt formations surround the dauntingly steep cove. To her immediate east, the smaller bread-loaf-sized rocks grow larger into formations that slant upward toward a rugged, precipitous rock face with tufted thatches of sea grass. Looking higher just above the cliff edge near the summit, Wire can make out the pointy outlines of green shrubs and trees. The whole shooting match is all so craggy with steep pitches, if the two did escape after they flipped and bellied out, with one of them wounded they would have had their work cut out; higher, drier terrain, *ipso facto*, would be tantamount to scaling a twelve-story building, and damn near impossible.

Wire pulls out her toasted coconut protein tarry from her pocket. She peels back the foil wrapping, tears off a large chunk, and chews. Had she been in Martstellar's position there's no question what she would have done.

Cut the dead weight.

Shoot the wounded.

She swallows a softened glob in her mouth as another even more distressing storyline weaves together. It might be that after they escaped the sub, Martstellar and Flynn got sucked out to sea and drowned. It's conceivable. Being forced aground and flipping over like this—it doesn't take a genius to figure out this was not what one would call a preferred arrival. Who knows what the storm or tidal conditions were at the time they made it to shore. Most likely bad. With the submarine weighing a conservative estimate of thirty-odd tons, even if it were disabled, only a massive ill-timed wave could have caused the catastrophic inversion. Survival after that? Pretty damn dicey.

Wire wraps up and stashes the rest of her tarry. After setting the multi-tool in her teeth, she drops back down into the sub and does an orangutan hang from the edge. Directing the torch beam with her head, she scans the brackish bilge and consoles and her speculative narrative of possible events thickens further. Several of the electronic modules and consoles are not only water-damaged but gutted. Big spaghetti spills of cables and thrown-open lockers. Fittings and bracing hardware has been pried off.

Scavengers could explain why the tracking beacon had been briefly reactivated. Maybe somebody found Martstellar and Flynn and rescued them, or worse (please, please not), killed them both and buried their bodies.

But scavengers out here? In the prohibs? Who? All that equipment, where would they go?

Wire immediately clambers out of the sub, drops to the beach, and starts looking for signs. All that removed equipment, it was likely heavy stuff. There have to be tracks, and there might even be a quicker way out of here without the climb straight up the cliffs.

Then Wire sees something. Ten meters above, along a sloped ledge, she sees what looks like a switchback trail carved into the cliff face. The trail is insanely sheer in sections, but portions of it lead upward to a crossover trail. Wire taps her temple to ocular implant enlargement and a bright, painful orb of light mule-kicks her square in the forehead.

Caterwauling, Wire falls down and rolls across the sand holding her head. The pain is penetratingly sharp and instantly she knows what's wrong. It's her new ocular—the one she replaced back in Surabaya. Half of her vision sears off in a dazzling wildfire of snowy code and then goes gray, then beet red, then black.

Crashed.

Wire rubs her head and gets a hold of herself. Wigging out like a maniac is not going to help her situation. In fact, if the sub was ravaged by scavengers they could still be close by. She might have already given her position away, and like an idiot she's out in the open like a sitting duck. As she pounds the heel of her hand into the side of her head several times in the lame hope to jar a reboot, blood leaks from her inflamed eye like tears.

Those scum-sucking cretins; if Wire ruled the world every last black marketer back in Surabaya and intern at the pop-and-op clinic would die a thousand slow deaths.

ON HIGHER GROUND

Not far away from the cliff and several hours later that same afternoon, the children's gathered information on the compound has Trick's mental bandwidth charged up.

"I know it sounds ballsy as all get out, but we'd be crazy not to give it a try. No weapons and a lousy lock on a gate? I'm tellin' you, this situation be riper than ripe."

The group is a gallery of slackened faces. Besides the occasional cricking snap of campfire embers, the only other noise in the camp's clearing is a large cast iron pot simmering with some of the recently procured dried beans. Trick crouches by the pot and jabs a stick into the fire.

"The key be we got to go tonight under cover of darkness. Move in and blitz 'em. Probably think we ain't got the chops because we sent the runts out to beg, and that rolls in our favor, right-right."

Someone mutters something about Sin Frontera, and Trick chucks his stick at them.

"Sin Frontera!? Ain't you been listenin'? Damn it, think for once, all of you. This be about our survival, not *theirs*. Just ask yourselves, did them people offer to take them runts in? No! And look at what they spared! Apples, a couple dozen hardboiled eggs, stale brown bread, and dried beans that look like they be takin' a year and a day to cook? Not even fresh water! Downright insultin'. Bet they be hopin' we don't push our luck and move along. They got more in there and I say we take it."

Trick's zeal leaves little room for discussion. Still, desultory reservations get mouthed. Maybe it would be safer to move on to Sin Frontera or even to the mountains. Either way, their group could stumble upon something else without taking such a chance. But Shirley's slit throat is still fresh in everyone's minds. Any reservations peter out.

"We'll take six," Trick says. "Me and Grum, Jasper, Foo, Mooch, and Ashida because we got the most scrap. Things wheedle hairy inside, we got to intimidate. Go brutal."

Grum raises a hand. "But you just said them be weak, Trick."

Trick wheels. "Shut up! Even the weak can go gonzo on you if you push 'em. No-no, it's settled. In a few hours it'll be dark and them'll be sacked out. We'll catch 'em off guard. All of you I just named, grab the sturdiest thing you can find."

SISTER MORPHEUS

Later that same evening and back in her room in Lodge Delta, Koko sits cross-legged on the bed and fumes.

Yeah, okay, maybe stealing a bunch of drugs wasn't the smartest thing to do seeing she's still on unfriendly ground, but for all this fishy bragging on about building a community or social petri dish or whatever, why didn't Sébastien or the doc bring up the fact that every place needs a damn watering hole? A little dive with some bung-nozzles of rotgut teat-hanging from the ceiling, maybe a couple of brew taps in the commissary, was that so much to ask? Pulling a vial from her pocket, Koko untwists the cap and shakes a few opioid gels into her hand. Of course she probably shouldn't, but given the facts that she has a knife now, that the transport is finally on its way, that Sébastien has been sufficiently warned, and that she's braced one of the room's high-backed chairs to block the door, Koko thinks a little stress relief is more than deserved. Swallowing two gels with a third bitten in half as a chaser, she doesn't even change out of her clothes, lies back, and soon, like a rising lake of the blackest mud, sleep overtakes her.

It seems like only a minute has passed, but hours later, an

impossibly loud scream rips her awake. Heart slamming, she wonders if it was her own scream, forced by a nightmare, but when a second scream pierces the air, instinctually Koko instantly rolls from the bed and sweeps her hand beneath it for a stowed weapon. Cursing and groggy, she then remembers where she is and reels toward the window. It's still dark out, but beneath the eerie glow of the solar-powered courtyard lights she sees an all-out argy-bargy along the westward wall.

De-civs.

Still dressed and in her socks, Koko spins around and tears out of the room. Ping-ponging down the hallway, she reaches the stairwell, gropes her way down the stairs, and crashes through the doors at the bottom. Looking right, the outlines of the attackers crystallize in her still-addled sights. Commonagers roused by the intrusion and the screaming, like her, do nothing to stop the invading de-civs, and most are being beaten savagely at every turn.

Koko rushes forward. Seizing the first de-civ she can by the shoulder, she jerks the man around and chops a hand across his windpipe. Gasping, the de-civ drops to his knees, Koko then pile-drives a second palm strike to the back of his neck to finish him off. Refocusing, she remembers the stolen paring knife in her pocket and draws it. The remaining de-civs whip their heads and Koko counts five. Fuck. Being outnumbered is never good, and with the opioids she's ingested, Koko is still half in the bag.

One of the Commonagers wobbles over to her, his face streaked with blood. Koko drags the man behind her back as the first two of the remaining five de-civs come at them both holding thick sticks out like jousting lances. When they're close enough, Koko leaps up, whirls her legs, and kicks both sticks from their hands.

The ground comes up fast, but Koko rolls and lands on her feet. One of the two disarmed jousters then makes a go for her shoulder, so Koko promptly knees him in the crotch and drives the paring knife into his ear. Blood jetting out over her hand, Koko is unable to free the blade and senses the second jouster coming at her. Bending, she uses the man's forward momentum and hurls the de-civ over her shoulder. When he lands on his back, Koko quickly drops on top of him, grabs his head and twists—*CRRRITCH!*

Three down, three to go...

Getting up, Koko roars, and the remaining three turn and hightail it for the access tunnel. Glancing over his shoulder, one of the de-civs—a wiry, dark-skinned man, stops and momentarily locks eyes with her as Gammy darts across the grounds at an insane rate of speed.

"They're taking the tunnel!" Koko yells.

Seeing the dog, the wiry de-civ takes off down the tunnel passage, and Koko bolts after him. When she reaches the tunnel's threshold, the three men have already cleared the passageway's length to the outer gate. Gammy is close behind, and Koko's earlier conversation with Sébastien comes back to her. There are more de-civs in the woods, and her paring knife is still back in that dead guy's ear. Without a knife, a broomstick, anything—Koko would be stone-cold nuts to follow, but then again, she's trained for this so she charges ahead.

Gammy slips effortlessly through the tunnel's open gate and seconds later, Koko reaches the same spot. Forced open with a crude log and rock fulcrum, the gate is off its hinges and Koko looks off just as a blood-chilling scream rings out deep within the fields. The screaming is hysterical and horrendous, and it ribbons into higher and higher octaves, until finally it's muffled silent by wet, gorging snarls.

Koko waits, and seconds later there's a rustling in the brush. Gammy emerges and with her thick blue tail wagging like crazy, she trots over and drops a mangled hunk of tendon and cartilage at Koko's feet. Looking up at her eagerly, Gammy sits and carefully Koko extends her right hand. When Gammy gives the blood on her fingertips a few slobbering licks, Koko takes a knee and scratches Gammy's blood-soaked ears.

"Aww, who's a good girl?"

* * *

With Gammy heeling proudly behind her, Koko struts out of the tunnel. Sébastien heads toward her and his face is an overheated radish.

"These three men are dead!"

"I told you giving de-civs food was a bad idea," Koko says. "And let's keep the body count straight. It's four dead. Gammy wasted one on retreat."

Mystified, Sébastien looks at Gammy. *"BAD DOG!"*

Gammy whimpers.

"Hey!" Koko snaps. "What's your problem, man? Gammy did great out there. If anything the big girl deserves a biscuit."

"A biscuit?"

"Yeah!"

"Don't tell me how to discipline my synthetic. And killing those de-civs, you'd—you'd no right to do that, not even in self-defense."

As Gammy gathers her dense frame at her side, Koko cruises right up to Sébastien. "Let me clue you in on something, chief. Despite whatever dove-like bosh you and your brethren here like to purport, de-civs are parasites and you damn well know it. You yourself called them miserable creatures before. True, the end results are rough to look at, but I've slightly more experience in dealing with their kind."

"Of course you do, massacring people for a paycheck."

"Oh, give me a break. You—glassing about here like some lofty paragon of virtue, reel in your phony outrage for a second and deal with reality. Stop being such a coward."

"Oh, and I imagine being a coward is something you know all about seeing that you're on the run from The Sixty Islands."

Koko doesn't flinch. She's not at all surprised that Sébastien has figured out her and Flynn's situation.

"Oh, now we're getting down to it. Great, how long have you known?"

Sébastien shoots his cuffs. "Shortly after your arrival. I'm not an idiot, you know."

"So what else have you got on us?"

"For one thing I know that your former employers, the Custom Pleasure Bureau, recently submitted an insurance claim indicating one of their maintenance submarines had imploded on a deep-water dive. They listed you and Flynn aboard."

Taken slightly aback by this revelation, Koko racks her brain. *What the—why would the CPB do something like that? Does that mean she and Flynn are off the hook*? No way, it couldn't be.

One of the fallen Commonagers has a compound fracture sticking out of his arm at a graceless angle and he screams. Koko sees Flynn helping Dr. Corella get the man up, and when he pauses to offer her a disappointed look, her stomach sinks. The adrenaline rush from the fight is wearing off, and the opioid gels' effects are now coming back, but hard. Hot-skinned and brain cotton-feathered, she gives her head a clearing shake. Ingesting two and half capsules—what was she thinking?

Sébastien starts to move away from her.

"Wait," Koko says, "those de-civs could launch another attack."

"Don't be absurd. That group is probably halfway down the coast by now."

"You don't know that, Sébastien."

Dr. Corella crosses over to them. "My God, how did this happen?"

"They levered open the tunnel gate," Koko explains. "Actually I'm surprised it hasn't happened before."

Dr. Corella stares at her. "Can it be fixed?"

Koko cries. "Fixed?! Oh, right. Fix a gate. Lah-dee-dah. Why don't you just hang up a big sign that says 'Come on in and eat us alive.' Your defenses need to be shored up immediately."

Sébastien addresses the doctor. "How many are hurt?"

"Six. I think," Dr. Corella replies. "Some larger cuts and a few broken bones, but most are just badly shaken up. Good God, Koko, you killed those de-civs with your bare hands?"

"Damn right, I did. And if your partner here hadn't destroyed my weapons, Gammy and I might've finished the rest of them off."

Dr. Corella swivels his head to look at Sébastien. There is a long, tacit exchange between the two men, and Koko waits for one of them to say something. When neither of them speaks, she throws up her hands and starts off.

"Goddamn it, I for one am not going to just stand by and line up for being a hot lunch."

Dr. Corella stops her. "Hold on…"

"What?"

"You're right," Dr. Corella says.

Sébastien's eyes darken. "*Doctor…*"

"No, Sébastien, she's right. We need to do something. We must. It's imperative, and we've come too far. There's too much at stake. And anyway, you told me you've arranged transport for Koko, did you not?"

"I did. What of it?"

"Well, I think we should listen to her. Ask for help."

Sébastien looks as if he's about to spew. "You want to take *her* advice?"

"Do you really think we can afford not to?"

"But we've never had an incident like this before."

"What if Koko hadn't been here? What if these de-civs do try to attack us again?"

"They're gone, this is upsetting the variables."

Koko looks at Sébastien. "What variables?"

Dr. Corella steps between them. "Koko, do you really believe those de-civs will attack us again so soon?"

"It's possible," she says. "Sébastien here said they were part of a larger group."

"Meaning?"

"Meaning this could've been a test to see if this place is adequately defended. I've seen the tactic before."

With his Adam's apple sliding, Dr. Corella cracks. "So what, ah, what do we do?"

"You mean other than overnighting a shitload of firepower

which, of course, isn't possible because of your stupid no-fly zone lift window?"

"Yes, other than that."

Koko blows out a breath. "At a minimum the gate needs to be refortified and barriers need to be put in place. After that… I don't know. Maybe cordoned barricades all the way around the walls."

"Can you show us?"

Koko tongues her cheek. *Well, well, well… you've got some nerve, you fucker*. To actually think when the shit is filling up hot and deep there's essentially something called fair equivalence in the world. What a load. Never one for philosophy, Koko's viewpoint (above portions of the private military code of conduct) has always been—me, mine, and screw the rest, no matter the outcome. Her priority is to protect Flynn and herself first. Maybe it's the drugs, but damn—it does feel kind of good to have the tables turned.

"Why should I?" she asks.

"Self-preservation? We helped you first."

"Immaterial."

"Please?"

Koko's eyes switch to Sébastien. "I'm going to need a lot of hands."

Dr. Corella looks gravely at his partner. "Sébastien?"

"What?"

"Surely we can get the Commonagers to pitch in."

"I can't believe we're even discussing this," Sébastien murmurs. He tries to keep his composure, but when he looks at the wounded, the trouble, fear, and irritation in his eyes belies what's left of his resistance. Begrudgingly, he nods.

Gammy circles, settles, and looks up at all of them. When Koko bends down to scratch Gammy's withers; the synthetic jumps up and gives her face a huge, happy lick.

"It'll be dawn in a few hours," she says, pushing Gammy down, "so we need to take advantage of daylight. It'd be stupid to try for us again tonight, and once we start on the barricades, who knows. Maybe Sébastien is right. Maybe they'll move off. Sébastien?

Whoever was in the initial search party that found us I want to talk with them. Get a feel for just how many of those de-civs are out there."

MEET THE NEW BOSS

It took Wire the rest of the afternoon to ascend the cliff face above the sub's wreck site and half of the night to clear most of the sawed-apart shells of the sprawling, overgrown ruins she discovered above.

She continues her advance carefully. As with earlier along the shoreline, she searches for clues and deliberates whether to hole up in the rubble and wait for daylight, but an inner nagging permeates. Whoever picked over the stolen submarine still has to be close by.

Checking the stars between drifting clouds, Wire ventures into the woods just after midnight. A scant five hundred meters in and her ears pick up distressed voices in the formidable growths. Wire promptly takes cover in a shallow, loamy gulch behind a tangle of fallen timber as the voices draw near.

"Trick! Wait! Trick, wait up!"

"C'mon, we got to fall back and regroup!"

Wire slides her Sig out of its holster and checks the readout on the housing—a cold, digitized green. The voices grow louder and branches crunch when two men crash past.

"So we southin' for Sin Frontera now?"

"Grum, will you shut up! I got to think!"

Sin Frontera?

Wire recalls something about the alleged independent de-civ settlements in the deserts in the southern prohibs—wild, spurious tales. But if these two galloping nitwits are talking about Sin Frontera, what in the hell are they doing way up here? They might be the scroungers who gutted Martstellar's sub, and one just said they had to fall back to regroup. *Fall back from what and regroup with whom?* Wire's cooked ocular is giving her a massive gem of a headache, so she downshifts her thoughts to immediate tactical concerns and tightens her grip on the Sig.

The two pass by oblivious, and Wire eases up from behind the fallen timber to track their movement. Two men for certain, one short and dark-skinned and the other outlandishly ursine and bushy-faced. The two move northwest, and when their lead increases to a safe trailing distance, Wire keeps low and follows. The bigger man carries on.

"We lost Jasper! That woman killed Foo and Ashida! Oh, man, poor Mooch! Do you think that dog be behind us?"

Dog?

"See? I told you that place was easy pickin's, didn't I?"

"Easy pickin's? They kicked our butts, Trick!"

"No, did you hear them? Practically begged us to stop. If it hadn't been for that split-tail and blue dog..."

Minutes later, Wire can see the copperish flickering of a campfire and she halts. Crouching low, she picks her way closer and the outline of a small encampment comes into view, set in a looped arrangement with draped plastic rain tarps and crudely patched tents. It's not a big group, maybe a couple dozen sallow-faced men, women, and children, but it's difficult to take an accurate headcount because everyone keeps shuttling in and out of the shadows. An afro of mosquitoes whines around Wire's head, and she fights off the urge to swat the cloud lest she give herself away.

Wire duck-walks right and hides in a fanning clump of licorice ferns. Fragments of fevered words filter out to her through the camp's extraneous background noises, and it's hard to hear everything, but soon she hears enough. The one named Trick strides toward the campfire and grabs a wooden spoon from a pot. He dips the spoon into the cauldron and shovels a sloppy, hot scoop of beans into his mouth, just as Wire charges into the clearing with her weapon up.

"Nobody move."

Stooped and careening around, the little man spits out the beans and drops the spoon. Pulling a knife from his waistcoat, he snaps it open and everyone in the camp freezes in mid-step. Wire steadies her aim.

"Drop it," she says.

"Who be you?"

"I'm the one with a pistol pointed at your face, that's who I be."

"I ain't droppin' diddly."

Wire eases her right index finger off the Sig's trigger guard. "Drop that knife or it's piñata-time, buddy. I won't say it again."

She watches as the man called Trick spreads his fingers and lets go of his blade. The jackknife impales the dirt at an angle.

"Good," Wire says, "now kick it into the fire."

Reluctantly, Trick does as Wire orders and the blade lands short of the campfire's rim of rocks. Wire's good eye slims.

"You can't be that dumb."

"Take it easy, lady."

"I told you to kick that knife into the fire."

"Okay-okay…"

A follow-up kick and the blade skips into the flames. Wire adjusts her stance.

"Who's in charge?"

"Depends on who's askin'. You be one of them?"

"One of who?"

"From that compound east of here."

Wire shakes her head.

"Okay, then I be boss here, right-right. Name's Trick. That burly lug be Grum. If you ain't from that compound, then who you be? You lost or somethin'?"

"Give me a weapon and headcount."

Grum blurts out, "Twenty!"

Wire and Trick sling their heads at Grum.

"We've just got some sticks and junk," Grum continues, "but we got no for-really weapons and such, not unless you count that knife Trick just kicked into the fire. We're northerners, out of the Canadian territories. Southin'."

"Sin Frontera, huh?"

Grum looks puzzled. "Um, yeah. We don't want no trouble."

Wire waves her Sig. "Everyone line up in rows in front of the fire. Get on your knees. Cross your legs behind you and lace your fingers on top of your heads. No sudden movements or I'll kill you all. Do it. Do it now."

No one waits for Trick's permission, and they all do as Wire says. Beyond their rank bodily odors, Wire can smell their fear. The one named Trick is the last to acquiesce. She's seen his kind of heart-eating arrogance before, and it's time to take out the alpha. Stepping forward, Wire backhands her pistol against his face and a wet crack seals Trick's compliance. He folds to the ground with a rasp.

Wire moves back and modifies her stance. When everyone is in place, she runs her eyes back and forth over the faces and then sets upon Grum.

"Twenty, you say? Looks like you're lying and lying to me right now would be a bad thing, big boy."

Grum stammers, "N-n-no, I swear, this be it. Be everybody or at least what's left of everybody. We lost a few people earlier."

"So, I heard."

"What?"

"I've been listening to you two imbeciles whinge on for the past ten minutes back there in the woods. For the record, when you beat a retreat keep your voice down. Everybody hold still and keep your mouths shut."

As the group attempts to remain as motionless and silent as possible, Wire fine-tunes her hearing for any movement in the campsite's edges. After a full minute without so much as a rustle or broken twig, she's satisfied no one is taking up flanking positions on her or hauling ass to escape. She relaxes her posture.

"I'll be the one asking the questions here out, got it? You scumbag de-civs play nice and answer true, nobody dies." Wire motions to Grum. "You. Yeah, you. Don't look away from me. Since you were so obliging before, I'm putting you on point."

Grum drags a finger down his chest. "Me?"

"Yeah. There's a lot of line with your tarps and tents, so I'm going to give you a job. Gather up as much of that line as you can and tie everyone's hands. Drag that knife out of the coals and cut the line into sections. That should speed things along."

Grum gets up and does as Wire tells him. After the jackknife is cool enough to handle, he cuts enough pieces and it takes him close to ten minutes to tie up everyone's wrists. Wire bird-dogs his movements the whole time and then double-checks his knots. After taking the jackknife from him, Wire pushes him down on his knees and pockets the blade. She then holsters her Sig and secures Grum's hands with an extra section of leftover line.

"Okay," Wire announces, "now that I've got you all formally arranged, tell me more about this compound you were talking about."

Grum steals a glance at Trick, but Trick's eyes are augering hot holes in the ground. "We don't know who they be," Grum says.

"Right. This is the Nor'Am prohibs. Nothing viable is supposed to be out here so I'll tell you what: I'm counting your lies from here on out. You only get three chances, so don't test me because three lies in a row and I'll shoot your balls off and stuff them in Trick's mouth."

Grum protests, "But I'm not lyin'! We don't know who they be."

"All right, then," Wire says. "So this compound, how far is it from here?"

Grum waggles his head. "Maybe a fifteen-minute that-a-way back through the woods."

"Corporate?"

"Corp-o? No, not that we gooned. Not natty-like neither."

"Guards?"

"Sort of."

"What do you mean 'sort of'? Is that another lie?"

"No! I mean, that's why we tried to get in there in the first place. Trick and me, we gooned them a while ago, right-right? And we'd some of the younger ones ask for food. When them gave the children some, well, Trick thought they be weak."

"So you mounted a raid."

"Six of us, right-right."

"What's inside?"

"Stuff, people. I don't know, it be so crazy. There's, like, structures and animals. Trick here thought it be bestest to go in at night and try to rob them when them sleepin'. It got out of hand."

"Out of hand how?"

"This wild woman and big blue dog came out of nowhere. We didn't know they'd no dog, and that wild woman? A hot meany she be."

Wire's lips twitch. "Describe her."

"Kind of small," Grum replies.

Wire points a finger at Trick. "You mean small like this piece of shit?"

"Kind of, but I didn't get a good look at her face."

Trick grumbles, "That's because you were too busy saving your own butt."

Wire pulls her Sig from her holster and hauls back to crack Trick's skull again, and Grum cries out.

"Dark hair!"

Wire whipsaws around. "What?"

"The woman," Grum says, "she got dark hair. And short. Not as short as yours, but she be meaner than meany, truer-than-true. Took out three of us all by herself."

"Three?" Wire says. "Counting you two that makes five. You said six before. Are you lying to me again?"

"No! The dog got the other one. Ate him all up."

"Ate?"

"Yeah, but that woman? She be a full-on wolf herself."

Wire's good eye narrows.

Martstellar.

THE DEFENSES BEGIN

Several hours later and little after eight A.M., Sébastien, Dr. Corella, Gammy, and Koko climb a set of stairs to a parapet on the western wall of the Commonage.

The late-night raid has everyone in the compound on pins, and word of the mandatory assembly spreads quickly. Restless and worried, the entire Commonage's population coalesces in the central courtyard. Up on the wall, Koko stands loose with her hands on hips and combs her eyes through the faces below. All seem present except, for some odd reason Flynn is nowhere to be seen.

Sébastien positions himself slightly behind Koko on her right, and Dr. Corella holds up his hands to quell the murmuring crowd.

"People, may I have your attention, please…"

Everyone quiets down.

"Thank you. We appreciate your taking time out of your daily obligations this morning to attend this emergency assembly regarding the events that transpired a few short hours ago," Dr. Corella says. "We know you're concerned, but we're here to advise you that there is an immediate action plan to address the issue."

Stepping back, the doctor looks at Koko before he joins Sébastien and Gammy sitting at his side. None of them have slept and Koko's nerves are ragged, so she runs a hand through her hair a couple of times before she steps forward. Blearily, she tries to recall the best way to address large groups and then remembers something about avoiding direct eye contact. Like most, Koko doesn't relish the prospect of public speaking as her only experience was when she pulled demonstration control at a port uprising in Maputo nine years before. A hostage standoff and nerve gas canisters had to be deployed, so no… her public speaking that time did not go well at all.

The pearly sun has risen higher over the eastern mountains, so shading her eyes Koko begins.

"Okay, let's not waste any more time. As most of you already know, my name is Koko. Because of that storm the other night my friend and I ended up here and while this was by no means our intention, right now you and I are in the same boat. What you might not know about me is that up until a short time ago I was a full-time soldier. Now, I know what you're thinking—her? Yeah, it's true. I'm not denying it, but since then I've left that part of my life behind."

Koko deliberately steals a glance back at Sébastien and then resumes addressing the crowd.

"From a resistance standpoint what I witnessed last night was pathetic. Those de-civs who attacked? Don't kid yourselves. It's likely they'll try to give the compound a second go, so with Dr. Corella's and Sébastien's consent, I'm going to show you how to secure this place. A full briefing with secondary labor assignments will begin in this courtyard in ten minutes." Koko adds a clarion note to close. "Thank you for your attention."

Sébastien steps forward and waves a hand at the gathered crowd as a signal that the address is now over. The people disperse into smaller groups, and with her tail wagging Gammy rushes over to Koko's side. Turning briefly to look out at the woods, Koko speaks quickly.

"I'm going to need help with subdividing Commonagers into construction teams for the cheval-de-frise barriers. It's better if there're two groups: manufacturing and placement."

"Pelham is good with organizing," Dr. Corella suggests.

"Good."

"Just how long should this take?" Sébastien then asks.

With her knee Koko bumps Gammy's hip. "Well, with Flynn getting fixed up I've already clocked most of your glaring vulnerabilities. After I give Pelham some instructions, and if things go well, we can work on more robust measures after that. Once the AA transport arrives though, you idiots are on your own."

Sébastien and Dr. Corella exchange pensive looks.

"What?" Koko asks.

"Nothing," Sébastien says.

Koko roasts the harshest of gazes at the both of them. "Look, right now I'm only looking out for my own best interests. You two might think you know all about me and Flynn, but I warned you earlier, Sébastien. Here on in, if you or the doc here even think about messing with me or that incoming transport, top down I'm clearing house."

Dr. Corella steps forward. "Koko, I'm afraid, well—I think Sébastien and I are both a bit frazzled. The events of the past few days, it's all been so taxing. But no… this is the right thing to do. We should get on these protections right away for all involved. We will oblige and accommodate your needs here on in."

All three of them move for the stairs and Gammy gambols ahead. Dr. Corella pauses before descending.

"Sébastien?"

"Yes? What is it?"

"I'd like to give you an in-depth prognosis report on the wounded, if I might."

"Now?"

Dr. Corella gestures with his head—yes. "I think we should. Oh, look. There's Pelham." He calls out, "Pelham? Could you come over here for a moment, please?"

The tall woman crosses over to the bottom of the stairs. Koko meets her and the two of them look up at Sébastien and Dr. Corella. Pelham shields her eyes.

"Yes?"

"Koko would like some assistance with organizing the labor groups, do you mind giving her a hand?"

Pelham looks at Koko. "Absolutely."

Across the courtyard, Gammy roots in some bushes and then barks. When Koko turns and looks back up the stairs, Dr. Corella waves at her.

"We'll be with you in a minute," he says.

Whispers.

"Sébastien, it's Flynn… the TAM cognitive reactions—they're extraordinary. His are some of the most remarkable I've ever seen."

Guardedly, Sébastien quickly steals a look at Koko and Pelham conferring at the bottom of the stairs. "But the incoming transport—"

"Remember your suggestion? Back in the alcove after their arrival?"

Sébastien's eyes widen. "You mean with Koko? But I thought—"

"No," Dr. Corella adds. "I was wrong. We'd be *fools*."

"When?"

"I was thinking tomorrow at breakfast. We should let her finish the fortifications."

Sébastien guides the doctor down the stairs.

BEANS AND SCHEMES

On her haunches in the camp just after sunrise, Wire shovels in spoon after spoon of beans from a tin cup. The beans are protein, but the taste is ghastly. Like half-hardened potato bugs simmered in swamp ass. Admittedly, Wire's had worse.

"I'll be straight with you," she says between bites. "I've no interest in who you are or where the hell you think you're going, because frankly? Your kind is nothing but a waste of oxygen to me. I mean, Sin Frontera? Good luck with that shit, suckers. Last I heard that place was nothing but a make-believe Neverland to winnow out the dumb. Seeing that you took on a walled compound without weapons, I guess I should expect as much."

Trick mumbles. "Hungry..."

"What?"

"I said, we be hungry."

"If you're reduced to eating this slop, I should say so." Wire drops the spoon into the tin cup and lobs the cup over her shoulder.

"So if you ain't got no interest in us, you goin' to let us go?"

"I haven't decided yet."

"Why not?"

"Two words, Trick. *De* and *civ*."

"Ain't that hyphenated?"

Wire pats the Sig on her hip. "And just as easily ventilated."

"Maybe you-me-you could help each other out."

Wire gets up and crosses to where Trick kneels. The fuzzy wash of light feeding in from her damaged ocular is still giving Wire a humdinger of a headache.

"Oh, yeah? Help me out how?"

"Well," Trick says, "that wild woman be the one you're after, right-right? You got your needs, and we got ours. Workin' together might be bestest."

Wire laughs and presses a boot into Trick's shoulder. Pushing him over in the dirt, she grinds the tip of her toe on his gashed temple like she's squashing an insect.

"Work together, huh? How?"

Trick moves his head away from her milling boot. "All I be sayin' is we got numbers. Plenty of us have seen our fair share of scrapes, and numbers can always give you an edge."

Wire scorns, "Numbers—don't make me puke. Alone I've waded in more blood and fought in more places than you can possibly imagine. If anything, you mangy degenerates are nothing but a bunch of liabilities to me."

"That may be," Trick counters, "but we still be hungry and willin' to fight."

Wire looks at the others in the camp. "Is that true? You all are that desperate you want to jeopardize your lives?"

At first not a soul presumes to look up from their sagging positions, but after half a minute the nods hesitantly begin. Soon one de-civ mirrors another and the answer looks unanimous, even with the children.

Wire sighs. Rank disgusting facial sores, and grotty to the letter, maybe it isn't such a bad idea. Maybe she could use them. Set up a diversion. Rouse up some distractive havoc. Hmm, she needs to check out the compound first. She orders Grum and Trick and one of the children, a boy, to get up. When the boy starts to blubber and cry for his mother, Wire jerks him aside and tells him to quit his fussing or she'll castrate him with Trick's knife.

"Look at me, kid," she says. "I might need an extra set of hands so you're going to do what I say when I say it, understand?"

After the boy nods feebly, Wire cuts off the line binding his hands.

Now on their feet, Trick and Grum turn around and offer out their hands for Wire to cut their bindings as well, but Wire ignores them. She folds and slips the jackknife into her breast pocket and then pulls her Sig.

"I'm taking you two and this boy to scope out the compound. If what I see jibes with your story maybe, just maybe, I'll consider Trick's proposal."

Trick pumps his legs. "Now you're talkin'. Hey, you got a name?"

"Wire."

"Wire?"

"Yeah, Wire. Now seeing that the rest of you mongrels are unreliable shit-stains, I fully expect one of you to try and save your own diseased skin once we head off. That's fine, and I guess it's your right. But if you do decide to run off, know this: I've no qualms about making this little boy's last moments alive ones of unbelievable misery and pain."

Using her Sig, Wire gives Trick and Grum hard shoves from behind.

"Let's move out."

It takes them a half hour to cut through the woods with Grum and the boy leading the way up front. Hanging in the rear, Wire prods Trick forward as he whispers.

"The bestest spot to keep low be just ahead, 'bout a hundred paces where the trees peter out. That be where we gooned the compound before."

Even with her hampered vision, through the trees and in

the distance Wire can make out the hulking white outline of the structure. Circular, the compound sits on a small rise beyond a large bramble-infested field and, as they draw closer, Wire blows a short whistle and gestures to Grum and the boy to hold up and stay low.

Kicking out both of his knees, Wire forces Trick down on the ground and studies the compound.

Trick looks up.

"What you goon?"

Wire thwacks the butt of her Sig on the top of his head.

"Shut up."

Without her ocular working, she takes things in slowly. Wire spots the tunnel entrance the de-civs used for their infiltration hours earlier, and the broken tunnel gate looks like it has been addressed with a quick wrap of thick rope. Raising her sights, she then scans the upper edges of the walls. The structure appears to have no recessed weaponry, electrified concertina wire, or obvious defensive measures of any kind. Outward appearances can be misleading, but damn if Trick and Grum weren't telling her the truth. Even if she doesn't end up infiltrating the compound through the weakly fortified gate, the walls are a farce. She takes a guess at a vertical reading: four meters. Using a swift sprint, Wire could clear the wall easily with a parkour *saut de précision* and follow-up *passement*.

Detecting movement, she then notices three bodies sorting themselves out along the wall's upper edges. The three are visible only from the waist up, and two appear to be male and the third looks female. It's hard to see much else because all three have their backs turned, and one of the men seems to be addressing someone farther inside the compound. When the female steps forward, Wire waits and then when the woman turns she chuckles softly to herself.

Bingo.

If only she hadn't lost the rest of her gear when the Goliath crashed. One well-placed shot with a rocket-propelled grenade and

Wire could easily take out Martstellar like a thunderbolt from the blue. Getting inside the compound will take some minor planning, but nevertheless Wire's mood has brightened considerably.

Grabbing Trick by the scruff of his neck, she hauls him to his feet. "Guess what? Today is your lucky day, maggot."

ON THEIR BACKS

Later that evening, after a long day of fixing the Commonage's blatant susceptibilities, fortifying the tunnel gate with additional chains, and helping the Commonagers build impromptu barriers and placing them along the outer walls of the compound, Koko returns to her room in Lodge Delta and is surprised to see Flynn sitting in one of the straight-back chairs beneath the window. Shutting the door, she quietly leans a newly fashioned wooden battle staff in a corner. Once the barrier assembly was under way, Pelham had showed Koko a pile of good unused lumber and Koko took a piece of the unutilized wood to hone down a battle staff. Intrigued by what she was doing, Pelham asked how she could make a battle staff for herself. Koko showed her how easy it was and suggested that later when all the fortifications were in place the rest of the Commonagers should make battle staffs for themselves too.

Flynn looks up. "Oh, hey there…"

Koko crosses to him. She pauses for a moment before she lowers her face and gives him a quick kiss on the cheek.

"Hey there yourself."

Achy and sweaty, Koko decides for now it might be better to just forgive and forget their blow-up back in the infirmary. Running a palm over a bothersome cowlick in Flynn's hair, she looks down at the object in his hands.

"Is that a book? Huh. You don't see a lot of those things around anymore. I hope you're reading something good."

Flynn turns the book over so she can see the embossed title:

The Arabian Nights: Tales from a Thousand and One Nights.

"It's kind of dense," Flynn explains. "And it's been slow going with only one eye, but it's not half bad. It's all about this guy with a mess of problems. Lots of betrayal, virgin executions, tragedy, the whole deal. I think you'd like it."

Koko strokes his hair some more. "I'm not much of a reader," she says. "Where did you get it?"

"Some Commonagers brought it here an hour or two ago when they came by to change the linens. I guess they thought I might like something to pass the time. Check out the cloth binding. Must be a couple of hundred years old at least. They said it came from Sébastien's private collection."

Koko then remembers her earlier infiltration into Sébastien's quarters, and thinks about the memory dot she retrieved from the crushed needle drive that she almost forgot is still in her pant pocket. She has a hunch that the memory dot might contain damaging information on the Commonage and exactly what Sébastien and Dr. Corella are up to, but seeing that she doesn't have access to tech at present and the transport is on the way within hours, she makes a mental note to look at it once they're good and gone. Flynn points to a teapot on the desk.

"Want some tea? It's jasmine, and it's really, really good. Nice to sip after a rough day."

"No thanks. So, how's the leg?" Koko asks.

Flynn beams. "It's good. Actually, Dr. Corella went so far as to show me all these trippy MRIs of my muscle tissue. I've got to stretch at least three times a day for the foreseeable future, but in no time I should have ninety-five percent mobility."

"Wow."

Koko deliberates whether she should bring up their leaving the Commonage again. Considering the fever of their spat in the infirmary and her epic loss of control shortly thereafter, she then reasons it might be best to skirt the subject for now. Flynn… he looks so mellow. Koko then wonders if there's something medicinal added to his tea. Man, when they finally get to wherever they're going she's definitely going to make it a priority to pour herself a tall belt of something strong.

Flynn sweeps his fingers lightly up and down her hip, drops his hand, and tries to find his place in the book. It's weird, but with him being beardless he looks almost five years younger, and despite his eye-patch a twinge of deep affection flickers in Koko's belly. Outside, a cloud change gilds out the room with a buttery, twilight glow.

"I think I'm going to have a rinse," Koko announces.

"Okay. Did you get anything to eat? We can grab a bite in the commissary if you want."

"Not hungry," Koko says, and then adds saucily, "not hungry at least for food."

Trying to read, when Koko clunkishly kicks off her boots, Flynn raises his head again and sees she's pulled off all her clothes.

"Are you really that into that book of yours, baby?"

Flynn's mouth drops open. Reaching the bathroom doorway, Koko turns and raises an arm up the bathroom's doorjamb. Flynn shuts the book and sets it down on the desk. Rising, his limp is slight, but when he reaches Koko he slides his arms around the small of her back.

Koko slips her hands down between his legs. Instantly she can feel him swelling beneath her fingers, so she presses her face into the space between his chest and his shoulder.

Flynn gulps. "Been a while…" he says.

"That it most certainly has."

Flynn angles his head toward the bathroom. "Kind of small in that shower stall for two."

Koko pulls his shirt over his head and unfastens the drawstring on his pants. "We'll see about that."

"Dr. Corella told me to be careful."

"Oh, I'll be careful with you, handsome."

"But I have to keep my bandage dry, and I'm still tender."

Flynn steps awkwardly out of his pants and Koko laughs. Like her, Flynn has opted against wearing the Commonage Farmer John undergarments.

"Tender right now sounds fantastic."

Turns out the bathroom's shower stall is too small for the both of them, and minutes later they end up tangled and wet on the bed. Minding Flynn's mending leg, Koko gently rides his damp hips as Flynn reaches up and lightly touches her face. It's a slow start, but soon they pursue familiar and trusted moves. The soft sweep of Flynn's hands moving over her sides and how he gently brushes her hair away from her forehead triggers a melty quiver, and, yearning to feel his heat and modest length, Koko takes him deeper inside. Damn, she'd wanted for them to take their time, but as the seconds pass they're quickly off to the races. Nerve endings awash in rhythmic sparks of pleasure, it doesn't take either of them long, and sensing Flynn is about to erupt, Koko lowers herself and twirls her tongue deep into his mouth. A clenched release—mutual and satisfying.

Koko rolls off him and catches her breath. Nuzzling herself against his side, she listens to the thrum of Flynn's heart and places a hand on his chest. His good eye has gone glassy, and when Flynn purses his lips he lets out a fading note—a bomb falling from above.

"That was great," he says.

Koko giggles. "That it was. Hey, Flynn?"

"Yeah?"

"I know now might not be the best time to bring this up..."

"I guess I kind of rushed it."

"Rushed?" Koko laughs. "Oh, that. No, not that. That was fine. That was more than fine. That was long overdue. No, it's something else."

Gallantly, Flynn adjusts one of the bed's pillows behind his head to support them both and strokes her back. "All right… what's on your mind?"

"Well, back in the infirmary, you know, when Dr. Corella showed up and I lost my head…"

"You want to apologize?"

"Yeah."

"I'm sorry too."

"But before, like before I went and lost control, I started to tell you… we're not staying."

Flynn goes still as a post and then sits up quickly. "I knew it—why do you always have to go and spoil everything?"

"Now, wait a second…"

"I mean, these people, they've got a good thing going here, Koko. Sure, I know it's not a tropical, kick back and watch the world burn and pour me another Mai Tai paradise, but why? Why do you want to leave? We're safe."

"Flynn, we're really not."

"Oh, c'mon, don't start with all that nonsense again. So what, we're just going to pick up and wander out into the prohibs on our own? That doesn't sound so hot to me."

"But we won't be wandering out into the prohibs. The transport is on its way. True, we might have to stay sharp when it arrives, but it's all been taken care of."

"But you've just spent the day helping them set up their defenses."

"Oh, that. That's not just for them. After those de-civs got in last night, for the time being that's for our safety too."

Flynn pauses. "So when?"

"The transport? Later tomorrow or the day after at the outside."

Flynn shakes his head sullenly. "Then I guess it's a done deal. Thanks for consulting me first. Thanks a lot."

Koko props herself up on her elbows. "C'mon, you ought to be relieved."

"Honestly, I don't know if I am. I'm just so sick of this, Koko."

"Sick? Sick of what? Sick of me?"

"No—sick of this, you and me, us being on the run. Killers hounding us, all the craziness that seems to follow you like a shadow you can't shake. And I have to say, this asymmetrical behavior of yours isn't exactly making me feel any better either."

"Last night this place was attacked, Flynn."

"Oh, I know... by de-civs. And you took care of them single-handedly. I saw the results."

Koko looks up at the ceiling. "God, can someone please tell me what happened to that great guy I used to know? I swear, he was plowing me like a champ just a minute ago."

"Har-har. Go ahead, make jokes."

Koko tries to rub his back. "C'mon, baby..."

Flynn jerks his shoulder away sharply.

"Jeez," Koko says, "did nice guy Sébastien tell you about the CPB filing an insurance claim on the submarine?"

Flynn turns his head. "What?"

"Yeah, the CPB claims the sub we stole was destroyed during a deep-water dive and said we died along with it. I was skeptical at first, but then when we were discussing the Commonage protections after last night's attacks I made Sébastien show me the documentation. It looks legit."

"But why would they do that?"

"Beats me," Koko says. "It could be they just want us to disappear, a cost benefit thing, but coupled with all this Commonage pap and de-civs outside the walls, it's got me on edge. Anyway, I think Sébastien doesn't care anymore. He and Dr. Corella just see us—well, me at least—as a destabilizing force. And while they asked that I help with getting some basic defenses in place, I think both of them have got a hard-on for a Koko-free Commonage."

"But..."

"But what?"

"But this... this could be a good thing for us, Koko. The CPB falsifying an insurance claim that large and asserting our deaths publicly is a major risk. If they're telling people we're dead, I think you're right. Maybe they really don't care about us anymore. This could be a perfect opportunity for us. We could—" Flynn stops and looks around the room.

"Oh, c'mon. You're actually telling me you're still keen on all this subsisting in the wilderness crap?"

"Well, it's not so bad."

"Flynn, we've only been here for a couple of days, and most of that time you've been getting put back together. You may think the Commonage is great, but it's definitely not. De-civs outside the walls, random incident or not, staying here unarmed is definitely not an option."

"God—you and the weapons thing again. Got to have my weapons, got to be armed—no one knows we're here, Koko! Commonage life, I know it might take some getting used to, but we could stay here. Back in the infirmary you said I didn't have my head on straight. Maybe you're the one who's not seeing things clearly."

Koko scrutinizes Flynn's face. Like a blizzard of puzzle pieces swirling finally into place, all at once everything gels together.

We've come too far... there's too much at stake...

I've taken great pains to alter the perceived hazards...

A personal investment?

A social petri dish?

The printout and data plug, how Pelham said that Dr. Corella used to be some expert in regenerative neuropharmacology, Sébastien's touted pharmaceutical and chemistry credentials, Kumari trying to leave, how the twins when she went off in the infirmary snapped to the doc's order and became bizarrely enervate, all of it suggests...

No. Could it—?

Flynn draws a hand across his face and wrestles his way out of bed. Hobbling toward the bathroom he picks up his clothes.

Fuck—they must've done something to him! To everyone!

Flynn looks back at her. "You know what? You do what you want, but I for one am not in any hurry to whisk off to C-GRAP or any place else out there and struggle to put my life back together yet again."

Blood boiling, Koko sits up. *Oh, God,* she thinks, *how could I have been so blind?* Dr. Corella and Sébastien—every nerve ending in her body is screaming at her to jump up, find them, and rip their shitsucking throats out. But then Koko cautions herself. She needs to tread very carefully here and stay calm. She can't betray any alarm to Flynn. She needs to keep him close.

"Look," she says. "I'm sorry I brought it all up, okay? I'm sorry."

"Don't patronize me."

"I'm not patronizing you, Flynn. Please, just come back to bed."

Flynn stares at her and then tosses his clothes on the floor with sudden disgust. When he plods over and sits back down, Koko crawls over and kisses his shoulder.

"Listen, why don't we just get some sleep, and we'll talk about it some more in the morning, okay? Fresh heads, maybe grab some eggs? I'm really tired, Flynn, and who knows, maybe you're right. Maybe I'm the one not seeing things clearly. "

"But the transport is already on its way."

Koko forces a smile. "Oh, transport… transport can be canceled, right? No biggie."

Flynn moves closer, and they both settle back beneath the covers. As the light from outside fades and the room darkens, soon Koko rolls to her side so Flynn can spoon himself against her back. Eyes open, Koko tries to allay her hypomanic dread and rage, but can't. She stares wide-eyed at the wall as Flynn yawns and rolls onto his back.

"Gosh, it's really hard for me to say this, Koko, but I wish you would at least try to show me some respect sometimes, you know? The truth is I do like it here. I can't explain it, but it feels like… I don't know… like I'm home somehow."

Oh, Flynn, baby…

What did they do to you?

WE'RE HAVING A WAR PARTY

Like before (only more aggravatingly so), the de-civs' second offensive comes in the middle of the night. This time, however, the first blow is announced by the telltale whump of a pulse explosion.

Leaping out of the bed, Koko has her pants and boots on before Flynn even has a chance to rub the sleep from his eyes.

"Flynn, get up! We're under attack!"

"What?"

Koko tugs her kurta tunic down over her head. "Get dressed, I need you."

And boom—like that, she's out of the room.

Gone.

On her way out the door, Koko snatches up her wooden battle staff. Ripping down the hallway, she raps the staff on the walls to sound the alarm.

"Everybody up now! De-civs! I repeat, de-civs in the perimeter! The Commonage is under attack!"

After the events of the previous night, Koko fully expects a mad spill of Commonagers marshaling behind her, but sadly this is not the case. The ones who do materialize in cracked doorways are terrified. Koko can't wait for them. When she reaches the stairwell, she drops down the steps, pouncing from one landing to the next like a leopard, until she reaches the bottom and throws herself out Lodge Delta's doors.

Once outside, it's painfully obvious who has the upper hand as the de-civs have doubled their numbers. Men, women, and even de-civ children are everywhere running amok; many of the marauders have torches and set fire to whatever they can. Few if any of the Commonagers attempt to stop them. When she sees Pelham across the courtyard tackling a de-civ trying to set fire to a trellis, Koko feels a brief throb of hope. The de-civ gets up and throttles Pelham's neck, but Pelham slaps the man's hands away and wrestles him to the ground again.

Muscle memory from t'ai chi. Maybe later Koko will compliment Pelham on her moves, but right now she's busy. As she sweeps the grounds for a target, a sharp pain bites Koko in the back of her head and looking down she sees a crooked wedge of rock in the grass. She sights the thrower: a boy transfixed fifteen meters off to her right. Koko promptly picks up the rock and flings it back at the boy. Clipping his knee, the boy drops with a yowl.

Behind Koko the doors to Lodge Delta bang open, and Flynn, half dressed in boots and pants, quickly gimps over to her side. Dabbing her fingers on the back of her head, Koko's fingertips come away scarlet and wet.

"What's happening?"

Koko grits her teeth. "Take out as many as you can."

Before Flynn can respond, Koko is off again, slaloming, running, and leaping through the fracas. She keeps wondering where the rest of the Commonagers are because the whole situation is deteriorating into a five-alarm mess.

A pulse explosion? Where the hell did these de-civs get explosives?

Beyond the administration building, the geodesic agriculture tents and livestock pens blaze. The petrified ensemble of animal cries is awful and sprinting toward the area Koko wields her battle staff in wide, debilitating arcs. A de-civ woman cradling a sheep runs past her, and Koko splinters the woman's shin. Using the battle staff, she follows through with a secondary swing and splits the woman's face. The sheep bounds away across the grounds just as a spear plugs the ground at Koko's feet.

Another de-civ, a man, steps out of the tunnel and readies to throw a second spear. Flynn lopes toward him and the man steps back. Flynn yanks the spear from the de-civ's grasp before he can throw, and when Flynn looks back at Koko she makes repeating stabbing motions. Flynn tosses the spear aside.

"This is what we've been reduced to?!" he yells. "Sticks and stones?!"

"Flynn! Look out! Behind you!"

From the smoky darkness and at speed, two de-civ children jump Flynn as the spear-thrower gets up. The two children pull at Flynn's flesh like rabid monkeys and the spear-thrower punches Flynn in the stomach. With his weakened leg and the blow, it takes little effort for the three to drag Flynn down like a roped calf.

Flynn covers up as best he can, but the de-civs pummel him. When the spear-thrower sees Koko rushing over, he warns the two children and all three take off. Koko skids and drops to Flynn's side.

"Are you okay?"

Flynn's forehead is gashed and his eye bandage has been torn off.

"Those were kids!"

"Not exactly a fair fight, is it?"

Koko helps him to his feet, and they push their backs together and circle. Koko points to a nearby apple tree with her battle staff and they dash for it. Outside the administration building, a few Commonagers—including Sébastien, of all people—have now finally appeared. A second explosion bursts on the opposite end of the compound, and Koko notices that the twins have joined the fight. But then a de-civ woman splashes some kind of accelerant on Bonn and Eirik and—*WHOOSH*!—the two brothers go up in tandem, screaming flames.

"Oh God, what do we do?" Flynn cries.

"They're setting fires to increase hysteria."

"Yeah, I can see that."

"They must've blown the tunnel gate's fortifications. This is why they probed the Commonage before, to see if we were ready to defend ourselves from a second assault."

"Oh, so it's 'we' now, is it?"

"Now's so not the fucking time, Flynn."

Flynn wipes some blood from his face. He touches his swollen eye and then squinting he scans the walls. A terrible, familiar shape moves fast along the allure up top, and his jaw drops.

"Koko?"

"What?"

"I think we've got a problem."

With the Sig in a two-handed downward-pointed grip, Wire hustles for a protective section along the top of the allure. Reaching it, she is pleased to discover the blockish architectural highlight bookends an open staircase that empties out into the greater compound area below.

In her half-compromised vision, she sees despite her instructions that the de-civs are already screwing everything up big time, and the raid is turning into a major-league Charlie Foxtrot. Breaking and smashing useful things, setting fire to structures willy-nilly—Wire specifically told them to torch the residential structures only, to draw out the occupants, and now they're setting fire to everything in sight.

No matter. Wire crouches behind the protective section and surveys the grounds. Botched instructions notwithstanding, within seconds what Wire hoped for actually materializes. Maybe seventy meters off from her position, Martstellar and that Flynn bastard are hiding behind an apple tree.

Wire sets up fast. Under normal circumstances her marksmanship is grade A-plus, but with her ocular being fried she reminds herself to compensate and stabilizes her forearms on the protective section. Taking a deep breath, she aims and eases her breath out.

Do it.

Take the shot.

Koko jerks her head.

"Where?"

As the bounty agent braces herself atop the staircase, Flynn throws an arm around Koko's shoulders and pulls her to his bare chest just as the impact of three quick, consecutive pulse rounds blister the apple tree on the opposite side. A follow up pulse blast rips the battle staff from Koko's hand.

"It's her!"

Koko glares angrily at her battle staff sizzling in the grass.

"Who?"

"The bounty agent! The one from The Sixty!"

Koko grabs Flynn's shoulders with both hands, mini ten-megaton explosions going off in her eyes.

FU-CHEW! FU-CHEW! FU-CHEW! FU-CHEW!

Four more rounds of blue pulse fire cross within fractions of the tree.

"Koko, what do we do?"

Koko has no idea.

Shit.

Shit, shit, shit, shit, shit…

Wire aimed for the edges of their bodies and compensated. Even so, she missed her targets by an embarrassingly wide margin and only managed to hit the damn tree. Fuck, she should've hit at least one of them. Bleakly she wonders if maybe the action on the Sig is off. Stupid. She should've sacrificed a couple of rounds before she and the de-civs set out. Then again, she thinks, the situation isn't totally roached, not entirely. The two are still pinned down. They can't stay behind that tree forever, and sooner or later they'll have to make a move. Wire contemplates unloading on the tree again until there's nothing left, when the sweetest of revelations hits her.

The two are not returning fire.

Not returning fire?

Wire rises.

They're mine.

Consider role reversal for a moment.

If Koko were in the bounty agent's shoes, she has no doubt of what she would do. Koko would just blast away at the apple tree until she and Flynn were exposed or until one or both of them caught a fatal round. The possibility that the bounty agent on the wall will do just that is leveling.

"Oh, Flynn, baby," Koko moans. "I think we're hosed."

Flynn stares at her. Whatever meager composure he has left evaporates.

"*Hosed!?* Goddamn it! I told you! You should've listened to me!"

"Listened to you?"

"Back on The Sixty—if you'd gotten rid of that woman in the first place..."

Koko's face warps. "Oh-ho-ho, don't even think of going there—you're saying this is all *my* fault?"

Flynn drops his face into his hands. Koko peers around the edge of the apple tree.

"How'd she even find us?"

"God, does it even matter?"

Somewhere inside one of the buildings a woman screams and the body of another Commonager pitches out of a smashed window. A gargantuan, thundering *KA-POW*! sounds, and a split second later a crackling fireball ascends into the night.

"The reactivated transponder," Koko says. "That bounty agent must've gotten wind of that intel somehow."

"Oh, perfect. A little late to do anything about that now."

"Will you quit your whining? Cripes, I'm the one she's after."

"You're the one she's after? God, could you be any more narcissistic?"

"I'm narcissistic? Maybe I should push you out there. You're the one who's so smitten with this place."

"I can't believe you're bickering with me at a time like this."

"You started it."

"We have to *do* something!"

Koko speaks fast. "Listen, we've got to move now and in separate directions before that bounty agent opens up on us again."

"Where?"

"Lodge Delta. It's closest. There's that wall near the side doors we came out of. Snake your way across as quickly as you can and try not to get shot." Koko then squats down and digs in a toe like a sprinter. Flynn bends next to her and clutches her arm.

"Koko, wait. If I—I mean, if we—"

"Flynn, this is *really* not a good time."

"I mean, yeah. Of course not. But I just want you to know—"

Quickly Koko cups Flynn's chin and kisses him. Hard.

"Get it together, baby. Ready? On three. One, two…"

Wire checks the pulse-round readout on the Sig's housing. Happily she sees there's plenty of power left to dismember Martstellar and her ex-sky-cop dreamboat, sweet and slow. Picturing them groveling for mercy after all she's been through makes her grin. It's going to be so choice. Maybe Wire will keep them alive long enough so they can feel it when she chews out their eyes. Wire starts for the stairs.

"Hey, Wire!"

When taken by surprise and from behind, only a chump hesitates. Pushing off and staying low, Wire propels herself forward and corkscrews her torso just as a large rock sails past her head like a missile. Swinging her Sig across her body, she fires twice in rapid succession just before her back crunches on the steps.

Almost getting struck by a flying rock was a close shave for sure, but then Wire realizes that was Trick's whole distractive point. When her shoulders hit the steps, she cranes her neck backward and sees the inverted wavering image of Grum running up the stairway from down below. Like a crazed Viking, Grum has a stick of rusty rebar hoisted above his head ready to split her head in two.

Instinctually, Wire tosses the Sig to her right and forces her feet over the rest of her body. It's a mindboggling feat of spontaneous gymnastics given her hearty physique, but as she completes her backward rotation and pushes off the steps, her shins land on Grum's shoulders and vise. Startled, Grum lets out a deep throaty sound as Wire yanks her body weight to the right. Together, she and Grum fall off the stairway and out into empty space.

The drop from the stairs to the ground lasts barely a second, but it is Grum who lands wrong. Horribly, horribly wrong. Upside down, the pile-driving, concertina crush on impact snaps Grum's neck instantly. Wire releases her legs before Grum's hulky mass lands on top of her and rolling over she sees Trick jump from atop the allure, a spread-eagled shadow of wrath.

When Trick hits, the collision is a shockwave. Fused together, Wire and Trick roll over and over in the grass, and before Wire can right herself Trick gains the advantage. Pinning Wire's chest, Trick lets fly a shower of fists and as he draws back to land a jaw-pulverizing right cross, Wire catches his wrist, digs in her thumb, and compresses the median nerve. Trick's fist splays apart, and Wire pulls his hand close to her face. Biting down as hard as she can, she rips Trick's index finger off.

"You bitch!" Trick screams. "You just ate my finger!"

Wire spits out the hot digit swimming in her mouth as Trick yells at Grum.

"GRUM, GET UP! HELP ME HERE GODDAMNIT!"

Popping up to a ready stance, Wire flashes her good eye around. Her thrown-away Sig is nowhere to be seen, but what she does see is Grum's dropped stick of rebar lying in the grass just off to her right. As Trick staggers backward and steps on Wire's discarded weapon, Wire lunges for the rebar just as Trick turns and grabs the Sig. With his ruined hand, the weapon's recoil herky-jerks his aim wildly and blue pulse rounds zing off in all directions. Gripping the rebar, Wire swings for the stars and connects. The single blow shatters Trick's elbow like a clamshell.

Shrieking louder this time, Trick instantly drops Wire's pistol and stumbles backward. Spinning right, Wire lunges and thrusts the rebar straight through Trick's gut.

A hiccupped transcendence siphons off the last of Trick's confidence. Wire waits and then yanks back on the rebar, pulling out a spurting gurgle of torn intestines. When Trick drops to his knees he attempts to stuff his guts back in the gushing hole in his stomach and realizes it's no use. Wire stands and cracks her neck.

"I swear, trusting de-civ trash like you… I mean, really? Attacking *me*? What, you've got nothing better to do?"

Trick looks up at her. Wire lines up the rebar on his shoulder, draws back, and cuts his head off with one magnificent, whizzing stroke.

Serpentining across the ground, out of the corner of her eye Koko sees that Flynn has successfully reached the garden wall by Lodge Delta. Astounded that neither of them have been cut to pieces by pulse fire yet, Koko glances backward and discovers the reason why. No longer atop the wall, the bounty agent is busy rolling around on the ground with the rangy-looking de-civ Koko remembers chasing into the access tunnel the night before.

Not knowing who'll win the battle, Koko hurdles the wall and lands next to Flynn just as several pulse rounds zip past overhead. Reading each other's thoughts, they both get up and rush for the Lodge Delta doors.

Seconds later Koko and Flynn are inside. Flynn yells at her to stay down, but she ignores him and edges up to the doors' windows. The unrelenting bloodbath outside continues to unwind in slow motion.

Koko sees two skinny women crosscheck Sébastien to the bricks. Gammy attacks the women viciously. Looking to the bounty agent, Koko sees the woman decapitate her opponent with a long rod. When the bounty agent picks up a weapon in the grass close by and checks it, the sepia glow of the spreading fires makes the woman look almost hellishly ascendant. But Koko detects something wrong. There's something off-kilter about the bounty agent's sway and gait.

When the woman homes in on Lodge Delta, Koko ducks down and instantly fears she's been made. Sitting on her heels and mamboing two quick fingers at Flynn to head up the stairs, Koko fully anticipates an explosion of pulse fire to rip apart the doors.

Flynn refuses to budge.

"God, don't be stupid, Flynn! Just go!"

"I'm not leaving you!"

When the door doesn't rip apart or blast inward, Koko hazards another glimpse out the windows. The bounty agent has now turned her attentions away from Lodge Delta to the rest of the chaos shredding the Commonage. Weapon up, straight-armed, and shooting indiscriminately, the woman's first eight pulse rounds miss her intended targets, but then a wild follow-up shot tags Pelham, who flies backward as if she's been hit by a wrecking ball. The bounty agent keeps firing and the sickening chorus of screams rises. Flynn scuttles over to her and tries to drag Koko down by her waist, but Koko tears off his hands.

Across the courtyard, Gammy whips up her head from Sébastien's cringing attackers. Stiff-spined and gumline bared, Gammy then rushes the bounty agent. A pulse round throws the synthetic sideways in a yelping whorl of white-hot sparks.

Koko can't bring herself to look away. When the bounty agent finally reaches Sébastien, she grabs him with one hand and lifts him up like a puppet. Koko can't make out Sébastien's frantic words, but to her it sounds like *cheese,* and *sky can gib-boo-bunny.*

Sébastien is pleading for his life.

Please! I can give you money!

Leaning in, the bounty agent bites out his eye anyway.

"Damn it all to hell," Koko says.

Stepping past Flynn, Koko kicks Lodge Delta's doors open and blows out a sharp, looping whistle. Dropping Sébastien in a squealing heap, the bounty agent turns.

"Martstellar!"

Koko hurdles the small wall and moves across the open ground.

"Yeah, we haven't been formerly introduced, fucker."

Not taking her eyes off Koko, Wire casually blasts a round into Sébastien's ruined face.

"The name's Wire."

"Wire?"

"Yeah, Jackie Wire. Do you have any idea how much trouble you've caused me, you little imp?"

"I'm guessing a lot."

"Veritable pantloads."

Flynn stumbles out of Lodge Delta. When he sees Koko closing in on the bounty agent he shouts.

"Koko, stop! She'll kill you!"

Koko hears Flynn, but it's too late. She's committed now, and there's no way she's going to back down, not from some butch-looking psychopath pursuing her halfway across the world like this.

"I sort of hoped you ate it big time back on *Alaungpaya,*" Koko says, "but then you showed up on The Sixty and now you're here. I guess you're some kind of super cockroach that just won't quit, huh?"

Wire gestures to Flynn. "I see you brought your boyfriend."

"Leave him out of this."

When Koko is ten meters from her, Wire lifts her weapon and Koko slams on the brakes. Taking a slow, Shaolin breath and lifting her arms above her head, Koko says, "I don't know what you're doing with these de-civs, but if you're here for me then let's do it. Leave the rest of these people be."

Wire fires a single pulse at the bricks, and red specks of rock sprinkle Koko's legs. The spray makes Koko backpedal a bit, but once again she notes a differential in the bounty agent's gloating, blood-splattered face.

There must be something wrong with her ocular, Koko surmises.

A malfunctioning ocular implant could explain the woman's piss-poor shooting, and the deficiency is definitely an advantage for Koko if she can stall long enough to get a chance. Wire then motions to the compound walls.

"What the hell is this place anyway?"

Giving their surroundings a brief commiserative look, Koko sighs.

"It's a settlement."

"Yeah, I can see that, but here? In the Nor'Am prohibs? The fuck's up with that?"

Koko bends a finger at Sébastien. "That guy you just smoked put it all together. He made a killing in pharmaceuticals and blew it all setting this place up. It's called the Commonage."

Wire scowls. "If this place is a settlement, then where are their defenses?"

"Would you believe they didn't think they were necessary?"

"You're putting me on."

"Nope."

"Wow," Wire replies, "what a bunch of goobers. They got transport?"

"Why, what happened to yours? I mean, I say yours because I assume you didn't just drop out of the sky."

"Funny you should say that because I had to ditch. Shelled out a ton of credits for a PAE Aerodynamics bird and the thing up and quit on me when I got within range of the area. Some prearranged restricted airspace agreement or something. I figured it was holdover quarantine nonsense."

Koko remembers the airspace restrictions. Bully for Sébastien for having the foresight, the fat lot of good it did him. Koko slinks a foot forward, and Wire adjusts her aim.

"You in some hurry to get dead, cupcake?"

"Not really."

"Then stand fast and answer my question."

"I'm sorry, which question was that?"

"Transport."

"No. There's no transport."

"None at all?"

"You actually think I'd still be here if they had transport?"

"Man, how does that even *work*?"

Koko shrugs. "It's hard to explain, but seeing that you're now leading this ad hoc slayfest, I'm sure you can hack *their* communication systems and work yourself out a lift. That is if your de-civ collaborators don't burn the whole place down first."

Wire levels her weapon. "Get on your knees, Martstellar."

Slowly, Koko does as she's told and keeps her hands high. "Listen, I know this might seem a bit much to ask, but I was wondering… maybe you could do me a favor before you take me out."

"A favor? For you? After everything I've been through tracking you down? Right now you're lucky I don't blast you in half."

"Well, immediate blasting in half aside, the way I see it, it's me you're after, right? I'm the one who took out the other members of your recovery team back on *Alaungpaya*. I'm the one with the outstanding price on her head. Think of it as a last request. These people, they've got nothing to do with you and me. Leave them alone."

Wire laughs. "Oh, that's rich. Leave them alone. That's really funny. Meat like this—what are these dipshits to you anyway?"

"They helped us out. Of course they also reactivated the transponder on the submarine which I'll figure is how you found me in the first place, and they probably messed with my lover's brain, but they helped us out nevertheless. They don't deserve this."

"Deserve. You know what? You know jackshit about what people deserve. I've studied your files, Martstellar."

"Oh, yeah?"

"Yeah. I guess you were a decent operator back in the day. Maybe a little below salt for my tastes, but still… you should know better how this sort of thing has to play out."

Wire then swings left and shoots Flynn twice.

OW

As the first pulse round hornets through his right pectoral and sneezes out of his back in a molten carnation spray of tissue and scapula bone, the good news is Flynn pirouettes clockwise with enough velocity to avoid Wire's follow-up shot.

The bad news, however, is…

Oh, c'mon—seriously? Again?

KOKO THE MIGHTY

If an aspiring combatant took the time to explore the literal scores of exotic martial arts, said combatant would likely be flabbergasted by the number of methods to disarm an active shooter.

Carpal crunching Nikkyo wristlocks, crippling two-point strike and kick Silat combinations, gnarly Malla-yuddha joint breaks—the list goes on and on with meticulous, debilitating nuance and mind-splitting pain. So go ahead, take your pick. In the end the common denominator to any disarmament method is invariably uniform: once you commit, you must commit completely. Second chances in hand-to-hand combat are nil.

In the shaved instant as Wire squeezes off her second blast at Flynn, Koko springs up and cuts the distance between them. Sensing her movement, Wire tracks back to respond, but Koko is already airborne. Wire fires and a pulse round slices past Koko's ear within a fraction.

In that fluky moment of midflight with her right arm crooked back, sadly Koko realizes she's already made a huge mistake. Then again, committed is committed so—fuck it. She's not going down without a fight.

Tucking her legs and spinning sixty degrees to her left, Koko talon-locks her hand on Wire's wrist before she can squeeze the trigger again. Mashing together the ulna and radius bones, Koko prays her counterweight will be enough to redirect Wire's line of fire, free the weapon, and possibly dislocate Wire's shoulder. When she doesn't feel a sudden give or hear a moist socket pop, Koko yanks hard and reverses her momentum anyway.

Wire wouldn't have lived as long as she has if she'd not been able to defend herself against such a predictable move. With jaded ease, she breaks Koko's hold and pitches her off her arm like an overgrown tabby. Landing on her back, Koko blacks out. A split second later and coming to, Koko is actually stunned that Wire isn't chewing out her eye.

Rally time.

Koko revolves over two fallen Commonagers and pulls one of the bodies on top of her. It's a last hope to shield herself, and when she sees that the empty-eyed corpse is actually Pelham, Koko's adrenaline spikes. Heaving Pelham up onto her back, she drives herself backward.

Be as small as possible…

…be nothing…

…be the…

Zero.

A pulse round slams into Pelham's body and the impact clobbers Koko back to the bricks with a grunt. Instantly Koko's shoulder burns with an incredible jag of cauldron-like pressure as the penetrating round melts into her own flesh. Mocking her with rough, wolfish mirth, Wire steps forward and hovers.

"Here's a last request," Wire says, pointing her weapon down at the back of Koko's thrashing head. "How about you come out from under there, and I shoot you in the spine. I'm told acute paralysis can abate some of the misery of being blasted at close range. Of course, I'll have to crank down the levels on this pretty Sig here to make it worth both our whiles, but to tell you the truth, in the end it might make things easier. I was planning on chopping you to itty-bitty pieces for fun anyway."

Koko claws forward with one arm, but Pelham's weight has her trapped. Knowing the warm pooling sensation beneath her chest is her own blood, the oncoming certainty of her death purifies her mind and her pupils dilate. Somehow she's always known that this was how it would turn out for her. Koko P. Martstellar? Grow soft-toothed, flappy, and gray? Not a chance. Everything has brought her to this moment like one achingly long joke. Still, Koko is determined not to give Wire even a morsel of satisfaction.

Bitch thinks she knows how this plays out?

Give Koko one chance.

Just one.

"Oh, well, have it your way..."

A wet, throaty snarl twists Wire's head and a radical vision of blue-furred bloodlust roars up.

Gammy!

Knocked sideways by the crippled dog, Wire brings an arm up across her face to protect herself. A frenzied mass of canine froth, Gammy scrapes wildly up Wire's body as Koko sweeps out a leg and hooks Wire's calf. Gammy's weight combined with the hooked leg takes Wire to the ground.

Koko wriggles out from beneath Pelham. Flesh thrumming, Gammy leaps on top of Wire who punches the dog's sides to no avail. Thrusting her saliva-drenched muzzle again and again, Gammy's fangs snap and Wire plants the tip of her Sig against the dog's skull. When she pulls the trigger, a jagged quarter of Gammy's head separates and lifts off like a pressure-cooker lid, but somehow Gammy's remaining circuitry appears unaffected. Her programming defaults go from protect to *kill*.

Gammy sinks her fangs into Wire's neck.

Clutching her shoulder, Koko scoots back and watches as Gammy and Wire gator-roll across the courtyard—a braided convulsion of rearing limbs. But then Wire manages to snake her weapon between herself and Gammy, and when she fires again flashes of blue-flecked viscera and fur fly outward. Gammy jiggers and carves apart in two hinged, flaming sections, but miraculously her jaws do not release their hold on Wire's neck. Now on fire herself, Wire spanks at the flames and her weapon clatters to the ground.

Wire grabs Gammy's head, and pulls her jaws apart. Clambering backward and kicking frantically, she sees Koko targeting her dropped pistol, and for Koko to grab it Wire knows she'll have to dive across Gammy's broken body, which is now a crackling electrical fire. Wire doesn't wait to give her the chance, and in the next instant she scoops up the Sig with one of her half-broiled hands as out of nowhere, a broken brick strikes her in the back.

Koko's heart soars. Across the courtyard in front of the burning administration building, she sees that someone at last is coming to her aid. Unbelievable. It's the little chicken swatter Koko noticed the day before with Sébastien. Chopping and wresting broken pieces of brick from a pathway with a shovel, the tawny-haired boy hurls his missiles in rapid succession as soon as each fragment is loosened from the ground. Soon other Commonage children join the boy, and Koko's sudden elation is cut short because the children's barrage is indiscriminate. Dark-red projectiles of all sizes hail down at every turn as a screeching pitch resonates from Gammy's burning body.

Both Wire and Koko look at Gammy, and the immediate forecast isn't good: the dead synthetic's internal batteries have superheated, and the lithium-ion cubes ignite in an effulgent belch of noxious smoke.

It's the chance Koko needs. Rushing forward, she seizes one of Gammy's forelegs just above the paw and swings the synthetic's disarticulated bulk at Wire like a hammer thrower. When bubbling specks of acid land on Wire's face, Koko releases Gammy's foreleg and charges. Wire lifts her weapon and fires. Both women collide just as everything for Koko jolts to an impenetrable, cold black.

TABULA RASA

Next to the last occupied gurney in the Commonage's infirmary, Dr. Corella pulls up a stool and wearily plants himself. Staring dully at the floor between his knees, for the eleven thousandth time in his career as a physician, Dr. Corella fails to understand the savagery of the human animal.

To say taking care of all the wounded has been murder and a half on his abilities is an irony of colossal proportions. It's been a non-stop, around the clock, nightmare of triage—twenty-one hours straight without a break. Swollen feet, fingers past numb, Dr. Corella did his best to save those he could, but the reckoning of just how many he's worked on vacillates. After the fires were brought under control and after the invading de-civs inexplicably turned tail and disappeared, at one point some of the children even dragged Gammy's smoldering body into the infirmary in the slim hope there was a chance at rebooting her. The synthetic Mastiff was hardly the most pressing issue, and with one look Dr. Corella knew a full operational mending was impossible. He located and removed the dog's memory stick anyway and assured the children that maybe Gammy would live on in another form, someday.

After all his work, now in the end, one thing brightens Dr. Corella's thoughts. With Sébastien's demise, the TAM research and its insanely lucrative applications are now his to reap alone. Thank goodness the fires were finally brought under control.

Rubbing his face, he compels himself to check the patient's vitals, displayed on a projection screen alongside the last occupied gurney. The graphs, columns, and assorted pings emanate a positive assessment. Miraculously, the patient has stabilized.

"Flynn? Can you hear me?"

Ever so slightly, Flynn's head moves but he doesn't respond audibly. Dr. Corella grabs the handles of the gurney and then leans over him.

"Koko is going to be okay. I've evac'ed her with two of the more critically wounded on the flight craft Sébastien requested. In an hour or so from now, the Akotitiwin Air transport will land in Calgary where Koko alone will be transferred to a second, larger transport. You're safe—and that lunatic who shot you? I ordered the same AA transport's pilot to drop her off in an isolated area several hundred kilometers north of here."

Flynn's eyelids flutter. "Where?"

"The woman who shot you?"

"No… Koko."

"My God, man, do you really want to know?"

Both of Flynn's eyes open and the dolorous anguish reflected within is incomprehensible.

"Just tell me," Flynn wheezes.

"It's a Mars Class transport called the *Omalhaut*," Dr. Corella says.

"*Mars?*"

"No, not quite. The *Omalhaut* was purchased by the Itokawa Corporation several years back. The *Omalhaut* is now refurbished as an interplanetary cruiser. It's primarily used for the Itokawa Corporation's lunar mining initiatives. I won't trouble you with the details, but I helped the *Omalhaut*'s chief medical officer during her residency and she owed me a favor. You see, before we operated, I took what we discussed seriously. I went ahead and made all the arrangements. In time Koko will be fine, but before you went under you insisted I get her as far away from the Commonage as possible before she received the news." Dr. Corella licks his lips tentatively. "This was your expressed wish, yes?"

Flynn nods.

Dr. Corella pats his arm. "Good."

Standing, Dr. Corella then notices the bandages around Flynn's midsection trembling. Flynn coughs and attempts to hide his face—a courageous effort—but the doctor knows there's no need for Flynn to hide his confusion or his pain, not anymore.

"Now then," Dr. Corella says. "I need to give you another shot in the eye."

EPILOGUE

THE HIGH AND BELOW

Twenty-three hours later…

Face-down in an elliptical zero-g berth aboard the Itokawa Corporation's interplanetary cruiser *Omalhaut*, Koko stirs and then wakes to the sound of classical piano.

The music drifts from a small speaker hidden somewhere above her. Ornamental in melody, the music is pleasant but it isn't a piece she recognizes. Later on, Koko will learn that the music is part of an aria composed many, many centuries ago by Bach, the Goldberg Variations.

Her focus gathering, Koko realizes she's no longer at the Commonage and appears to be in a cramped, windowless, sickbay compartment. With insulated cream-colored ribbed walls and limpidly lit, there is no one else in the compartment and a console on her immediate left senses she's awake. The zero-g berth rotates one hundred and eighty degrees, and an indigo-colored projection screen materializes two feet in front of Koko's bandaged head.

As the screen concentrates, a logo for ITOKAWA CORPORATION appears with the word *OMALHAUT* refracted as shadow in the background. Koko tries to touch her face, but she can't. Once again within a week she fumes at the fact that she's secured down by restraints. There are hundreds of pressure pins and tubes plugged into her arms and directly into her shoulder.

An ether-like disruption to her vestibular system makes her feel nauseous and when the aria in the background abruptly clips silent, the projection screen above her head goes blank. After a pulse beat, Dr. Corella's face appears.

"Hello, Koko," Dr. Corella begins. "If you're watching this, you'll be pleased to know the recovery monitors have assessed it's safe to revive you from your tranquilizers. This means you're recuperating well from a parietal fracture in your head and from your shoulder wound. At this point you've probably guessed you're no longer at the Commonage. I know this may come as a shock, but you're now aboard a vessel known as the *Omalhaut* and you're in lockdown on the *Omalhaut*'s medical deck. In a few days your final destination is the Itokawa Corporation's lunar mining facilities located on the outer rim of the moon's Copernicus Crater."

The Copernicus—wait—what?

Koko tries to sit up, but the restraints immobilize her. A woozy reel sloshes back and forth in her stomach, and the metal sutures beneath her shoulder dressing start to strain.

"After everything that's happened and not knowing who else may be looking for you, for your safety I felt it best to dispatch you on the *Omalhaut* once your initial surgeries at the Commonage were completed." Dr. Corella's sunken eyes look up as if he's searching to pull down the right words. "The events of the past few days have been exceptionally trying, and honestly, I don't know what else to say other than you did what you could for us, and for that I thank you. The Commonage as a whole thanks you. Much to his chagrin, I believe if Sébastien were still alive he might even find the will to thank you as well."

Koko heaves hard and her shoulder sutures start to bleed.

"I know you're not completely one hundred percent yet, but

since the monitors feel it's fit to revive you, I believe you deserve to know. I'm sorry to have to convey this, but Flynn did not survive his injuries."

All at once it is as if the air has been sucked out of the tight compartment. The news of Flynn's death collapses Koko to a cold and infinitesimal pinprick before atomizing outward.

Koko can't breathe.

No, she heard that wrong.

No, she's hallucinating.

He's lying.

Koko's stomach convulses and one of the stressed metal sutures in her shoulder rips. She dry retches again and a second suture tears, then another and another. Like quills swept by the blackest of winds, the pressure pins across her body chatter together.

"Flynn's penetrating injury had complications. Combined with the immediate dramatic blood loss and the tenuous state of his physical being after his previous infection, hypoxemic shock led to a cardiac arrest and it couldn't be helped. Please know I did everything I could to bring him back, but Flynn remained unresponsive. I'm sorry."

With all her strength, Koko heaves herself upward until the restraints across her chest give way with a stiff snap. Trailing a shower of pressure pins and tubes, half of her lifts up in weightlessness. The console next to her starts to beep urgently. Bending over in dizzying pain, Koko seizes the last restraint holding down her legs and wrenches it off. Grabbing the gown covering her by the collar, she shreds the fabric in two and screams.

Lifting higher off the elliptical berth and her gown dropping away, Koko's torment is all consuming. Pin-balling from wall to padded wall, her mind floods with confusion and sadness, anger and disbelief. She kicks and punches the air and it feels as if her head is about to blow apart. Sobbing, Koko beats and smashes everything within reach.

It can't be.

It can't be, it can't be, it can't…

* * *

Meanwhile, four thousand and twenty-seven kilometers back down on Earth, Wire hikes across the North American prohib border into the Canadian Territories.

Bandaged and dehydrated, Wire still isn't sure how she ended up wrapped in a solar blanket inside the ruins of a roofless church three hundred and fifty kilometers northeast of the Commonage. The last thing she remembers is that massive blue dog on fire, the acid, and Martstellar getting knocked comically out of the air by a flying brick. After that—everything is a concussed curtain, an unexplained blur.

Wire figures Martstellar must have fed her a line about those people in that compound not having transport. After all, someone must have dropped her off in the middle of nowhere. The same someone must've taken her weapon too and even relieved her of Trick's jackknife. To her astonishment, whoever it was, however, left her other things. Her multi-tool, three days' worth of water in a large plastic canteen, a solar blanket, and a few fat apples. It's unsettling. Why didn't they just finish her off? Goddamn, doesn't anybody know how to fight dirty anymore?

Like an oozing saddlebag, the carcass of a jumbo-sized wood rat she snared earlier that morning is now lashed to Wire's waist. She plans on roasting the creature over a fire as a protein treat on her next rest, a fine comeuppance to the late rodent's Surabayan relatives.

Hiking on a northwestern heading, Wire estimates she'll reach the fringes of the New Vancouver supercities in three or four days, tops. Those environments will present their own brutal challenges, but for now she concentrates on the task at hand, keeping one foot in front of the other. The densely forested relief grades upward and Wire stops to consider the terrain. Once part of a major interstate, the impression between the trees snakes through the wreckage of a large, overgrown town and through the sloped wedges of ruin, she studies the mountain peaks beyond. Yeah, it's going to be a hell of a slog to clear those higher elevations, but if she keeps moving she should make the foothills by nightfall. Pulling the solar blanket from around her waist, Wire drapes it over her shoulders. A waxing crescent moon rises in the east, sharp as a scimitar.

Taking a deep breath, Wire picks up her pace.

THE END

ACKNOWLEDGMENTS

Sequels can be angry circus bears. Briefly I want to thank all those who helped me hotwire the clown car to avoid being eaten alive by this book: my wonderful agent Stacia J.N. Decker at the Donald Maass Literary Agency; my incomparable editor Cath Trechman and all the enthusiastic cats over in London at Titan Books; all my crime and science fiction writing compatriots; my ever mystified family; and (of course) fans of Koko P. Martstellar both near and far. Finally, a special note of gratitude goes out to Commander Peter D. Quinton USN (Ret.) for his input and guidance on extra-tropical weather systems. As my late uncle always used to say, I'll see you in the funny papers.

ABOUT THE AUTHOR

Amongst other things, Kieran Shea once posed as a Secret Service agent protecting JFK on the cover of fictional news tabloid the *Weekly World News*. He prefers red wine over white, sunrises over sunsets, and is convinced that sooner or later we've all got it coming.

ALSO AVAILABLE FROM TITAN BOOKS

NO HERO

JONATHAN WOOD

"What would Kurt Russell do?"
Oxford police detective Arthur Wallace asks himself that question a lot. Because Arthur is no hero. He's a good cop, but prefers that action and heroics remain on the screen, safely performed by professionals. But then secretive government agency MI12 comes calling, hoping to recruit Arthur in their struggle against the tentacled horrors from another dimension known as the Progeny. But Arthur is NO HERO! Can an everyman stand against sanity-ripping cosmic horrors?

TITANBOOKS.COM

ALSO AVAILABLE FROM TITAN BOOKS

OBSIDIAN HEART

THE WOLVES OF LONDON

MARK MORRIS

Alex Locke is a reformed ex-convict, forced back into London's criminal underworld for one more job. He agrees to steal a priceless artefact—a human heart carved from blackest obsidian—from the home of a decrepit old man. But when the burglary goes horribly wrong, Alex is plunged into the nightmarish world of the Wolves of London, a band of unearthly assassins who will stop at nothing to reclaim the heart. As he races to unlock the secrets of the mysterious object, Alex must learn to wield its dark power—or be destroyed by it.